The Iron Bridge

Also by Anton Piatigorsky

Plays

Breath In Between

The Kabbalistic Psychoanalysis of Adam R. Tzaddik

Easy Lenny Lazmon and the Great Western Ascension

The Offering

Eternal Hydra

ANTON PIATIGORSKY

THE IRON BRIDGE

Short Stories of 20th Century Dictators as Teenagers

STEER
FORTH
PRESS

First published in Canada in 2012 by Goose Lane Editions

For information about permission to reproduce
selections from this book, write to:
Steerforth Press L.L.C., 45 Lyme Road, Suite 208,
Hanover, New Hampshire 03755

Book design by Chris Tompkins

Cataloging-in-Publication Data is available from the Library of Congress

ISBN 978-1-58642-218-9

First U.S. Edition

1 3 5 7 9 10 8 6 4 2

Everything inhuman is senseless and worthless
—Vasily Grossman

TEA
IS BETTER
THAN PEPSI

Just inside the threshold of the company mess hall, wearing an apron smeared dark with Worcestershire sauce, maize meal, and other detritus from the evening meal, stands Idi, tall and slender — the newly recruited assistant cook. He's watching the rowdy *askaris* from Company E of the Fourth Battalion of the King's African Rifles as they laugh and kick a soccer ball around the dusty main square of the Jinja barracks. With their black chests exposed through open, untucked shirts, the enlisted men plow through beers purchased in the company canteen and top them off with sips of their forbidden *waragi* liquor.

It's the last Friday of the month. Payday. There will be no sleep tonight for this weary young assistant cook. The yelling and kicking mass will storm around the field for hours, keeping everyone awake. At dawn the drunken soldiers will stumble back to their huts, crooning and cursing each other, vomiting in the bushes, just when *dupis* like Idi have to rise for their kitchen duties. He has finished cleaning dishes and wouldn't mind a beer himself, but a *dupi* can't drink all night. He has real responsibilities, as the platoon sergeant has made perfectly clear on several occasions. Who else will cook for the fighting men?

The camaraderie of these soldiers — heavy drinking and informal soccer — that's Idi's idea of utopia. The cook submerges himself in shadow so the others can't see him. His pinched eyes follow the game's every turn, an eager child in silent study of the adults he longs to join.

Idi's big greasy hand clutches a bottle of cola. He gulps a mouthful of sweetness and fizz, the carbonated tingle rising through his nasal cavity and exploding inside his nostrils. He burps and opens his wide mouth to let the gas escape. Holding the bottle before him, Idi studies the distinctive red-and-blue logo that proudly declares the brand. He can't read the words, but he knows what it says: Pepsi-Cola. Same as her. All those years ago. That woman who, along with his own mother, ruined his chances. Together, they got him cast out of paradise. Together, they destroyed his future.

Pepsi-Cola was dragged before Mama during that blissful summer when they lived in Corporal Yasin's tiny hut in the Nubian compound outside the gates of Magamaga barrack, no more than a few kilometres from this same mess hall. Pepsi had a torn pink shirt, blackened and unwashed, and knotted cords of thick hair, red from *murram* dust. Sunglasses with one lens that she refused to remove, a skirt sewn together from a discarded burlap sack, and all those dangling, clanking, cracked bottles of Pepsi-Cola attached by little nooses to her frayed rope belt. Did her father bring her to them? No, she was too old for that; it must have been her brother. Yes, Pepsi was hauled before Mama by some ashamed and angry sibling, whose tight fingers dug into his sister's forearm as he meekly inquired whether

Mama was indeed Assa Aatta, the famous Lugbara sorcerer, as all the rumours declared. Idi remembers his mother's proud confirmation: "Yes, I'm full Lugbara. Yes, I'm a true diviner"—for God had visited her in adolescence and cast her trembling and naked out of her tiny village into the wild fields of the West Nile for three whole days and three whole nights—"And yes, although a female, I'm a competent oracle who can, as the rumours claim, determine the source of your Pepsi's illness—be it simple ghost vengeance or the more mysterious work of *adro yaya*, the one who makes humans tremble—and prescribe a proper treatment for any debilitating disease." If only his mother had turned that woman away. Idi, ten years old, stood on the porch of Corporal Yasin's dim hut, holding a tray of sweet *mandazi* biscuits that he'd intended to sell by the roadside, thinking: *This client, this Pepsi-Cola, is worth waiting for.* He followed them through the front door of the hut and stood in darkness by the wall.

He remembers the horror and shame on that poor brother's face when Pepsi sat on the earthen floor and parted her cola bottles to either side, flipped up the front of her skirt, and began to twiddle and whack and flick at her vagina with surprising aggression. She spread it wide, stuck her fingers inside, and extracted them with grunts and howls like a screeching monkey. Idi laughed so hard his small, bony shoulders shook and his biscuits fell to the ground. His mother silenced him with a wave of her hand. Pepsi hunched over, chanting a garbled and curious mixture of Lugbara and English and some entirely made-up language into that open vagina, as if it were a separate sentient creature that needed convincing.

"She has shamed me," said the brother. "She has shamed my kin."

Pepsi confirmed his claim by waving desultory arms and hissing through closed teeth and letting drool slide down her chin.

The brother's eyes implored Idi's mother for answers. Assa Aatta dropped to her hands and knees and peered intently at Pepsi-Cola as if there were a door between them and the patient could only be seen through a tiny keyhole. "It's possible," said Assa, "that it's a case of ghostly vengeance. But then it's the worst I've ever seen."

"Hyenas come," howled Pepsi, either to her brother or to herself, no one could be certain. "Bite and rip to bits! Hah hah hah!" With the rounded base of a cola bottle, Pepsi rubbed her clitoris and moaned.

"Ack," winced the brother, turning away in pain. He kicked Pepsi, knocking her over. "You can have her. I don't want her! She has brought shame to my family. My own daughter is barren because of her sins. This woman is not my sister!"

"Shhh!" commanded Assa, still on all fours, studying the strange possession of Pepsi-Cola. The brother quieted down, but he was unable to bear the sight of his sister. He turned to face the wall.

His mother's first interrogation of Pepsi-Cola's brother amazed and impressed Idi. Assa Aatta seemed so wise—that she could find such significance in a string of seemingly pointless questions posed to an enraged relative. She inquired into some disagreement between a grandfather and great-uncle. "These are clues," his mother said, "clues to the trauma in lineage that resulted in this curse." Idi had faith that his mother would deduce the problem. He assumed she would solve the case quickly.

Now he knows he was wrong. Now he knows the truth: that drawn-out investigation was the beginning of the end. As the days passed, his mother learned nothing. She used every technique at her disposal, from rubbing-stick and chicken oracles to spittle application with *larigbi* and *ajibgi* leaves to procedures of more dubious origin, such as the study of the victim's excrement. "I think she was poisoned with snake-head powder," his mother said one morning. "Or maybe a tincture extracted from rotten placenta." Uncertainty began to infect her voice as the patient's illness progressed. There was an all-night shrieking fit outside Corporal Yasin's hut, an episode of stone-throwing that blinded a private's left eye, continuing bouts of public masturbation, and the capture and near strangling of a neighbourhood dog. *Why doesn't she cure this woman?* Idi wondered each day, as he left to sell his biscuits. People were starting to talk.

Days stretched into weeks. Although Idi's mother flashed lights and rang bells and induced trances inside Corporal Yasin's darkened hut, nothing worked. Pepsi emerged each night from her treatments to loiter in their rocky yard, mumbling to herself and threatening passersby.

Several weeks later, Mama called in Pepsi's distraught brother to inform him that all was lost. She said that his only hope was to assemble the scattered members of his ruined family and journey en masse back to their abandoned village just beyond the Sudanese border. There, at the family shrine, they could sacrifice a goat and hope that the resulting meat and blood would appease whatever irate ancestor was behind this unyielding plague. Young Idi knew, as he stood by the wall with his tray of biscuits listening to his mother, that she was an utter failure. He'd heard Corporal Yasin and his friends mocking Mama and her failed sorcery, as they got drunk on the porch. Idi was ashamed of her. He stopped meeting his customers' eyes.

Nine years later, as Idi sips his Pepsi and studies the soldiers playing soccer on the dusty field, he doesn't know why he ever expected anything better from his crazy mother. He watches a trim *askari* kick the ball into an ad hoc goal and hoot with drunken pleasure. All Lugbaran people are frauds. They always have been and always will be.

As a child, Idi never fully understood his mother's Lugbaran ways. He didn't grow up in Assa Aatta's West Nile village, never made an offering at her family shrine, and, as the spurned child of a Kakwa father, could never have made a reasonable claim to her Lugbara lineage even if he had wanted to. He held no sway with her revered ancestors. Idi knew that he was worthless to his mother's people, superfluous, not even human. "You are a thing to me." That's what the *'ba wara* said to him on his sole visit back to her arid village. "A *thing*," that village elder had said to the gangly adolescent.

"Never mind him," his mother replied as they walked away. "You're my son and you're Lugbara no matter what the *'ba wara* says."

"No," Idi says out loud, to his memory of her comment.

One morning, six weeks after Pepsi's arrival, Idi's cursing and bawling mother kicked the rough pallet on which he was sleeping and commanded the boy to pack his bag. In a drunken fit the previous night, Corporal Yasin, his mother's lover, had ordered the sorcerer and her idiot son to leave the Magamaga barrack. "We have to leave?" Idi mumbled, as a pit opened in his stomach and swallowed all his strength.

"I'm sick of this place and these stupid soldiers," his mother tearfully replied. "We're moving back to Bombo to live with Uncle Yusuf."

Idi knew it was a lie. He knew that his mother's failure with Pepsi was at the root of their dismissal. For a moment he stood stunned, but when she repeated her command, Idi stood his ground, scowling and refusing to pack a bag, his arms crossed against his chest. Although he had never before acted with such disobedience, Idi suddenly felt ready to abandon his failure of a mother, ready to live on his own—if only he could remain here, in the barrack, where men wore clean and pressed uniforms, sometimes festooned with medals and ribbons and fancy regalia, and not the rags and filthy shirts worn everywhere else in East Africa. He didn't want his life ruined by his mother's absurd and fraudulent sorcery, behaviour that seemed all the more strange and embarrassing when juxtaposed with the military precision of the finest troops in the British Empire—the King's African Rifles.

Idi told his mother that he would rather stay with Corporal Yasin and all the other proud *askaris*, but she only laughed at him. "Good luck," she said, as she threw her things into a beat-up suitcase. "Go on and try. See what happens. Yasin won't let you sleep here for one night."

Idi knew she was right. The gruff corporal had never made any attempt at hospitality and would surely have rejected a plea from Assa's tall and plainly stupid son. Still, these were men here in the barrack, real men, brave and strong and competent, all of the *askaris* in the ranks of the King's African Rifles. Idi had lived amongst these soldiers for so long, had been so steeped in their ethos, that he'd begun to think of dark-skinned Africans outside the grasp of the British military as uncivilized, apelike creatures—primitives, for lack of a better word—even though he was one of them. They could not walk, sit, or speak with any dignity. They were wild animals, never comfortable outside the forest, desert, or grassland of their birth, whereas *askaris* might travel to Kenya or Egypt, or even someday north to the great city of London, where they would have tea with the King. No matter, Idi couldn't stay with them.

When Idi and Assa Aatta lugged their few belongings onto the Bombo bus, the boy could see through the rusting barrack gates the elaborate drills and marches and exercises of the Fourth Battalion, the only men in his life, his spiritual fathers. Already, on that bus to Bombo, Idi knew that the Magamaga barrack in Jinja was more of a home than any place he'd ever lived. He vowed to return.

Now, in his dirty apron at the mess hall door, Idi knows that if his mother had turned that Pepsi woman away, he'd be an *askari* by now, not just some miserable *dupi*. His mother ruined him. Idi downs the remaining cola and tosses the empty bottle into the rocks and dry dirt outside the mess hall, not unaware of the symbolism. He resolves to return to his barrack and spend the night polishing his boots and steaming his cook's clothing so that when morning comes he will look more like a soldier than any of these disheveled *askaris*, despite his lack of a proper uniform. He removes his apron and returns to the kitchen to hang it on a hook.

"Amin," calls Joseph, the senior cook on duty. "Don't you take that apron off." Joseph approaches with a plate in one hand and a scowl across his lips. "Look at this," he says, as he holds the filthy dish inches from Idi's nose, exposing bits of drying beef and mashed cassava stuck to the porcelain. "Are you trying to give the *askaris* dysentery?"

Idi, who can barely comprehend the man's rapid Swahili, clutches his apron and shrugs.

"You can answer my questions with either a yes or a no."

"No," says Idi.

"Are you sure about that?"

"I am sure."

"Then get back into the kitchen and wash this one and the others. Now, Amin! I want to go home."

"Yes, sir," says Idi, as he grabs the plate from Joseph's hand. "I'm sorry. I'll do it."

Idi fills a bucket of fresh water from the faucet behind the kitchen. He pours it into the sink and then adds a kettle's worth of hot water and soap. His eyes sting from the chalky cleaning powder wafting into the air. As he sifts through the clean plates, sighing and extracting the dozen or so that need to be rewashed, he wonders if there is any job less fierce or manly than his. With his forearms and elbows submerged in sudsy water, his aching back bent at a sink built for short men, Idi can't resist comparing his life as a *dupi* with that of a real KAR soldier. Instead of a gun, a sharp panga, and proper training with mortars, signals, and bayonets, he has a sponge, a spatula, and complete knowledge of the evening's routine for sterilization.

Two years ago, when the young *askaris* of the Fourth Battalion battled the Japanese in the thick jungle of Burma's Kabaw Valley, Idi owed his allegiance not to glorious King George or any of his colonial representatives, but rather to the balding and bespectacled manager of Kampala's Imperial Hotel, a coward known more for his oversized paunch and squeaky voice than any proficiency with a Sten gun. Idi's uniform in those days was the standard red jacket and juvenile cap of a common bellboy, an inherently comic outfit that looked outright absurd on a teenager of his immense stature. His major responsibility during that great war of the world was lugging Europeans' trunks up the stairs for a spare coin or two. Now he's nineteen, almost twenty, cleaning dishes in the heat. Is this a man? Is this a Kakwa? Not at all.

He overheard a conversation earlier in the evening between several older *askaris* and a recent recruit that emphasized the difference between an assistant cook and a soldier. Idi lingered in the dining room, clearing dirty plates and filing standard-issue cutlery, drawing out each of his motions so he might extend his opportunity to eavesdrop on their tale.

"He wore blackface," said the sergeant, who crossed his legs under the long table just like an Englishman. "It came from a special cream—very dark and very sooty—so the Japanese couldn't tell who was the European in charge."

"He's always the one to kill first," explained a corporal.

"It's something they made in England especially for that occasion," added another.

"It made them look silly," the sergeant chuckled. "Bwana Robertson, with his English blue eyes, but his face as black as any Nubian."

"So what happened?" asked the recruit.

"On patrol that morning we reached the river, which was wide and deep and fast—and remember, the jungle was so thick in that valley that the river was the only place where we could be seen by the enemy. They set up their ambush beside it."

"By the bridge," said a corporal. "The little rope bridge."

"Which we never used," added the sergeant. "We always waded. But halfway to the other side, the Japanese started shooting."

"They had their trench thirty feet away."

"Thirty feet!"

The *askaris* broke their conversation to sip their tea from European cups with handles. Idi could barely resist turning to regard those brave corporals and sergeants, their faces weathered by gunpowder, disease, and exploding shrapnel, one with a nine-inch scar in his cheek that extended all the way down to his neck.

"So Bwana charges the river and we follow," continued the sergeant. "All leaping into the mud on the other side."

"Except Nabugere," whispered a corporal.

"Yes, Nabugere. He got hit."

"And on the other side," continued the sergeant, "just when he's in a most desperate fix and should be taking cover in the monsoon mud, Bwana Robertson stands up screaming and waving his arms and jumps back into the river."

"No!"

"Yes!" confirmed a corporal. "With the enemy firing all around."

"And then he runs up the river screaming bloody murder, ordering the others to stay put and return the enemy fire, except for me — *only me* — to follow him into the water. This crazy man, I think. But what can I do? If my lieutenant orders me to follow, I have no choice but to follow."

"And then," picked up the corporal, "in the middle of the river, with bullets flying all over, Bwana Robertson yanks off his webbing and drops his rifle, pulls down his pants, and sticks his white ass into the air."

"And with his black face turned back and his blue eyes pleading with me and his white ass up in the sky to get shot by the Japanese, I suddenly see that his whole backside is *covered* with biting red ants."

"Oh, Lord almighty," groaned the new recruit, echoing a phrase often heard from British officers.

"He's screaming, *Get them off, sergeant! At once! That's an order! Off!*"

"Oh Lord," laughed the recruit.

"So with the enemy hollering *Banzai! Banzai!* and bullets

all around—and for certain we'll be shot—I start brushing ants off what must be the whitest ass in all of Burma."

"His testicles, too."

"And his cock."

"Oh Lord!"

The *askaris'* roaring laughter infected Idi Amin. He chuckled openly, his thick fists clutching cutlery, his wide back rising and falling with each sucked breath.

"If I had had a camera, I think I might have given myself up for dead just to snap a picture of Bwana like that. Black face, blue eyes, white ass, red ants. Oh, and the welts rising! Bwana clutching his balls. And his ass the biggest target in the world."

"How did you survive?"

"How?" The mirthful sergeant shrugged his shoulders. "I don't know how. Ask God that question. We survived, that's it. Got the ants off the Bwana's ass, picked up my gun, and fired back."

"Bwana Robertson still laughs about it. You can ask him. He'll tell you everything."

It was all too magnificent for Idi to comprehend. He shakes his head at the sink, wondering at the *askaris'* bravery and sense of duty, their humour and fatalism. These are the very models of men, with their amusing recollection two years later, here, in the safety of the company mess hall. And the way they genteelly sip their tea—such sophistication for Africans; so worldly and European. As the soap bubbles swallow Idi's giant hands, he resolves to absorb and mimic everything he can about these soldiers. He'll learn how to sit and walk and speak like them. He'll shine his boot caps into shimmering black diamonds and stiffen his crisp khaki shirts with so much starch that they'll stand by themselves, their creases capable of cutting any finger that dares touch them. His Sten gun—is it possible he will ever hold his own?—will be so thoroughly oiled and cleaned that the others will have to ask him just how he did it. He will shoot straighter, run faster, sing *tu funge safari* with more strength and clarity than anyone in the battalion, even twenty miles into an all-day march through the jungle.

His glorious fantasy is interrupted by a nearby voice, just outside the humid concrete-block kitchen. "They're animals," a man says. "I know that for the truth."

Idi wipes his brow with the back of his hand and looks up from the dishes. Outside a tiny barred window beside him, a couple of *askaris* have stopped to have a smoke or take a piss by the wall. They can't see Idi.

"I also know it for the truth," says another.

"They're like a plague, ripping you off."

"That's all they know how to do."

The soldiers are talking about Asians. Although he's rarely given East Africa's Indian merchants much thought, Idi has often heard soldiers complaining while standing outside the local tin-roofed *duka* in the compound, which is owned by an Indian merchant—as are all the *dukas* in the land. He's heard the *askaris* cursing their inflated prices and their monopoly on purchasable goods.

"I saw them in Kohima, you know," says the first voice.

"Oh yeah?"

"Here in Africa they think they're such big men, but in their own country they live no better than goats."

"In their own shit," says the second.

"I'd never make my goat live like them."

"They're some kind of Asian animal."

"I saw them with my own eyes."

The voices fade as the soldiers move away. Idi finishes washing the dishes, dries them off with an old towel, and stacks them on the metal shelves. The head cook nods his approval and Idi removes his apron at last. He returns to the threshold and stands partially outside, watching the increasingly violent game of soccer that's being played by the drunken soldiers.

"I was open!" screams one *askari* at another.

"But you can't get anything."

"Why don't you kick me the ball?"

"I'll kick it up your ass!"

One of the grumbling *askaris* spits in the dust and walks away. The game resumes, harder and faster, charged with an aggression that wasn't present before the latest confrontation.

A British NCO cuts past the mess hall and catches Idi's eye. "*Jamba*," he says in passing.

"*Jamba*," Idi returns, as he stiffens his posture and salutes. The NCO smirks at this *dupi* who salutes as if he were a soldier.

Idi catches the smirk and knows exactly what it means. You can't play at being an *askari*. The British have a keen smell for fraudulence. They court-martial cowards and liars, sentencing offending *askaris* to lashings with a *kiboko* or, if the offence is committed in combat, to death by firing squad—as well they should.

Idi chews his bottom lip, peeling swatches of black skin off with his white teeth. He recalls his father's scorn on the only occasion he's seen the man in the past ten years. His father was employed in Bombo by the military police. When he saw Idi and his mother ambling up the road for a visit, he pointed his gun at them and shouted: "Get away, crazy lady, and take your stupid Lugbara son with you!"

That crazy lady never stops, thinks Idi, as he leans against the threshold and watches the soccer match. She kept trying to win Idi over, long after he had given up on her. He recalls the morning he finally left home, two years ago, for Kampala and his awful stint at the Imperial Hotel. That was the last time he'd seen his mother. She panicked at his abrupt departure and made him sit down in their dingy hut, demanding to know if he'd had any dreams recently.

"Mama, please," Idi said, "I have a bus that—"

"*Sssssswhit*," she interrupted, scratching her cheeks and bugging her eyes. "Tell me your dream, son of Amin."

"And why should I, Mama? It's not like you can do anything with—"

"*Sssswhit!*" shouted his mother, louder this time, and pounding the ground with her palms. "I will tell your future, don't you know? I will let you understand the danger that is coming and how you can avoid it."

He dug his mammoth heel into the dirt and sighed at his infuriating mother. She had turned into such a slob. There were rags and old bottles lying on every exposed surface, chicken bones and lanterns, other oracles strewn across the ground, and the whole hut smelled vaguely of rotted fish. Idi had to escape. After everything that had happened to them, all the disappointment brought on by her failure, how could this woman still trust in her own powers? But the quickest way out of hell, Idi knew, would be to tell a dream to the crazy old lady one last time. He could add a few tantalizing details, sure to interest and delight her, to make it easier for him to escape without a scene.

"A few nights ago," Idi began, "I dreamt I was naked and shivering in Jinja, on that old wooden dock a few miles from the Magamaga barrack—do you remember? That dock on the shore of Lake Victoria?"

"Naked on the dock," whispered his mother, her eyes shut, body swaying in a pseudo-trance.

"There was a sprawl of stars above me. And shadows of towering trees. And all the flowers there, remember? The coffee flowers and the frangipani. I was scared. There were hyenas growling nearby and I couldn't see them, but I knew they were fighting over a human carcass. I backed up on the dock, closer to the water, to get away from them, but I was trapped. And then there was this *askari* of the Fourth Battalion who appeared but wasn't alive. His sockets were soulless and hollow. And he was standing on the grassy shore, clutching in one hand the company's forest green colours, and he was wearing high socks and that strange skirt they all wear, you remember?"

"Kilt," said his mother. "Mmmm..."

"The *askari* held out another piece of kilt cloth with identical markings and said: *Take this, Idi.*"

"And did you take it?" asked his mother.

"I knew what it was and I wanted to, but for some reason I said: *No, sir, I won't take it. That is a dress and I will not wear it.*"

"Ah," said his mother, as if this information were especially important. Idi rolled his eyes at her portentous nodding.

"I turned away towards the lake, turned my back on that soldier, then saw rising from the water, distant and very far, this enormous and pure-white half man—I don't know how to describe it—"

"Half man?" asked his mother, her eyes shooting open and staring at Idi in terror. "Was he split down his middle, as if by machete? And was he very white? And with one half taken away?"

"Yes," said Idi. "That's him."

"One ear, one eye, one leg, one arm? Half a mouth with razor teeth? One testicle and half a penis?"

"That's him," said Idi. "And that horrifying man floated towards the dock—whistling *wheeee wheeeee wheeeeeee*— faster and faster, coming closer, until at last he stopped before me, just hovering there. He must've been over ten feet tall."

"*Adro yaya,*" said his mother. "It was *adro yaya* come to eat you."

"And he was transparent—"

"Of course, of course."

"And hollowed out and ghostly white—"

"He always is."

"And he slit his one eye and grinned his half teeth and

laughed in a hyena's distinctive voice. It was only then that I realized *he* was the hyena I'd heard."

"You see?" cried his mother. "You are Lugbaran! I told you!"

"I got down on my knees and prayed like Mohammed Al Ragab showed me. *Allah is great, Allah is great…*"

"And that did nothing, of course."

"No," said Idi. "*Adro yaya* stayed right there. Then I woke up."

His mother roared with laughter and fell onto her back. She convulsed in some entirely fake fit, sat up suddenly, and pounded the ground in front of him. "You," she hissed, pointing at her son and trembling her hand as if it were possessed. "Idi Amin — *ssssswhit!* — you turned your back on the *askari*. You must never do that. Never forget you are an *askari*. You will be an *Effendi*. And then *adro yaya* will not touch you; he can never touch you, not unless you turn your back on the other soldiers. You have to go and join the soldiers. Do you understand? You cannot wait or you are in grave danger from *adro yaya*. You are master of men, butcher, strangler. Your lineage is Lugbaran. You are not Kakwa like your father! *Sssswhit!* You are blessed and you are chosen."

His mother nodded to announce that she was finished, and then she laid her palms on the dirt and closed her eyes. Idi stared at his mother, thinking that this advice was not at all what he'd expected. He was amazed that she was encouraging him to return to Jinja, that she read his dream in that way. For the first time in years, Idi realized that his mother wanted him to succeed. She wished the best for her son. Suddenly, he had mixed feelings about leaving. He scratched his heel in the dirt and didn't know what to say.

Idi watches the game. Out on the field, while lunging for the ball, one of the drunken players involved in the recent altercation rams his opponent with such force that he knocks the latter over and sends him tumbling through the dust, wailing in agony. Battle lines are immediately drawn, the *askaris* bumping chests and shoving each other. At first the divisions are clear and easy and a product of the team's rosters — a skirmish over soccer — but when the racial slurs begin, the division spontaneously reorganizes along ethnic lines. The Acholis and Langos condemn the small brains and backward ways of Kakwas and related Nubians. The Kakwas, in turn, threaten their eastern Nile foes with astonishing acts of violence, such as the puncturing of their lungs with sharpened bayonets and the severing and raw consumption of their weak Acholi hearts. Idi smiles at that last threat, wondering if the soldier who uttered it is serious. You can never be certain with a Kakwa. The young *dupi* steps out of the mess hall to observe the ruckus more closely.

A punch is thrown and returned. A Kakwa hits the dirt. Amidst equal-part cheers and jeers, he rises and charges, dive-tackling his Acholi opponent. The two men grunt as their fists pound into each other's ribs. The opponents stand and separate, and then the Kakwa kicks the Acholi's shin with an audible *crack*! The Acholi howls and rolls in the dirt, but gets up on his one good leg to re-engage his enemy. Auxiliary battles erupt across the field, but it somehow remains clear that the real war will be won or lost by the original two combatants. A Kakwa and an Acholi: tribal representatives. An enterprising soldier could have sold tickets to the fight for a healthy chunk of the *askaris'* monthly pay.

Adrenalin now pulses through Idi's limbs. His breath quickens, his pupils dilate. He wants to get in the middle of the battle, no matter which side—skulls need to be cracked with his fists. He's hungry to participate in the skirmish, in an event that actually *matters*, a test of his strength and endurance. Idi wonders for a moment if he is strong enough—these *askari* have been to Burma—but then decides that it doesn't matter, he is most certainly strong enough; he has won all his fights in every town he's ever lived: Jinja, Bombo, Semuto, Kampala. He won that scrap with Akello behind Garaya mosque—the man's hand was dust inside Idi's—and there was also the time Idi beat Mukasa unconscious with a sugar stalk in Mehta's fields. Was that not *askari* material? Idi steps from foot to foot, side to side, but he can't seem to find the confidence to propel himself forward into the fight. His skin prickles. Part of him wants to turn away and head back into the mess hall.

Idi hears his mother's voice, so shrill and easy to conjure: *Never forget you are an* askari. But his mother was crazy when he last saw her. Her trance was fake, her dream interpretation fraudulent. His mother is nothing more than a shrill screeching monkey, responsible for getting him expelled from heaven, a powerless woman who can't even cure a simple lunatic like Pepsi-Cola. And yet he hears her voice: Adro yaya *will not touch you unless your turn your back on the other soldiers.*

The fighting in the dusty soccer field has grown fiercer.

It is a good thing these men have left their pangas in the barracks and brought with them only beer. Still, the glass bottles are thrown and cracked, their shards used as makeshift knives, so far with little effect. It won't be long until there's a rifle crack in the sky and a firm order to halt, and then an angry march of white officers storming onto the field to scold their black charges.

Idi's fingers touch the Yakan water in his pocket.

For some reason that he couldn't understand, this morning, as Idi was getting dressed, he picked up the small bottle of Yakan water that he always keeps on his shelf in the *dupi* barrack behind his two pairs of underwear, and stuffed it into his pants. He's never sampled it before, never even been tempted. His mother pressed that little bottle into his hands two years ago, the same morning that he left her for his new life in Kampala, just after she interpreted his dream. It was her final offering. The Yakan water was given to him a moment before he stepped onto the bus. Her bug eyes were wild and her throat punctuated each of her crazy commands with those high and purposeless whistles: "Yakan, my son, to make you fierce and frenzied — *sssssswhit! sssswhit!* — touched with the *kamiojo* herb that I myself have picked from our village, yes, and you will hear your ancestors calling when you take the Yakan to your lips and they will call you — *sssssswhit!* — and they will show you the enemy and whisper their names and it will not matter if they have guns, for when you charge against them — and charge you must, after you have drunk the Yakan! — their bullets will not puncture you, and their pangas will not slice you and even if they are Karamajong with their eight-foot-long spears, they will break and crack against your body and you instead will cut their throats, *sssswhit!* But you must be careful, Idi, and only use the Yakan for battle."

He takes the bottle out of his pocket and stares at it incredulously. Did his mother know the future? And did she somehow send him a secret message this morning from wherever she might be in the world, a message that Idi didn't even know he was receiving? He unscrews the metal cap of the recycled brandy bottle and knocks back a mouthful of its clear and potent fluid. He could use its power now. As soon as he drinks the water, Idi feels that he is invincible, that Allah and Yakan are behind him now.

He stuffs the half-empty bottle into his pocket and charges the field with long and steady strides, his lean belly unburdened by the girth that will plague his later years, his gigantic fists clenched into powerful iron balls. He ignores the secondary skirmishes and goes for the original two. They are now at midfield, locked in an angry embrace — the Kakwa's arm formed into an unloving vise around the Acholi's head, the Acholi's fingers carving parallel red chasms into the Kakwa's bare chest. Idi's forearms pierce the tight crevice between the two pulsing bodies and wrench them apart. Although there's only a half-second equilibrium, as Idi stands between the two bloodied combatants, most of the spectators register the traditional Kakwa scarring on the big *dupi*'s forehead and therefore assume that he'll turn on the Acholi with all his fury. But, to everyone's surprise, Idi hops to his left, pulls back his right fist, and releases it against the Kakwa's face, cracking the man's nose and sending him hurtling off his feet in an almost exaggerated tableau, as if the scene were an animated frame from the Superman comic that the soldiers keep passing around the barrack. The spectators freeze. Acholis giggle; several Kakwas gasp. But while the broken soldier moans in the dirt, darkening the orange dust with his copious red blood, Idi now moves against the Acholi. He grabs the back of his neck with one hand and, with the other, wraps his mammoth fingers and wide palm around the man's genitals, pressing his five fingertips into the base as if that package were a ripe fruit easily picked and tossed away. Idi is at least six inches taller than the Acholi, so he's looking down at the soldier.

"If you touch a Kakwa again," he tells the trapped Acholi, his voice loud enough for all to hear, "I will rip this little thing off you and shove it down your throat."

"Yes, yes, I understand," whispers the now-submissive Acholi, a response that garners laughter from the crowd.

The ancillary skirmishes break down and split apart; the wounded cluster in tribal groups. Although not everyone has witnessed it, the fighting soldiers have all sensed Idi's intervention and have silently and unanimously agreed to respect its result. There's no need for the approaching British officers to fire any shots into the air. Major Mitchell, commander of the Fourth Battalion, trots awkwardly onto the field, leading four junior officers. The *askaris* stand at attention. Some wobble in place, threatening to fall over, far too drunk to keep steady.

"Would someone care to tell me what you think you're

doing?" says the major, so drunk himself that he's almost slurring his words. No one dares answer. "Fighting again, are you?" The major sighs and shakes his head like a weary parent, not offended himself but determined to show some disappointment as a means of bettering his children. His eyelids are heavy and he smells of whisky; he too has been enjoying his night off. "My goodness," he continues, "what are we going to do with you men? Are we not all Ugandans, here? Are we not all servants of His Majesty the King? This is preposterous. *Askaris*, I tell you once: you are all equal and the same in service to the King's African Rifles. Sergeant, corporal, private—it doesn't matter. I will have no more of this foolishness of Kakwa versus Acholi, or Iteso versus Madi. It's entirely ridiculous! Do I have to take away your beer and *pombe*? Must I forbid you leisure time? Do we need to pay you on Monday mornings and then not let you off for a whole week? Have we indeed come to that? Listen to me, men: no more fighting amongst yourselves! Everyone understand?"

"Yes, Bwana," say the *askaris* in unison.

The pacing major halts before the wounded Kakwa. Despite his broken nose, the blood dripping off his chin onto his chest and into his stained pants, he stands at attention. The pain he must feel does not alter a muscle on his stoic face. The major snorts, swallows hard, and peers into the *askari*'s eyes for some sign of his fear or agony, but finds only the blank stare of a soldier's abnegation.

"Private, who did this to you?" asks the major.

The soldier is silent.

"Tell me, private. That's an order."

"The *dupi* did it, Bwana."

"The *what?* The *dupi?*"

"Yes, sir," says the soldier.

"Are you kidding me?"

"No, sir, I am not."

The major swivels and searches the crowd until he finds the one big man who wears long trousers and a cook's white shirt. He raises his brow in surprise at the size of this particular *dupi*. Idi is standing at attention like all the other soldiers. The major swaggers towards him and stops, regarding the man with his hands on his hips.

"What is your name?"

"Idi son of Amin, Bwana."

"Did you break this man's nose, Idi son of Amin?"

"Yes, Bwana, I did."

"Why?" asks the major, as he leans closer to Idi and blows his whisky-tinted breath up at him.

"He was fighting with the other *askari* and I was trying to stop them."

"So you broke his nose?"

"Yes, sir," says Idi.

"Do you know that it's a serious crime for you to strike an enlisted man?"

"Yes, Bwana, I know."

"Are you aware that this man fought bravely for the Crown with C Company in Burma?"

"Yes, Bwana."

"And that didn't bother you any?" presses the major. "It didn't stop you from attacking him?"

"No, Bwana," answers Idi, his calm voice unwavering.

The major regards the three narrow, parallel lines scarred into either side of Idi's temples. "Triple ones," he says, pointing. "You're Kakwa."

"Yes, Bwana," says Idi, touching the lines with pride. "I am Kakwa."

"But that man whose nose you broke is Kakwa as well."

"Yes."

The major, whose dour brow and crossed arms have made him seem until now nothing but grave and solemn, lets his mouth relax into a smile. "I see you hold yourself above this sectarian nonsense, then," he says.

"Yes, Bwana. We are all Ugandan in this barrack."

"Indeed, Amin, we are. I was thinking the very same thing."

"I did not think they should be fighting," says Idi, now gaining a bit of confidence.

"You're quite right about that."

"Yes, Bwana."

"And I see you're not afraid of battle, either," continues the major, as his drunken eyelids droop for a moment and he seems to stumble ever so slightly on his feet.

"No, sir. I am not afraid. I am a man."

"A rather big man at that."

"Yes." Idi beams. "A very big man."

"Part rhinoceros, I would even say."

Idi chuckles his jolly, shoulder-shaking laugh. "Except, Bwana," he says, "I think it's not very smart for you to say that to my face. I am known to break noses."

The nearby *askaris* can't help but chuckle at Idi's audacity.

The major raises his brow in surprise. "Why, you're quite right," he says. "I think I shall retract it."

"That is very wise of you, Bwana."

The major laughs in staccato, an innocent chuckle of real joy, a release he usually only allows himself with close friends and family. He shakes his head, obviously surprised by his own candour with this African underling.

"You're a funny chap, Amin," he says. "And you have very big hands."

"Good for fighting."

"Yes." The major smiles. "It seems you're good at that."

"I enjoy it."

"Well, then, given your considerable skill in combat, why have you remained a mere *dupi*?"

"I do not know, Bwana."

"Wouldn't you rather be a soldier in the King's African Rifles?"

"Oh yes," says Idi, smiling. "I would like that, Bwana, very much."

"Then come with me to my office and we'll enlist you anon," says the major, waving his arm towards his office and residence. "How does that sound?"

"That is my dream, Bwana. Exactly my dream."

"Good. So come."

"Yours is the office with all the butterflies on the wall stuck with pins?" asks Idi, still standing at attention.

"You know it?"

"I brought you tea and *mandazi*."

"You did?" The major squints and looks away, searching

his memory. "Oh, yes, of course. Last week. I remember. It's true, Amin, I have many specimens on my walls. I am quite partial to the butterflies in this part of the world. Especially the extraordinary variety of the *Charaxes* genus. Splendid creatures. I'm a bit of the amateur lepidopterist, I would say."

"Yes," says Idi, still smiling.

"That means a man who studies butterflies."

"Yes," agrees Idi.

"Do you like butterflies, Amin?"

"I will eat anything, Bwana."

The major, roaring with laughter, slaps his thigh and steps back. "Then I will have to be sure to command the new *dupi* to cook you some, Private Amin."

"Private?" asks Idi, his eyes widening like a child's.

"Correct. But listen, man, you do not have permission to eat the butterflies on my wall, understand?"

"Don't worry, Bwana," says Idi, as he reaches out and grabs the major's shoulder with his mammoth hand, another act of pure audacity that he somehow gets away with. "I already had my dinner."

"If you so much as try to eat my butterflies, I'll have you court-martialled!" laughs the major. "Even if you break my nose!"

"I would not do that, Bwana," says Idi, wisely removing his hand. "I love the King's African Rifles."

"Yes, I can see that you do. All right. Come on, then."

The major turns too sharply, trips over his foot, and nearly tumbles to the ground. He catches himself and stands tall, smoothing his shirt, pretending his slip never happened and that he's had nothing to drink all night. He waves Idi on. The excited young *dupi* breaks his attentive stance and moves beside the major. The silent *askaris* remain at attention, since the company's lesser officers continue to linger in the field, but they watch in astonishment as Major Mitchell and the brazen *dupi* march back to the commander's office, side by side, as if they were equals, as if there weren't an entire military hierarchy and colonial history separating one from the other.

Idi has never walked taller, never felt stronger or braver or more worthwhile than he does right now. He's approaching the timber frame of the major's office — that oak desk, the butterflies. Idi's fingerprint will stain the KAR's official enlistment paper and he will be one of them. In five minutes, he'll be an *askari*, a soldier, a comrade. *Mama*, he thinks, *where are you?* The *kamiojo* herb from the Yakan water is pulsing through his veins — his Kakwa veins, his Lugbara veins, his distinctly Ugandan veins — strengthening him and making him feel invincible. Or maybe it's just the adrenalin and the thrill of his unprecedented success. *Mother, look at me,* he thinks as he moves swiftly through the *murram* dust next to the grinning major — an actual commander of an entire KAR battalion. *I am a big man now.* Yes, a genuine big man, a *'ba wara* of more value and worth than that one who called him a *thing* back in his mother's miserable West Nile village. He is a big man who can break the nose of a real *askari* with a single punch, who can reduce an Acholi brute to a whimpering woman by grasping his balls and spitting a sharp phrase in his face. Has there ever been a more innate soldier in the history of the entire world? Idi knows that not only can he join these men in their barrack, sit with them at company mess, drink their tea with his legs crossed like a European while they tell their tales of Burma, but he can also participate in their next conflict, wherever it might be, and with a little luck could someday pace before them in the field as they stand at attention as their superior, their *Effendi*. Someday he will lecture these *askaris* on what it means to be a soldier, on how they're supposed to do it, on how to punch, how to shoot, and how to kill. Why not? Doesn't he know the facts as well as anyone? Is he not walking beside the major like the Englishman's equal? Can't he lead inspection and parades and tell them what's right and wrong and good? They will call him Bwana Amin. Yes, he will be an *Effendi*. Dreams do not lie. His mother does not lie. And could he rise higher, even to unprecedented heights? Could he someday be a major? Idi suppresses a smile as he opens the commander's door and lets him proceed before him. And if these damn *askaris* don't like a Kakwa-Lugbara for their supreme commander, Idi will find some thick white cream to spread on his face and hands, and then they'll know he's to be taken seriously, that smart people do not mess around with Idi son of Amin. Idi decides that's exactly what he'll do, as he steps into the major's office to seal his fate. He will coat himself in leadership. If they make a black cream for officers, then somewhere back in England they must also make a white one for that same purpose.

A PLAYTHING FOR THE KING'S SUPERFLUOUS WIVES

The city, stuffed with greenery, gently steams. If wrapped in bamboo leaves, these buildings would soften like gluten and stick to each other. Saloth Sâr has no idea that someday he will devour them.

The boy's entire body pulses with desire. He is standing on the street corner before the École Miche, savouring the wet heat trapped inside his thin shirt. The back of his neck is sticky. A slow-moving rickshaw rounds the bend, drawn by a half-naked Vietnamese driver and carrying a mustachioed gentleman in a cream-coloured suit, obviously in no hurry to reach his destination. The gentleman stares at the pink-cheeked and newly virile Sâr, whose wide face has flowered into a smile. A photograph of the smooth-skinned fourteen-year-old boy could grace the cover of any travel brochure for Indochina. The gentleman sucks his cigarette and tips his hat in greeting, but Sâr doesn't acknowledge him. Instead, he watches the rickshaw bump north towards the colonial villas in Wat Phnom. Arrogant Frenchmen are of no concern.

School has ended for the day. His friends, like vapour, have reabsorbed into the humid air. Sâr has declined their persistent invitations to visit the market en masse, where the giddy teenagers will play at boldness, trying to hide their Cambodian features and pass for Chinese, snacking on fried crickets and unripe bananas, goading each other into haggling with the Vietnamese merchants. On most days the central market is Sâr's favourite destination, still a novelty with its art deco dome, peculiar chevron-shaped windows, and four corridors extending outward at slight angles like a heron's foot. He loves the diesel fumes, the scent of coriander and lemony rice-paddy herbs, the magical wristwatches on display between bits of junk on the pavement, and the overheard phrases of incomprehensible Mandarin spoken by the foreign merchants. Still, he can't go today. The heat is too intense, too distracting.

He is picturing Chanlina, a palace dancer, one of the King's lesser wives. He sees her full-moon face, popping lips, and dark, coy eyes. He can't stop thinking about her, although he's only met her once, when there were other people around. Sâr's sister Roeung, who works in the palace, introduced him to the dancers. She told Sâr that he could visit any time, but he's not sure if he should take her at her word. Roeung never specified if those visits had to be *with* her. He wonders if the dancers would mind him dropping by, just a friendly visit to say hello.

As he starts towards the palace, Sâr realizes that he's made his decision, and his stomach tenses. The combination of heat and anxiety makes his legs feel weak. Sâr walks on, taking cover from the sun beneath the inconsequential shade of high palm trees and the thicker foliage of the odd teak or rosewood. Even so, the heat is too much to bear. The sky is blue and nearly cloudless, as it's been for months. When the New Year arrives next week, greeted with festivities at the palace, and familial gatherings and games in the park at Wat Phnom, it will usher in the seasonal procession of cooling monsoon clouds. Such relief seems improbable today.

It's a stupid plan, destined for failure. He'll never get to see them. The guard will never let him venture into the compound without Roeung, which is for the best, Sâr thinks, as he passes the surging *naga* heads and French balustrades on the National Museum. He has no business among King Monivong's lesser wives, distracting them from their sacred duties. The guard will save him great embarrassment if he refuses to let him pass.

He passes coolies repairing the sidewalk and weaves through a group of monks dressed in saffron robes with white parasols. He steps over a pile of fish bones and fruit rinds someone has dumped in the street. Chanlina and her roommates will be grumpy and exhausted from practising the particular hand gestures needed for the upcoming New Year's dances. Sâr dodges an ox cart laden with orange flowers, green mangoes, and rotting jackfruit. He reaches out and scrapes his fingers along the plaster-grit of the mustard-coloured wall surrounding the royal compound, doubting that the dancers will want to see him even if the guard lets him into their compound. He wishes he could will himself to turn around.

But now it's too late, Sâr knows, as he stands before the sentry box beneath the gate's white spires and ornate festoons, a rucksack over his shoulder, one of his wooden clogs tapping the concrete in anticipation. He watches a lacquered black Renault with curtains over its windows roll down the wide avenue. At last a Khmer guard emerges from the sentry box, wearing a hard white helmet and epaulettes reminiscent of the French Foreign Legion. The guard recognizes Sâr and smiles at him. Sâr presses his hands together before his lips and bows the respectful greeting appropriate for his elders.

"Is Roeung expecting you?" asks the guard.

"Yes," answers the lad, his voice a near whisper.

It's a good-enough answer for the guard, who slides open the copper gate and, with a short nod, lets the boy enter the forbidden palace compound without the accompaniment of his powerful sister. Sâr grows dizzy as he passes through the gate, his heart pounding so hard he can feel it in his neck.

He skims along a path beside the low wall enclosing the Silver Pagoda. He quickens his gait into a trot as he crosses the manicured garden and lengthy driveway before the Throne Hall. He's quietly whispering a sutra he learned during his year-long immersion at the Theravada monastery, five years earlier. In the past, the memorized chants soothed him when he'd grown too excited or impassioned, but today he can't find a rhythm strong enough to relax him. Sâr needs a plan, he realizes, as he tucks his shirt into his baggy pants. He should say hello and then leave, appreciating the dancers' responsibilities and not imposing himself. Yes, he will be brief and polite, and the dancers will see that he's kind, and be happy that he hasn't overstayed his welcome. Still, his cheeks redden, as if the four serene faces of Brahma were judging him from their mounts on the Throne Hall's tallest spire.

The path splits in three directions outside the King's residence. Sâr is about to head south at the crossroad — towards the cramped enclosure housing royal dancers, serving girls, and other wives — when the Khemarain Palace's main gate fans open to reveal Princess Kossamak in quick departure from an audience with her father, King Monivong. Wrapped in a shimmering green and gold *sampot* and painted with Parisian cosmetics, the future Queen Mother is a living doll of brocade, jewellery, and cascading hair. She draws behind her a wake of aides: native servants, enormous guards, tailored Frenchmen. Sâr stops so suddenly that he nearly trips over his feet. He drops his rucksack, collapses to his knees, and prostrates himself, his nose pressing against the hot pavement. It won't be long, he knows, before he's accosted by these guards, questioned and roughed up a bit, certainly thrown out of the palace compound. But Kossamak and retinue charge past Sâr's fallen body without giving him a glance. He raises his eyes in disbelief, just in time to witness Kossamak's skittish sixteen-year-old son in military dress struggling to keep pace with his bustling mother.

Sâr rises to his knees, wondering why the guards have again left him unattended in the compound, why someone won't prevent him from courting disaster. He detects the lingering floral scent of *Calotropis* from the Khmer princess's European perfume, and wishes it were stronger. Sâr rubs his tongue along the inside of his teeth as he stands, brushes off his pants, and hurries along his original route.

The dancers' compound lies on the far side of a sturdy brick wall, entered by means of an unadorned gate. All of the King's secondary wives, including Sâr's sister, live in this austere zone. There are no manicured lawns over here, no topiary trees or gilded fountains, no golden roofs or tapered spires. Dirt pathways weave between the two dozen unremarkable wood-and-brick homes, most of them no taller than a single storey. Windows are scarce and small. A few gardens contain mango and mulberry trees, but otherwise there's a noticeable dearth of greenery. A garbage pile rots near the northern compound wall.

The front door of Chanlina's house swells and retracts before Saloth Sâr as he licks his lips and tries to regulate the pace of his breathing. He knocks. Inside there's shuffling, a baby's wail, the gentle banging of pots.

"Get that, will you?" He recognizes Kiri's voice, one of Chanlina's roommates.

The door quivers, unstable, more liquid than solid.

"Veata!"

There's further shuffling inside, and the low gurgle of boiling water. Kiri is singing a high-pitched phrase extracted from the chorus of a popular Reamker dance. They don't want to answer, Sâr realizes, as he shifts his weight and groans. If he doesn't run away this instant, he will embarrass himself.

"Veata, answer the door!"

The baby's wailing grows louder as someone approaches from inside. At last the front door opens, revealing a woman with unkempt hair and a noticeable sag beneath her eyes, holding a scruffy baby. Sâr clutches tight to his rucksack and lowers his head. A musky burnt-leaf odour wafts from the enclosure.

"*L-Lok,*" he begins.

"Well," says Veata, cutting him off. "It's Roeung's little brother."

The wailing, naked baby wraps his plump legs around Veata's hips, clutching her shirt with one hand and a large wooden spoon with the other. As he fixes his gaze on Sâr, his crying stops and he stuffs a portion of the spoon into his open mouth.

"*Lok Srey,*" Sâr greets, pressing his hands together and bowing with composure.

The spoon falls from the child's mouth, and he giggles.

"*Lok,*" says Veata, regarding her son's change of mood. "I think Nhean likes you."

"I am very sorry to bother you," says Sâr. "I was visiting my sister and...and thought only that I'd stop by for a minute and...I don't know...say hello."

"Hello," says Veata, grinning.

Sâr looks down at his clogs. "I hope I'm not bothering you."

"What's your name again?"

"I'm Saloth Sâr," he answers, his gaze still averted. "I'm Roeung's younger brother, Saloth Sâr."

The baby on Veata's hip grins, tenses his body, and releases a high shriek of joy.

"I know who you are," says Veata, rubbing the baby's back. "Just not your name. Come in before anyone sees you."

"Who's there?" asks Kiri from the small kitchenette, as she shovels rice from a steaming pot into a bamboo bowl.

The young woman puts down the pot and shuffles over to see. "Is that Roeung's little brother?"

Sâr offers Kiri a second deep bow. "*Lok Srey*," he says.

"Don't stand there. Come inside and close the door."

Veata and Kiri giggle and step back to let the thin teenager enter their tiny home. Although the curtains have been pulled to counteract the sun's strength, the brick walls have trapped the day's warmth like an oven, so that now, late in the afternoon, with dinner still simmering, the heat is at its worst. Both women's faces are flushed. Besides an indoor sink and gas stove, there's a circle of mats in the middle of the floor where the women can eat their meals and relax. In the back of the room, raised a step, is a compact sleeping section separated by traditional partitions of dried palm. There are two high windows on the southern wall, both missing glass, but with screens for the bugs and drawn curtains, each no bigger than a square foot.

"Take off your shoes," says Kiri.

Sâr slips off his clogs and lays his rucksack on the floor. Veata places her now-squirming baby onto the ground. Nhean crawls onto a mat, sits tall, and munches his spoon, happy to study the enchanting face of young Sâr. Veata straightens her *sampot* and rubs her hands through her long hair, trying to tame the tangles. She's a high-cheeked, handsome woman, bustier than her friend, no older than twenty-one.

"We're having rice and *prahoc*," says Kiri, referring to the traditional fermented fish paste. "Do you want to join us?"

"No, no," whispers Sâr. "I don't want to impose."

Veata laughs at the boy's politeness.

"You're not an imposition," says Kiri with a grin.

"I should've never come," says Sâr. "I owe you my sincerest apology."

"You don't want to join us for dinner?"

The boy's face lengthens and furrows, and again he stares at the floor. "Of course, I'd—I'd...but I should never, and it's—"

"You'll join us for dinner," says Kiri, turning away to settle the matter.

Kiri returns to the stove, where she finishes transferring the rice and dressing it with fish paste. Sâr steals a glance at her smooth legs in motion, her calves taut and strong from hours of gruelling rehearsal. Kiri's younger than Veata by a couple of years. She wears an identical dark *sampot*, a golden necklace, and a tight white shirt with many small buttons up the front—the standard practice costume worn by all royal dancers.

"Chanlina," calls Kiri. "Do you remember Roeung's younger brother?"

Sâr watches the palm partitions in the back of the house for any sign of Chanlina, but there's no movement on that side of the room.

"How's school, little boy?" Veata teases.

"School is good."

"Roeung said you go to the Catholic school."

"Yes," says Sâr. "The École Miche."

"That's strange," Veata giggles. It seems she's letting her hair flop forward against her cheeks on purpose. "What do you do all day in Catholic school? Pray?"

"Yes," says Sâr. "That's all they have us do. Pray and pray and pray. But their prayers are not like our sutras. They don't focus your mind or anything else."

"Why do you go there?" asks Veata. "Isn't it very expensive?"

"I don't know," he says, shrugging.

"Did your parents become French and Catholic?" she giggles.

"No," says Sâr, growing embarrassed by the line of questioning.

"That's where all the rich kids go to school," calls Kiri from the kitchenette.

"Tell me a prayer," says Veata. "I want to hear one."

Nhean shrieks in apparent agreement.

"Um," says Sâr.

"Go on," commands Veata. "Teach Nhean a prayer."

The authority in Veata's voice relaxes Sâr, making him feel as if he has no choice but to comply. "All right," he says. He kneels and looks into the baby's wide brown eyes, and then chants: "*Our father, who art in heaven, hallowed be thy name.*"

Veata and Kiri laugh, their giggles girlish and playful. "Art in heaven?" one of them repeats.

"*Thy kingdom come, they will be done, on earth as it is in heaven. Give us this day our daily bread.*"

Nhean lowers his wooden spoon while his mother and Kiri tremble in paroxysms of laughter. As Sâr speaks these incomprehensible words before him, the child struggles to comprehend, sensing a swirl of excitement and mischief rising in the room. He can only try to join it by widening his bursting face and shrieking in a hearty combination of frustration and joy.

"*And forgive us our trespasses as we forgive —*"

"You're wrong," interrupts Kiri. "Nhean's father is not in heaven."

"*Art* not in heaven," corrects Veata.

"His father's over at Khemarain," says Kiri. "Probably halfway through the act of fathering another."

Sâr stands and blushes.

"He's the lucky one, isn't he?" Veata asks.

"I don't know," says Sâr.

"He *is* the lucky one."

"Well," says Sâr. "He's the King."

"Do you want to be lucky like the King?"

Veata is approaching him, a slow and rhythmic walk, her eyes intense, lips pressed together.

Sâr opens his mouth but can't bring himself to reply. He's hypnotized by the soft pulsing of her steps.

"I asked you a question, little boy."

"I don't know," says Sâr. "I'm not the King."

"Don't you want to be lucky? Didn't you come here to be lucky?"

"I don't know," says Sâr, backing up a step. "I just came to say hello."

"Hello," says Kiri, the corners of her lips rising. "Lucky boy." Now she's approaching Sâr too, staring at him with a mischievous grin.

"What's your name again?" asks another soft voice. "Roeung's little brother?"

Chanlina has pushed aside her palm partition and stepped down into the main section of the room. Sâr gazes at her, wide-eyed, for she is as beautiful as he remembers. Her lips are so plump and full. With her hair tangled and her pupils constricted, wearing the standard white dancer's blouse — with six or seven buttons undone — and a pair of skimpy underwear, she is far more languid than the others. Chanlina's feline padding as she moves towards Sâr has a dancer's natural grace, but it's undermined by the way she scratches a patch of inflamed skin on her ruddy upper thigh. Her colouring is dark. She looks no older than eighteen. On the steel-framed bed behind the partition, Sâr notices Chanlina's discarded *sampot* and a small wooden pipe.

"Sâr," he whispers to her. "My name is Saloth Sâr."

He's been cornered by Kiri and Veata, and now the grinning third dancer slips between them into their tight semicircle. Chanlina rests a hand on Kiri's shoulder and lets her fingers drape over her roommate's collarbone. "Saloth Sâr," she repeats, almost singing his name. Her long and bare legs electrify the room, although Sâr doesn't dare to look at them.

"That is my…yes…"

"Are you hungry?" Kiri asks, prompting Chanlina to giggle.

"Yes," whispers Sâr.

Nhean drops the spoon from his mouth. His enormous cheeks sag into saddlebags, the envy of any ibis or other fish-hoarding bird, and his eyebrows rise in curiosity as he glances from Sâr to Chanlina and then back to his mother. The adults seem so grave and solemn and possessed, but the boy does not understand the magic transpiring in the room. Nhean's groan this time is extended, ambiguous, and low.

"I think the baby needs his nap," says Veata. She scoops Nhean off his mat and hurries him into his bamboo crib, hidden behind one of the palm partitions. He lets out a holler as his mother lays him down. "Shhh," says Veata. "Sleep!"

She pulls the partition forward so Nhean won't see them and rejoins the others. The child's groans of complaint transform into shrieks of real protest.

"Never mind him. He'll sleep soon."

Chanlina leans forward to touch a button on Sâr's shirt. Her hair is saturated with the musky odour he detected upon entry. She reaches down and clasps Sâr's trembling hand. Her fingers are warm—he feels his hand could melt in her grasp. All up his arm, the muscles relax.

"Are we eating?" he whispers.

"Later," says Chanlina.

As Chanlina holds his hand—her grin wide, her eyelids drooping—Veata moves to unclasp the buttons on his shirt, pulling at the fabric. Kiri drops to her knees, unfastens Sâr's belt, and shimmies his pants down his skinny legs. In a fit of panic, Sâr reaches down with his free hand to pull his pants up, but Kiri halts him with no more than a simple touch to his forearm. Veata pulls open his shirt and rubs Sâr's sticky, hairless chest with the palms of both hands. Her touch is staggering, somehow soothing and igniting Sâr's skin all at once. Now Kiri finds the soft skin on the underside of his testicles and strokes it gently with the tips of two fingers. Sâr can't believe the sensation; nothing in his life has ever felt like this. He does not have the words to describe or the thoughts to comprehend it. He does not look at either Veata or Kiri. His gaze is fixed on Chanlina who, standing before him, doing nothing other than clutching his trembling fingers in her own steady grip, remains by far the most erotic of the three. Sâr closes his eyes and moans, and then blushes at the realization that he's made a sound. Chanlina releases his hand, brushes the hair away from her sleepy face, and reaches down to palm his penis. She begins to stroke him off with long, slow movements. It is another unexpected sensation, even better than the first, adding intensity and drive to his pleasure. Chanlina steps close to the boy, letting her sleek thigh touch his, gently laying her other hand on his forearm. When she plants a tiny kiss onto his mouth, Sâr tastes smoke on her lips.

The others move to help her, planting feather-light kisses on his soft belly, letting a stray finger reach up to tickle the protrusion of his nipple. He's swimming in a sea of hands that paw and rub, clasp and squeeze. Nhean's screams flatten, as soft and diffuse as if they were filtered through water. If that child is still in the room, he must inhabit another dimension. A wayward thought crosses Sâr's mind: *so much better than a sutra.* The pulsing of his body, the incessant throbbing that's plagued him all afternoon, shortening his breath, running his heart ragged, blurring his ability to perceive the division between things liquid and things solid, has now concentrated acutely in a single clutched, stroked, and teased part of his body. For a second he thinks he's going to lose control of his bladder and piss everywhere. He doesn't even care. He bites down hard and moans, touches the silky knots forming in Chanlina's hair. Somewhere through the room's thin haze of opium smoke he detects a wall of brick, an old gas stove, a faded gingham curtain, a steaming pot of rice. That mundane world: distant, forgotten, and irrelevant. Someone's hand squeezes his buttocks. Another's nails scratch ticklish roads into the skin of his leg. His testicles are gripped and released, and then gripped again. The crown of his penis is rubbed, possibly licked. He's pressing his eyes closed; he can't bear to watch. He can't believe this is happening. This couldn't possibly be real. Too much awe, too much energy, too much heat in one place; it's like staring straight into the Cambodian sun.

Someone giggles and another moans. Someone whispers his name. All this skin, so much silkiness around him, rubbing and enveloping him, all these muscles toned and firm from a decade or more of precise training. With his eyes shut, Sâr forgets the women's names, forgets the details of their faces, and sinks into a pool of bliss. When he rouses long enough to let himself glance downward, he's rewarded with the sight of Chanlina's conical breast through the unbuttoned top of her blouse. The image fires his desire in new and unexpected ways. He feels a surge, a tensing, a longing that breaks boundaries. He suddenly needs them to stop. He doesn't know what's happening to him; he's sure he's going to piss himself. Sâr's moan is almost a plea. The women, who don't seem at all confused, concentrate on stroking him off—stronger now, quicker, using longer gestures—and the pleasure's too great for him to bear. "Stop," he whispers, but too softly for it to matter. A white-hot firecracker explodes in his head, blinding him from inside, bouncing light off his skull and shooting down his neck and surging into his limbs and at last escaping in hard contractions that are met in the outside world with a giggle, a gasp, and a groan.

Sâr's whimper of pleasure silences Nhean in his crib.

For the first time in hours, the young teenager sucks in a full inhalation. Every cell in his body feels oxygenated at last. His scrawny chest heaves. Sweat trickles down his brow, framing his face and wetting his cheeks. He blinks and focuses his gaze, observing the young women around him. Kiri has risen, and now leads her gooey hand over to the sink as if it were a wounded animal that she's picked off the road. Chanlina rests on her heels and giggles, her fingers sticky and glued together in a viscous web, and holding in the cup of her palm a teaspoon's worth of semen. Veata is sitting on the floor, leaning her weight onto her palms, hyperextending her elbows, and smiling at Sâr.

"Roeung's brother," she says. "What a nice boy."

"I'm sorry," says Sâr through his long gasps. "I think I...think—"

Veata laughs and shakes her head. Over by the sink, a chuckling Kiri waves a soapy hand and calls out: "Yes, you did!"

They're laughing. This seems to be what they wanted, what they'd expected of him. It's not a surprise to them.

Sâr turns and grins at Chanlina. Now that he can breathe, he suddenly wants more than anything to speak with her. He wonders if there might be some intimacy, a special connection between them, different from what he feels with Veata and Kiri. But Sâr's favourite dancer has unexpectedly turned sombre. Without matching his smile, she stands and goes to the sink, using her hip to nudge Kiri aside. Chanlina cleans the semen off her hand. It seems so perfunctory. Her cheeks are red and her breathing's clipped. She needs something—but what? Sâr knows she's unhappy and unsatisfied, but he's incapable of detecting the signs of her own longing.

"Chanlina," he says—the beginning of a question he can't complete.

She doesn't try to draw him out. Chanlina returns to her bed, picks up her pipe, and pulls the palm partition, but not quite far enough to hide herself completely. Sâr's cheeks droop. She strikes a match, lights the pipe, and inhales. Chanlina leans back on her *sampot*, holding her breath for five seconds and then—as the opiates relax her muscles and frost her gaze—expelling the dark smoke. It forms an ominous cloud in the air before thinning and scattering. The room's musky odour strengthens.

Sâr snatches his pants and pulls them up. He's so quick to button his shirt that he fumbles several times before closing it askew. Chanlina inhales a second drag, lies back on her bed, and stares at the ceiling with blank eyes. It doesn't look as if she has any intention of moving.

Now Nhean's crying resumes and Veata hurries to the boy, withdrawing him from his crib and plopping him down on the floor. The baby stops crying, gapes at Sâr, and crawls to his favourite spoon, which he resumes munching as if no time has passed at all. In the kitchenette, Kiri stirs their meal, fluffing the rice to make it look more appetizing. She lays the bowl in the middle of the floor and takes a seat on one of the woven mats.

"Come," she says, nodding at Sâr. "Eat."

Eating is the last thing Sâr wants to do.

"Come on," Kiri commands with some irritation.

He moves to sit beside her.

Both Veata and Sâr scoop glutinous clumps of rice into their hands, and Nhean, smelling the *prahoc*, moans with hunger. Veata grabs the baby, lays him sprawled on her lap, and lets him suck on her breast.

No one mentions Chanlina or asks if she wants to eat. Sâr steals furtive glances at the almost closed partition and the enticing sliver of flesh that remains exposed. The girl is prostrate and submerged in some sort of dark reverie, her eyes open but empty, her mouth parted with a bit of drool pooling at the corner. He wants to say something but doesn't know what. Between bites, Kiri half-heartedly sings the musical phrase that Sâr heard earlier through the door.

Without his furious charge of desire, the dancers' small home now feels dingy and overheated, stifling and depressing. He doesn't want to be here. He grabs some rice and takes a bite, but his eating lacks joy. The young women have abandoned their perfect postures and atrophied into older figures, more slumping grandmothers than strong girls. Veata rubs her lower back and sighs. The diffuse opium smoke irritates Sâr's eyes. He rubs them dry with the corner of his shirt. He feels like a captive in this stuffy room. When the silence grows too awkward, Sâr forces himself to speak.

"I suppose," he says, "you've been practising dances all day?"

"All week," replies Kiri.

"*All life*," corrects Veata.

Kiri chuckles bitterly. "Yes, we practise all life."

"Is it especially difficult to prepare for the New Year's dances?" Sâr asks the question quietly, his eyes downcast, head barely raised, knowing full well the answer.

"Of course," says Veata. "Very gruelling. Your sister's hard on us."

Sâr's cheeks flush with shame.

"But the New Year is not half as difficult as the Water Festival," says Kiri.

Veata groans in remembrance of last November's dances.

"I'm never more tired than I am each year after the Water Festival," Kiri adds. "We sleep for a month after that. I mean, when we're not practising."

Nhean chokes, coughing sharply, spraying droplets of breast milk all over his startled mother.

"Aayh, Nhean!" Veata cries as she pulls him away. Kiri chuckles while the boy wails in his mother's arms. Veata brushes off the milk, pats the baby on his back until he's calm, and lets him return to his meal.

"That sounds very difficult," says Sâr. Each word sprouts thorns that torture his throat. His politeness feels grotesque—a trite and obvious dressing that can't cover the crude purpose of his visit, the nakedness of his now-fulfilled desire. Sâr's delicate hand reaches for another ball of rice in a gesture that feels forced, stupid, and obscene. He imagines a machete falling, slicing the hand off his arm, the severed limb bleeding and pulsing beside the rice — he believes he deserves this fate. He scoops a ball of moist rice with his fingers and brings it to his lips, forcing himself to chew and swallow. The rice is thick and flavourless, a mass of glutinous paste, more like mortar in his mouth than food. The hunger he's identified as his own feels remote and obscure. Nhean's slurping makes him want to vomit. He has to get out of here.

Saloth Sâr. He can still recall Chanlina's smooth voice, singing his name.

There's a hard rapping on the door. As the women widen their eyes and turn, Sâr's body surges with adrenalin. Outside, Roeung calls to the dancers.

"Girls! Open up!"

Chanlina rouses from her drugged stupor and jolts up. "What?" she cries, blinking fast, trying to force her eyes to function.

"Evening practice in ten minutes. Have you eaten? Open the door!"

"The fan," says Chanlina in a panic. "And the curtains!"

"One moment, *Lok Srey* Roeung," calls Kiri as she stands. She runs to the window, opens the curtains, tries to fan some fresh air into the room with her hands. "We're just cleaning up."

Sâr stands, checks his shirt, and notices that it's fastened incorrectly. He frantically re-buttons it while trying to slip on his clogs. Chanlina has managed to stand. She tucks her pipe beneath her pillow and works to tie her *sampot.* She represses all signs of intoxication; her motions are precise and deliberate. Veata fans the air with her hand as she moves towards the door.

"We're just finishing dinner, *Lok Srey*," she calls.

"Let me in," commands Roeung, her voice lacking menace.

Veata checks to make sure Chanlina's dressed and Sâr's prepared before she opens the door. Roeung steps inside and immediately scowls at the opiate smoke she can smell in the air. She opens her mouth to speak, but as soon as she sees her younger brother standing in the centre of the room, her expression freezes in blank astonishment.

"What are you doing here?"

"He just came by to say hello for a minute after school," answers Kiri.

Sâr shifts his rucksack to the opposing shoulder and forces a smile for his sister.

"He said he was looking for you," adds Veata, "and that you must've been with the King. We gave him some dinner. He played with Nhean. He's very good with babies!"

Nhean, on the floor, blinks at the intruder.

"You should be home for dinner," Roeung scolds Sâr. "Your brother expects you right now. He will be worried."

"Yes," says Sâr. "I was just going."

"Well, go on, then. Go!" Roeung turns away from her brother and fans the air, giving Chanlina a hard stare. The dancer, standing motionless by her palm partition, regards the floor in a failed attempt at appearing innocent. "I hope you're ready, Chanlina," warns Roeung. "Lady Meak expects a full practice this evening."

"I am ready," whispers Chanlina. "I am always ready, *Lok Srey* Roeung."

"I am going," whispers Sâr as he stands by the door. "Goodbye, and thank you." He stands tall, presses his hands before his lips, and bows so deeply to the women that they can't help but giggle. Such reverence is more fit for the King than for his lesser wives, this group of common dancers.

"Bye," says Veata, offering the boy a smile and a little bow.

Sâr scurries out of the house and quietly closes the door behind him. Although the sun is nearing the horizon, it still beats down on him with vengeance from its extreme angle. He squints, sighs, and wipes his sweaty brow. To stand in this open-air compound, despite the garbage pile by the wall, the grungy stone, and the weedy path — it is a real liberation. The expansive Cambodian sky is a welcome contrast to the compact darkness of the dancers' home. Sâr hurries away, hoping he won't encounter anyone else he knows.

He marches towards the nearest exit from the royal grounds, which is through the eastern wall facing the river. His eye muscles twitch and his jaw tightens, but Sâr fails to relate his tension to the fact that he's passing the royal monastery, Wat Botum Vaddei. He reaches the exit and knocks on the copper gate. The sentry, rooted in a stance of gruff suspicion, leans out of his guardhouse and asks: "Who's there?" Dancers, of course, are not allowed to depart. When Sâr bows in respect, the sentry abandons his aggressive posture and smiles. It's only Roeung's little brother. He has seen him before and, like everyone, he enjoys the boy's wide smile. The sentry opens the gate and lets Sâr exit without comment.

Now, out in the street, Sâr thinks about Wat Botum Vaddei. The pagoda and its sealed compound loom ominously behind him. He imagines its pointed, bluish-grey stupas toppling over and crushing him, a gruesome death beneath the heap of ruined beams, shattered and splintered *naga* heads. As if to escape the improbable threat, he jogs across the wide avenue and enters the expansive manicured park that hugs the riverbank.

The change of location doesn't clear his thoughts. The royal monastery continues to irk him, fuelling his shame, funnelling Sâr into a state of limb-weakening emptiness that can only be described as despair. Although he hated his long year as a novice in Wat Botum Vaddei — but what nine-year-old boy would enjoy the rigid prescriptions and denials of monastic life? — that time now stands in stark contrast to his present, decadent existence. The bitter memory of the monastery's privations and restrictions has faded with time, leaving Sâr with a distilled recollection of that period in his life: the pride warming him each evening as he lay on his thin pallet, staring at the ceiling's wooden slats, weary from hours of prayer and study, from washing and sifting rice, from sweeping courtyards covered in banyan leaves, from countless mundane but purifying tasks that were executed in an air of enforced silence, that were always done with great awareness of right conduct, right diligence, right motivation. His muscles ached each night inside his red novice's robes. Goodness, wholesomeness, and purity filled young Saloth Sâr all throughout that year. Yes, there was the constant threat of beatings — and the pain of actual abuse — but that was nothing compared with this present torture, this pointless life of filth and shame.

Sâr walks towards the water, conscious of his body, all too aware of how his muscles move his legs. All around him the grass is mowed, the paths paved, the weeds pruned. Tall trees, mostly palms, spot the terrain. This pseudo-French park, extracted from a south Asian jungle and groomed into compliance, is located on a protruding elbow of land that marks the merging point of the powerful Mekong and Tonle Sap rivers. The wide blue sky above is fermenting into a longer spectrum of orange, yellow, red. The sun moves to kiss the horizon. An almost imperceptible breeze dries his skin. A distant *kahark* escapes from the throat of a grey heron riding the air currents above the river. Each step on the downy lawn forgives the trespass of his foot. Sâr wants none of this worldly stimulation. This body, this fleshy thing that pulses incessantly, that eats and ejaculates, imprisons with its various hungers, is not a welcome home. At this moment he would very much like to do away with it.

He finds a wrought iron bench beneath an ornate lamp-post and takes a seat. The water passing before him is calm, almost still, and the far shore is imperceptible in the distance. *The Chaktomuk*, he thinks. Sacred Four Faces: the confluence of Cambodia's two powerful rivers, merging, mixing, and splitting again into two separate entities.

He knows it was not right to visit them like that, to arrive at their small home fuelled by such desire. It was not proper at all. He must resist thinking about their bodies. He must not submit. But even now the boy can't stop the flood of images, can't stop his recalled bliss—the unimaginable pleasure, the way they stroked and pawed him, those gentle kisses delivered with smoky lips, the long scratches from hard fingernails. All of it makes his ears grow hot. His stomach churns rice and *prahoc*. Digestion seems a base and loathsome thing. An image of Chanlina, glassy eyed and recumbent, too intoxicated to get herself dressed, steals across his mind, and he clenches his teeth in an effort to make it go away. "You must not visit those dancers again," he says out loud. "You must begin to foster a pure consciousness." If he does not think in a pure way, how can his behaviour be pure?

Now, closing his eyes, sealing them tight, Sâr tries to recall the sutras he memorized years ago, the ones he repeated by rote every day for the holy purpose of erasing himself and suppressing his desire, but the only thing he can manage to recall is the thrilling swelter of the dancers' dingy room, the hot flush in their cheeks, the moisture of their brows, Chanlina's smooth skin and tapered breasts, and the way her palm enveloped and cupped and stroked his—

No!

He knows sutras of great austerity. He knows antidotes to desire. His Pali, however rusty, allows phrases of extreme admonition to slip from his lips. He will loop them, repeat them, ad infinitum, until his need is gone, his desire abolished, his body lost in rhythm. "*The eye is to be abandoned,*" he chants in a steady and monotonous tone. "*Forms are to be abandoned.*

The ear is to be abandoned. Sounds are to be abandoned.
The nose is to be abandoned. Aromas are to be abandoned.

The tongue is to be abandoned. Flavours are to be abandoned. The body is to be abandoned. Tactile sensations are to be abandoned.

The eye is to be —"

"*Sra-thnot?*" interrupts a craggy voice.

Sâr twitches with surprise and opens his eyes to an old, twiggy Vietnamese man in wide trousers and a full-body robe standing too close to his bench. His turtle-like face is withered and toothless. From a long bamboo yoke draped over his narrow shoulders dangle a dozen or so hollowed sections of cut bamboo, fastened with twine. They bump and bong against each other like a pagoda's wind chimes.

"You want some *sra-thnot?*" the Vietnamese man repeats. His broken voice, husky and soft, implies a larynx riddled with cancer, as well as a more rudimentary geriatric decay. "It's very good *areng* palm. The best and strongest. Try it. I think you want to."

The man has already tilted his yoke and started to untie a hollowed bamboo section filled with rich palm wine.

"No," says Sâr, "please."

The vendor holds a pungent cup of syrupy liquid beneath Sâr's nose. "Here," he says. "Take it. Very strong. You like to be drunk? Only one piastre."

Sâr bows his head in deference. "Thank you," he whispers, "but I don't want any wine. Thank you very much, but I will say no."

"It makes you laughing drunk. You don't like that?" The man's tone has grown more aggressive. "Why not? You've never had it maybe? It makes you laugh. You understand?

It's fun. It's very funny. If you'd had it before, you wouldn't refuse."

Sâr bows his head several times, exaggerating his respect. "That's very kind, thank you. But no, I am sure. I must say no."

The vendor grunts and retracts the wine. He takes a moment to study this mysteriously sombre boy, assessing whether or not he can push him into a sale. Conceding defeat, he ties the bamboo section back onto the pole with the twine. When the yoke is balanced on the vendor's shoulders, he digs his hand into a hidden pocket and extracts a small packet of tobacco wrapped in banana leaf. He peels it open, takes a pinch, and packs it into his cheek. As he regards the grand scope of the riverscape before them, he gnaws at the raw leaf with his toothless gums.

The sun is half hidden behind a strip of foliage on the far shore. A jumping fish breaks through the surface and then cuts back into the deep. An egret flaps its wide wings and floats across the sky. Smooth water reflects the increasing orange of the sun.

"Very pretty," says the man. "You like the sunset?"

"I do," whispers Sâr.

The vendor spits a thick gob of tobacco juice on the manicured lawn. "Why not have a cup of *sra-thnot* to better enjoy this pretty dusk?"

Sâr, in lieu of another denial, presses his hands to his lips. "Thank you," he says. "It's kind of you to offer."

The vendor grunts his disapproval and wanders along the path in search of other customers. His upper body remains a fixed support for the seesawing cups of palm wine, his thin legs absorbing the shocks of the sloping pavement.

Sâr watches the vendor depart. *The Vietnamese are disgusting*, he thinks.

The air has cooled. The sunset stretches brilliant fingers into the sky before him. The intruder has disrupted Sâr's attempt at equanimity, and now there's no chance he will lose himself in sutra recitation. His skin tingles and his heart thuds. Desire is already recharging inside him. He tries to empty his mind, but his sharp and electric thoughts crack through that failed void like lightning. They were using him, of course. All they wanted was for him to put in a good word with Roeung. They read his desire — because it couldn't have been more obvious — and found it innocent enough, maybe even charming, or amusing. *You are a fool, Saloth Sâr. Why did you let them know what you wanted? Why did you ever tell them your name? You are nothing but a plaything for the king's superfluous wives. They will tell your sister Roeung. They know all your secrets. They know you.* Sâr's face heats into crimson red; he wishes he could rip the sod beneath his feet and bury himself inside it.

Although his humiliation is complete, the desire to return to those dancers surges through him, churning his blood and swelling his veins. His feet are tapping inside their clogs. Were it not for the evening's rehearsal and his sister's interruption, Sâr knows he'd be crossing the wide avenue again right now, en route to the royal compound. "I am weak," he says out loud. His desire dampens at the acknowledgement and his eyes fill with tears. "I am weak and exposed."

Despair nails him to the bench. He regards the serene vista before him. How wide the river is. How slow and peaceful. Sâr pans north and spies dozens of covered boats permanently moored at jutting angles along the shore of the river. He sees the peasants' tiny plots of cultivated riverbank, their tobacco and vegetables. These are seasonal gardens, since that coastal slope will be submerged a few weeks into monsoon season, when the swollen Mekong River overwhelms the Tonle Sap and—amazingly, majestically, almost incomprehensibly—reverses the flow of the Tonle Sap away from the sea and back into the great lake. The river's reversal is the origin of much of his childhood joy. Days upon days of sweet torrential rain, cooling the air, burying whole villages, transforming the dusty roads of his hometown into deep canals. He loved the way his parents' home, raised on its mangrove piles, became an island every year. He recalls sitting on their porch in early monsoon season, watching the water encroach and bury the earth. Now, thinking of it, Sâr begins to feel a vague hope. Can't his desire, like the April heat, be quenched by a change of season? If the rain can reverse the flow of a wide and mighty river, why can't he change his personal direction? His decadence is no more solid than the ground beneath his parents' home. Why can't he also flood his path and flow in reverse?

Sâr leans forward and bites his lip. Maybe it's possible. Maybe he can do it. The sole requirement, it seems, is a proper loss of self. Don't monks achieve nirvana? Didn't the Buddha achieve nirvana? There must be some means for a layperson to disappear.

He recalls the previous November's Water Festival, when his cousin Meak and his sister Roeung invited him to the open-air Chan Chhaya Pavilion to witness the annual dances. Sitting on one of the raised viewing platforms, his back pressed against the balustrade, Sâr absorbed the light of a thousand candles—although he himself, outside their range, was bathed in the more diffuse glow of the evening's full moon. The scene impressed him deeply. He remembers how King Monivong daintily extracted an Abdullah cigarette from a bejewelled tin on a side table and offered it to a nearby guest. He remembers the king's wide-brimmed crown and sacred sword, his rigid posture in the large throne underneath the interior arch, while the muscular arm of a statuesque servant held the royal seven-tiered parasol (about which Sâr had heard so much) above his head. He also remembers, to the right of Monivong, displeased like a child by his less ornate chair, the Résident Supérieur dressed in a European suit. He wore gaudy insignia on his breast to designate his authority as colonial governor of the Cambodian protectorate of French Indochina. He sipped gin and quinine with his legs crossed effeminately, waiting for the evening's dances to begin.

That dance was the first time Sâr had seen Chanlina. She was stunning, no older than seventeen. At first he could only look at her, although she was merely one of the seven motionless background Apsaras, each frozen like a chiselled figure in an Angkoran relief. Then came the lulling and enchanting music of the *pin peat* orchestra: the wailing, nearly vocal line of the wind instrument, the *sralai;* the multi-rhythmic clangs and pings of the xylophones; the throbbing pulse of the *samphor* and *skor thom* drums beneath. And when the central dancer, in a bodysuit and brocade skirt as white as her foundation, stepped forward to play Mera and the xylophones and high flute promptly dropped away and the vocalist's mournful lines soared like a night insect, Sâr's skin erupted in goosebumps. But what Sâr remembers most, right now, sitting on the park bench, is how the background dancers, with their peaked Apsara crowns and strings of jasmine flowers dangling from their ears, stepped forward to move in unison with their leader. It was only then that Sâr realized the full value of the event, the personal religious significance it would secretly hold for him.

In the synchronicity of music and movement, the dancers lost their individuality and moved as one. Their pigeon-toed feet tapped on the pavilion's smooth tile, sliding and pushing against the hard floor in syncopated steps. Their heads waved in almost imperceptible figure eights. The dancers kneeled on one knee, with their hands extended in superhuman contortions and the flattened soles of their back feet facing the ceiling, as if they were indeed goddesses soaring through the sky. The music exploded into a frenzy of atonal xylophones and pounding drums, led by a single, screaming flute. Yes, they were goddesses, their boundaries blended by music, their individuality lost in their precise movements, in routines that had been passed down for generations. They were no longer women with concrete histories but, in fact, Apsaras.

A total loss of self: that is the true value of the dance. It induces proper consciousness and right thinking. Humans are better creatures, Sâr knows, when they have lost their egos and desires, when they have abandoned themselves. Saloth Sâr, sitting on the iron bench in the park by the river, recalls his blissful engrossment in that performance, how he forgot which dancer was Chanlina, how it no longer mattered. He recalls how, with his knees tucked up against his chin—for he was already embarrassed by his egregious desire and brash humanity—he longed to disappear into the collective nothingness like one of those beautiful dancers before him, how he longed to annihilate himself through performance.

"So it can be done," he says, sitting on the bench. "It can happen."

He watches a fluffy white cloud block the sun over the river, casting the park into shadow. *Could there be*, he wonders, *somewhere in the world, a special dance to erase me, Saloth Sâr?*

THE
CONSUMMATION

The clap of firecrackers precedes her. Hired labourer Wu has been given the important task of igniting these mini-explosions, and his gap-toothed smile as he steps away from the black smoke indicates his pleasure with the assignment. A giggle whistles through his nose as the unnamed woman of the Luo family, riding inside the Maos' frayed sedan chair, arrives in their open courtyard. It's been a long and bumpy ride on the shoulders of four dangerously thin peasants. The perspiring men groan as they lower her sedan onto the gravel.

"She's here," says Jen-sheng, the Mao family patriarch. He's a short and skinny man, dressed in a new cotton robe that stretches down to his ankles. His tiny eyes regard the arriving party through the front window. Madam Mao, the local matchmaker and a distant relation, stands outside beside the sedan, waiting for the next phase of the ritual. She spies Jen-sheng through the window and responds to his fierce squint with an unimpressed nod. Madam Mao is a dour old lady who smells of rancid congee and sweat. Nuptial families throughout Hsiangtan county gossip in the packed tea houses about the odorous matchmaker, how she devours their egg noodles and taints their otherwise fragrant ceremonies.

Jen-sheng notes the red lacquered box tucked underneath her arm. Empty. Luo has accepted the contract and gifts. The deal is done. "Come here," he commands his eldest son.

"No," replies the tall boy standing firm in the corner. His slender shoulders are pressed against the two whitewashed mud walls as if his body were a post holding up the roof.

Jen-sheng turns to face his child. "Tse-tung, your bride."

Tse-tung cups one of his thin hands around the fingers of the other and looks at Jen-sheng, scowling. He too is dressed in a long cotton robe that stretches down to the floor. His back is rigid and his body still, which accentuates his height.

"Now!"

"She's not my bride," Tse-tung says calmly.

Jen-sheng's small eyes widen for a moment. He knows what's coming. He's seen this behaviour from Tse-tung on previous occasions and has secretly feared for weeks that he'd see it again today, when the boy is to be married against his will. Still, he catches himself before he shows too much anxiety. Jen-sheng's brow falls and his eyes darken. His tight-lipped frown is exaggerated by the descending tails of his moustache, two misty waterfalls plunging off either cheek. "I am your father," he says. "Come and do your duty."

The boy lowers his chubby cheeks and stares at a small pebble on the ground, hiding his blatant defiance. "No," he repeats. There's no wavering in his voice.

Jen-sheng's shoulders sink and lock, as if he were a large-enough man to pop his chest out and intimidate his opponent. "Come here now, you unfilial beast."

The boy, still staring at the floor, grunts in revulsion. "Who are you to say unfilial?"

Jen-sheng squints at the gross impertinence of this child, this *insect*, and he bares his few remaining black teeth. He cannot accept rebellion on such a solemn day. The boy should be bowing to his father, as would be proper for a respectful eldest son. Instead, Tse-tung remains locked in the darkest of the room's corners, ready to fight. It will take more than a few harsh commands or even a sound beating with the switch to pry him from that position. Jen-sheng doesn't know what to do.

"You let Grandfather rot in his chair without ever once *k'ou-t'ouing*, or asking his opinion, or serving him tea or deferring," says Tse-tung. "A thousand times you mocked him with Li by the pond, calling him lazy and worthless. I heard you. You cannot deny it. And stupid for pawning his land. Tse-min heard you too. And yet you call me unfilial?"

"I always do my duty," hisses his father.

Tse-tung forces an artificial chuckle. "That's another one of your futile farts."

Jen-sheng lunges a step, but balks. He blinks and sucks his cheeks around his decaying teeth. Jen-sheng wants to hit Tse-tung, but there are too many people around and it is too formal an occasion. All he can do is stomp his foot on the earthen floor, which has been brushed as smooth as tiles. The gesture's nothing more than a pitiful tantrum, as the hard-packed ground absorbs any sound his foot makes and resists the imprint of his heel. In his embarrassment, the old man glances around to see if anyone other than Tse-tung is openly mocking him. He finds only the dead stare of his rotund wife, Wen Ch'i-mei, kneeling on the ground beside the ancestral tablets, and the wide-eyed shock of his second son, twelve-year-old Tse-min, sitting near the table with his chair against the wall as if he's hoping to disappear in the shadows.

Wen Ch'i-mei pushes herself off the floor, her hand on the wooden table to relieve the pressure from her ruined left knee, her pear-shaped face lowered and expressionless. She shuffles into the kitchen with a slight limp. Tse-tung watches her go.

"Are you sick?" Jen-sheng asks his eldest son.

Tse-tung smirks, but tries to hide it with the heel of his hand. Rivulets of sweat drip from his temples along the ridge of his jaw, falling onto the rough spun cotton of his robe. The base of his small silk hat is stained dark with sweat as well.

"I don't think so," continues Jen-sheng. "No, you're perfectly well. So why don't you remember your duties? Remember the Master's saying: *Give your father and mother no cause for anxiety other than illness.* Your bride's locked in the sedan. Waiting is not the rite."

Tse-tung doesn't say anything. An iridescent dragonfly, which has found its way into the dark room, now circles wildly in the stifling space between father and son in its confused search for an exit. Tse-tung follows the insect's trajectory with a squint, his grin unyielding. There's something maddening to Jen-sheng about how his son watches this dragonfly in the midst of their confrontation, his ability to be distracted by something so ordinary, and smirking all the while.

"I said waiting is not the rite."

"It's true," Tse-tung retorts. "But then the Master also said: *If one is guided by profit in one's actions, one will incur much ill will.*"

"Your wedding's decreed by heaven," insists Jen-sheng. "The contract accepted. Eight characters matched."

"You don't believe in that old superstition."

"It's heaven's will," repeats Jen-sheng. "The old man in the moon has knotted the threads."

Tse-tung tilts his head and laughs, high-pitched and girlish. "Oh yes!" he cries. "The old man's threads! This, from you: a father who hasn't made an offering to his ancestors once in his life. Now it's 'the old man's threads' and 'a marriage decreed by heaven,' like some peasant girl. That's really too much. You're full of gall."

The dragonfly buzzes near Tse-tung and he swats it down with a flip of his wrist. The insect hits the earth and lies stunned for a moment before testing its wings and rising into the air again.

"A marriage for your son precisely when it's too much for you to manage all the new land by yourself," he continues. "How thoughtful of heaven. How fortunate the eight characters have matched so seamlessly at such a good time for your profit. With the laundry and the sewing, and the pigs bursting from their sty, and the rice milling more labour than Wu can handle by himself. Are you sure heaven hasn't decreed a wife who can also work the abacus? That would've been thoughtful too. You miser. You can't bear to part with even one extra tael to pay for more help. And you quote the Master at me? Believe me, I know what Confucius says. *The gentleman understands what's moral. The small man understands what is profitable.*"

The farmhouse's mud-brick walls, sturdy by village standards, are nowhere near thick enough to mute this family dispute. Outside, in the courtyard, with the heat still oppressive although the sun's nearly down, neither the malodorous matchmaker nor the thirsty peasants nor the grinning labourer Wu show any signs of overhearing this eldest son's scandalous rebellion, but no doubt they're already dreaming of returning to their homes and local tea houses, where they will gossip in earnest about Jen-sheng's unfilial boy in Shaoshan. Woman Luo, the only hidden one, sitting in her locked and oven-like sedan, is especially attuned to every word of the fight, since the moods of this father and son control her fate. Each harsh phrase stabs her like a knife. His mocking grunts, his taunting laughs, the blunt refusals of a future husband are jabs to her inner organs.

Inside the house, Tse-tan, a plump two-year-old naked but for a pair of thin cloth shorts, marches into the central room and baldly stares at his brother in the corner, his face full of open curiosity.

"I think the little one's also ready for a wife," says Tse-tung, gesturing at the boy. "Are you sure heaven hasn't decreed that as well?"

"Wen!" shouts Jen-sheng.

The boys' mother scampers into the central room and awaits further instruction.

"Get him out of here."

She scoops the child over her shoulder and takes him back into the kitchen. Tse-tan regards his furious father as he departs.

"Your problem," says Tse-tung, "is that you've only eyes for money. Is eighty-four *tan* of rice not enough for you? Still hungry for more? You want to be really fat? You think I can't see your intentions? You tell Luo you're pious, that this will be a pious home for his daughter, but your sons know better. Don't we, Tse-min?"

Tse-tung turns to his brother for reinforcement. Tse-min, who has remained hunched and motionless in his chair by the wall, now sits up in shock. The younger boy is thin-faced and scrawny, tense and insecure, almost a clone of his father in both appearance and attitude, except for his timidity in place of Jen-sheng's brashness. He doesn't know how to answer his brother; Tse-tung almost never speaks to him, let alone asks for his support. He stutters some inaudible phrase, shifts in his chair, and darts his eyes back and forth between his brother and his father. While Tse-min has enjoyed the candidness of this battle, he has also been dreading the possibility of being used by one faction or the other, of being forced to take a side, since he's sure he'll be destroyed for his participation by either his father's blunt diminutions or his brother's sly logic.

Tse-tung rolls his eyes, refusing to wait for an answer from his cowardly brother, a lackey to his father. "You can't order me around," he tells Jen-sheng. "I'll throw myself into the pond before I'll ever follow you."

Jen-sheng winces at the painful reminder of last year's fight. It was a humiliating afternoon when Li and Yang and the three elder Wens from his wife's village over Tiger Resting Path came to his house for tea. Tse-tung ambled home midway through the visit with *Three Kingdoms* tucked under his arm, his girlish hands clean and unblemished, not a second worked in the fields that morning—a shameful display before their guests. Of course, the boy received a public berating from his embarrassed father. But then, to Jen-sheng's horror, Tse-tung did not respond with the submissive *k'ou-t'ou* appropriate to his filial role. Rather, he threw his book in the dirt, cursed his family blasphemously, and stormed out of the house, threatening to throw himself into the lotus pond. Jen-sheng and Wen Ch'i-mei followed their son to the shore, with Jen-sheng demanding a *k'ou-t'ou* in apology. Tse-tung adamantly refused out of nothing but spite. Jen-sheng had no choice but to back down and change the subject in front of all his horrified friends.

Now Jen-sheng recalls the sharp taste in his mouth as he stood by that lotus pond. That same metallic tang is currently spreading across his tongue. His throat constricts and he thirsts for public affirmation, some definite confirmation of the indisputable fact that he, Jen-sheng, is the Confucian father, the elder, the leader of the Mao clan. He knows his thirst will only be quenched by the transformation of his stone-like son into liquid. Tse-tung must melt. It's not even a question of what Jen-sheng wants; his role in the family demands it. Tse-tung must kneel before his father with his head touching the ground, absorbing into it like water. After so much defiance, the boy must show complete submission—spineless and limp. But Jen-sheng knows his present command will be as futile as last year's. Still, he can't help trying; he deserves an act of obeisance. The demands of his status are imprisoning and compelling.

Jen-sheng points sternly to the ground. "*K'ou-t'ou* before your elder," he commands again.

Tse-tung purses his small mouth and straightens his long back. When he stands at full height, he's a good head taller than his father. How the young Tse-tung inherited such height, no one knows for certain. Maybe it comes from his mother's grandfather, rumoured to have towered over his kin. With his high and broad forehead and his mother's sweet and taunting eyes, two rainbow-arched lids with flat walls underneath, Tse-tung looks as sturdy as the wall behind him. He's intimidating in size and in his precocious daring. Four tutors the boy's been through since the end of his public schooling, but not one could temper him. Not that he hasn't learned his texts. Jen-sheng is well aware that his eldest son's command of the classics is better than his own, for on every occasion when he corners Tse-tung with some saying from Confucius or Mencius, the child turns the Master back against him.

Jen-sheng wants to keep fighting, but Tse-tung can't be out-reasoned, can't be physically beaten, can't be married off like a normal son or made to work the fields or the abacus or anything. It's an intolerable bind: Jen-sheng loses in every way, either by fighting or by capitulating to his son's insubordinate behaviour, especially here and now, in front of Tse-min and Wen Ch'i-mei and the child, and with Madam Mao and her loose tongue loitering out in the courtyard, and Wu and those damn sedan transporters pricking their ears. Heaven knows what they'll say about Mao Jen-sheng back in their tea houses. He'll be mocked. That woman Luo is stuck in his sedan, affronted by her impudent groom. If Jen-sheng dares to send the bride back to Luo, the powerful father will call him a fool, an ignorant old fool, incapable of controlling his own boy.

"*K'ou-t'ou* this instant," he shrieks, one last time.

Jen-sheng's voice cracks. He smoothes the ends of his moustache and tries to appear magisterial. Tse-tung smiles but gives no sign that he'll lower himself in obedience. Jen-sheng's cheeks are darkening, sweat has ringed the collar of his robe, and his legs feel weak. He can't stay here. He hurries through the kitchen and into the bedroom behind it.

Moments after the man's departure, Wen Ch'i-mei re-enters the room and approaches her son, who remains pressed into the corner with his hands cupped together. She puts fidgety Tse-tan on his feet. The small boy wanders off to investigate a centipede crawling on the room's central *k'ang*—a brick- and wood-planked platform for sitting with a cooking stove built into the earth beneath it.

"*Shisan yazi*, what is this?" Wen Ch'i-mei asks Tse-tung as she shakes her head mournfully. "Don't you know heaven's involved now, the date's decreed, it's out of your hands?"

"Heaven has nothing to do with it, Mother," replies the scowling Tse-tung. His eyes are lowered, but his lips are twisting in paroxysms of confusion and despair. He doesn't look so strong and confident now. "She's not my bride. She's just another person around the house to clean pig shit. Another woman to wash underwear and get commanded by Father. You, of all people, should know that."

"Ogh," moans his mother. "How you're killing me, Tse-tung. This behaviour, it's not right. Left in limbo out there, the spirits will devour her."

Tse-tung's eyes moisten. All day it's been easy for him to understand the stupidity, greed, and small-mindedness behind this wedding. He can see it in the smug expression on his father's face. Tse-tung knows he's capable of standing firm against a demand that's so obviously wrong, regardless of the consequences. But now that he hears the anxiety and fear in his mother's voice, now that he feels her panic, he's not so sure what's the right or wrong thing for him to do. Tse-tung regards his mother and squints to prevent his tears from falling.

"How can you make me," he starts, "after all that you—"

"No."

"I won't have her," he whispers. "I can't have her. Send her back."

"She's not going back."

"Then let her rot in that sedan! She can burn up in the heat, for all I care. I hate her! I don't want anything to do with her."

"Shhh! Tse-tung! Shame on you. They can hear."

"I don't care! She's a rotten bride and I don't want to get married."

Tse-tung is surprised by the vehemence of his resistance. He thought his rebellion was a principled stance against the avarice of his father. Nothing more and nothing less. It shouldn't have anything to do with him personally. He shouldn't care so much. But now the tears are flowing freely down his chubby cheeks.

Wen Ch'i-mei touches her son's face, still so much the baby's, and straightens his silk hat. He'd acted like a man against his father, tall and strong and unyielding, but this person standing before her seems to be a confused child. He's trembling and biting his lip, terrified and blubbering.

"Mama," he whispers. "I don't want to."

"Dry your tears, *shisan yazi*. Everyone must get married. It's duty. It's good for the family, and for me. She's welcome here. I could use her help. And it's a marriage decreed in heaven, you already know. The ancestors did not object to the eight-character match. So the thread is tied and it's all set."

"No," he whimpers.

"No more, Tse-tung. You're still my eldest." She hesitates and shrugs, peering up at her tall son. "That is, if you'll continue to have your poor mother as your own..."

"Of course I will," says Tse-tung, cupping his slender fingers around his mother's face.

"All right," she replies, stepping back. "So don't worry. You'll have many sons. And I won't work Miss Luo too hard.

Just the help I need. I will speak kindly. She's lucky to have a mother-in-law like me."

Tse-tung grins and nods his agreement. "Very lucky," he says.

"She could've gotten a monster."

"Everyone but you is a monster."

"Dry your face. Today is *ch'in ying*. You're very fortunate. You're getting married."

He brushes away his tears and sniffles. "She'll be ugly," he whispers. "I'll find her repulsive."

"She's pretty," says his mother.

"How can you say that? She won't be beautiful."

"She's waiting too long in that sedan. The longer she's exposed, the greater chance the evil spirits will have her."

Tse-tung moves to the threshold and gazes into the courtyard, taking stock of the situation and wondering if he's really going to go through with it. The matchmaker glares at him, her lips curling in disgust. Tse-tung's protestations have made this match seem less than ideal, which is very bad for her credibility. The sedan carriers stand at quasi-military attention, fighting off grins. He scans their rough and sun-drenched faces, registering the mockery in their eyes, the way they're resisting laughter. It's clear they think this boy-husband is an embarrassment and a joke.

Tse-tung hardens with anger. The challenge of the sedan carriers burns away his weakness and childishness as quickly as it flooded him, and now he sees all these smirking peasants before him as hypocrites and narrow-minded slaves, made in his father's mould, more worthy of shame than he will ever be. They are stupid peasants, with nothing but their blind acceptance of a superstitious rite. They can't read a book, but still they think they know the proper way to behave?

Tse-tung's anger and hatred forge inside him an iron will, but he doesn't yet know what he'll do with it, what he wants to do with it. His vision clouds over with white rage and he feels himself stepping out into the yard, ready to stand face to face with these peasant cowards but unsure how exactly he's going to act on his indignation. He approaches the closed sedan.

Before he's made any decision about what to do next, the matchmaker removes a small key and inserts it into a tiny lock on the sedan's door. The lock's purpose is clearly symbolic; a single hard tug would break its clasp. Tse-tung kicks the bright red door, announcing his presence and his command over his bride, while the matchmaker turns the key. The sedan opens.

On the far side of the courtyard, Wu lights another string of firecrackers to ward off any lingering evil spirits, and then steps back to watch them explode. As the firecrackers belch black smoke, the labourer grins with unrestrained glee. Tse-tung realizes that he's just begun the ceremony. Two of the nearby carriers reach inside the sedan and withdraw the unnamed woman of Luo, her face covered by a worn piece of embroidered red silk dangling from a large phoenix crown. She wears a red dress made of rough homespun cotton and her hair is fastened against her head. The two carriers heave as they lift the young woman into the air, and then across the stone threshold of Mao Jen-sheng's home. Inside the farmhouse, they set her down upon her tiny, crushed feet.

Tse-tung forgets his rage as he follows his bride to the threshold. He is standing on the cool earth, unable to take his eyes off those feet. He didn't expect this. Could they be real? Is this woman standing before him, this actual living person, really his intended bride? A foot-bound woman for a wife would indeed befit a family of increasing economic station like the Maos, a family in possession of many paddies, of twenty-two *mou* precisely. Woman Luo's heavy cloth shoes are drawn into points at the toes, as if the flesh inside were shaped like ducks' bills. Although her footwear is fashioned from rough red cotton and sealed with bulky metal clasps—entirely lacking the silk-and-flower elegance of a rich lady in Peking—and her feet remain a few inches bigger than the three-inch lotuses of classical perfection, still this young woman's bindings are unspeakably exotic.

Mao Tse-tung's hungry eyes feast on these delicious morsels. His legs tremble and his throat constricts. Is he really to be as indulged as the Hunanese governor in his Changsha *yamen*? His heart is pounding so strongly he's losing breath and growing dizzy. How does he even imagine touching such little jewels?

For Tse-tung, the wedding is no longer a theoretical possibility, not just another in a long string of battles with his infuriating father, but an actual ceremony between him and this foot-bound woman. Still, the groom can't seem to move from the threshold. The nakedness of his surprise transforms his features into the open stare and slack mouth of an innocent child.

Unnamed woman Luo wobbles from side to side like a gradually slowing top. She walks on her small feet towards Jen-sheng, who has re-emerged from his bedroom to stand regally beside the earthen *k'ang* with his proud chin raised like a pompous governor, his moustache imperial and his frown foreboding. He waits for her to reach him. The bride's arms are swinging like frantic pendulums to balance her precariously shifting weight. When she reaches her father-in-law, woman Luo tucks her crisp cotton robe beneath her knees and kneels before him. Three times the young woman knocks her forehead against the brushed floor. Jen-sheng offers a thin smile in acceptance of his daughter-in-law's *k'ou-t'ou.*

Tse-tung is playing with the split hairs at the end of his long queue, the hairstyle mandated by the Manchu authorities. His braid stretches from the ridge on the back of his skull down to the top of his buttocks, while the rest of his head is shaved. Roused from stunned incredulity by the hissing of his mother, he looks towards her. His mother is widening her eyes at him and he realizes — yes, of course — that it's time to perform the next action prescribed by the rite.

He moves to woman Luo's left, and together the bride and groom *k'ou-t'ou* towards the entrance. Tse-tung fires a quick glance at his bride's covered face but catches no glimpse of her, no indication of her appearance. They step before the ancestral tablets mounted against a small wall and again kneel in obeisance. Neither the sweet incense burning nor the bride's faint smell of pomelo wash can mask the encroaching putrid odour of the old matchmaker, who has entered the room behind the couple and now lingers by the front door, awaiting the festive meal. The couple bows to the tablets of the Mao clan's ancestors, to heaven and Earth, and again to the altar of the Kitchen God, Tsao-Chün. All as prescribed. All as expected.

Now unnamed woman Luo shuffles into the kitchen. The perspiring boy's parents pull out their chairs and sit beside each other, near the ancestral wall. The bride boils water and prepares the cups. When Luo re-enters with the formal tray and ceremonial tea, Tse-tung concentrates on remaining motionless, on keeping his legs from trembling, his teeth from grinding.

Woman Luo performs the tea ceremony impeccably. Tse-tung can see she's been well trained. She doesn't have to sacrifice her dainty steps for additional stability. She executes a *k'ou-t'ou* before his parents in one smooth movement. Her wrists, as she hands them tea, bend at a pleasing angle. Tse-tung observes his father's wide grin at the success of this wedding, and although he's partly enraged by Jen-sheng's ownership of the event, he's also proud of his bride. The tea is sweet, perfectly saturated with lotus seeds and red dates. Both parents lick their lips. It's true, this Luo woman will make a perfect wife. Tse-tung can't help but regard the half moon of her behind through her tight-fitting dress.

Tse-tung has been entitled to expose her face since the moment she entered their home, but only now, as the bride and groom bow to each other, ending the ceremony, does he recall his right. He watches his trembling hands lift the phoenix crown off her head, the veil rising with it. The metal decorations along the crown's fringes tinkle and ring; Tse-tung can't keep his arms still. Unnamed woman Luo stares demurely at the ground. She's a beautiful girl—a small mouth, wide-set eyes, full cheeks with high bones, smooth and unblemished skin—but the deadness in her expression astonishes Tse-tung. She's blinking, but otherwise shows no sign of life. The groom places the wedding crown on the table.

She's like a statue. Nothing there.

The sun is setting outside. The farmhouse, though still scorching, is slowly growing dark. Unnamed woman Luo returns to the kitchen to prepare the festive meal as Wen Ch'i-mei lights a lantern. Jen-sheng pulls out a chair at the table for the village go-between. Jen-sheng ventures into the kitchen and returns, grumbling curses, carrying several bowls of rice. He goes into the courtyard and pays the sedan carriers and his labourer Wu with the simple dinner. He's about to come back inside, but then changes his mind and offers each man a single tael without meeting their eyes. They k'ou-t'ou gratefully, puffs of dust rising when their foreheads touch the dry earth. Woman Luo brings out bowls of noodles, an earthenware jug of water, and, for a treat, a glutinous rice egg-cake.

But for the clicking of chopsticks and the occasional slurp from the patriarch, the newly expanded Mao family eats in silence. Tse-tung doesn't look at his bride, nor does she regard him. Jen-sheng, however, glances under the table at unnamed woman Luo's magnificent bound feet, his eyes bright with the pride of being able to afford a wife of such limited mobility. The matchmaker, as expected, eats her portion in large mouthfuls and taps her chopsticks on her bowl in a blunt request for more. Woman Luo is quick to stand and give her a refill. No one else dares to take seconds. Other than the sweetened egg-cake, consumed at the end, their meal is squalid, gone in minutes.

Wen Ch'i-mei clears the bowls and takes them into the kitchen. "Tse-min," calls Jen-sheng, snorting. He spits on the ground.

The groom's heart thuds.

Tse-min enters the central room holding the small hand of his younger brother.

"It's time for *yuan fang*," says Jen-sheng.

The two younger boys skip out of the room, Tse-min almost dragging the toddler behind him.

Tse-tung and woman Luo rise solemnly and follow the boys. Tse-min and Tse-tan lead them into Tse-tung's room, where the mattress has been re-stuffed and new cotton sheets laid on the bed. There are two fluffy feather pillows that the groom has never seen before. Several candles placed around the room cast a dim glow. Tse-min hauls his younger brother up onto the mattress, grabs the child by both hands, and begins to bounce with him. Tse-tan squeals with open-mouthed laughter. They hop for several minutes, shrieking with glee, but there are no smiles on the lips of either the bride or the groom.

The younger children finish their fertility rite and climb off the bed. Tse-tung and woman Luo sit on the new sheets, each taking a cup of wine placed beside the bed for them. They sip and exchange glasses without looking at each other, and then finish off the other's wine. Tse-tan stares at his oldest brother with a frown, unsure why Tse-tung appears so serious and ill. He is unable to understand what could've gone wrong. Tse-min leads his younger brother away, closing the door behind him. The bride and groom are alone.

Yuan fang. Now.

Tse-tung, unmoving, can only listen to the sound of his own breathing and the faint rasp of his bride beside him. He can't seem to move. He can't do anything at all, because he's clumsy and awkward—this he knows about himself—and because he has no idea how to touch a woman, or how he's supposed to handle his slowly engorging penis, and is certain if he tried to put it in her he'd do it wrong. Woman Luo, who has the clear sophistication of bound feet and perfect features, would not be able to suppress the crushing laughter at her idiotic husband. And then, in the morning, when Tse-tung's mother comes to fetch the sheets so she can scrub away the blood in the yard, she will learn of her son's failure and know that he's not a man. And, worse still, Wu or some other labourer will also see the crisp white sheets and know his failure as well, and all the peasants in Shaoshan and beyond will laugh at Tse-tung, and mock him to his face in the fields, and again at the village store, and again at the tea house.

Unnamed woman Luo emits a tiny, muffled cough from

deep inside her chest. She lies back in bed, careful not to rustle the sheets as her body meets the mattress. Tse-tung clenches his teeth but remains upright. In his peripheral vision, he sees his wife's knees and firm thighs through her red dress. He leans forward to spy her tiny feet, but they're hidden at this angle. Now that she's moved, Tse-tung tells himself that he can do more, that he can look directly at her body—yes, anything he wants. He can take off her shoes if he so desires. He can touch and squeeze her, seize her with all his strength.

He musters up the courage to turn and regard his new wife. In his youth and inexperience, he sees a landscape, the rolling field of a recumbent belly, breasts looming like forbidden mountains. Farther beyond that range, woman Luo's dark eyes lie open like two gaping mine shafts, plundered and glassy, staring at the ceiling. She does not acknowledge his glance, although she must be aware of it. She is waiting for him, but still somehow dead to the world.

Waiting for me, thinks Tse-tung. *That body, so easy to touch. So easy to reach out my hand and feel that rough cotton. Unfasten the buttons on her dress. Pull it apart and see what's beneath. Smooth skin. Lift her leg and peel the shoe. Touch the turned-in foot. Right there: yours. Climb on top of her and press her arms into the mattress and push yourself deep inside her. You must act like a man. You are her husband.*

Tse-tung's arm feels trapped under a heavy stone. He wants to beg her to show some sign of life, a twitch in her fingers, or, better yet, a glance in his direction. Why won't she acknowledge him?

"Miss Luo," he says—but he's shocked and sickened by the sound of his own voice. The tone, so much lower than usual, is the same as his father's.

It's enough to turn Tse-tung away from his bride. With his weak body leaning forward, he thinks, *No, not Father, never be like him—cruel and callous and violent.* He tucks his hands into the tight crevice of his lap. Luo's presence in this room, lying on his bed, sucking in the humid air that should be reserved for his use alone, and mocking him with all her fancy sophistication, suddenly enrages Tse-tung. Get out of here! He wants to scream at her, out of the marriage dressing, out into the courtyard! He clenches his teeth together and crashes back on his bed, his hat tumbling onto the sheets. Although he's lying next to his wife, staring at the same ceiling as her, Tse-tung might as well be in Peking.

A mosquito taps and taps against the ceiling, pulling away each time as if the boards were made from heated iron.

If only Tse-tung could melt into the mattress. He doesn't know what he should do now; he can't lie here forever. He is as trapped as the tiger the villagers caught last month in the pass. He knows he has no choice. His duty is *yuan fang*. He has gone through with the marriage and now it *must* be completed. But the thought of reaching over to touch woman Luo's breast instills such panic that it halts his breath and makes him nauseous. Tse-tung raises his hands to his face and presses his palms into his eyes. He feels that the torrential downpours of planting season are now swirling inside him, a confusion of contrasting forces—the heat of his desire rising, the hail of his shame falling. He knows that his father wasted no time fucking his mother on their wedding day. He surely took what was his without a second thought. *Yuan fang* in one greedy minute. He plunged into her, fast and hard, careful not to waste time on the deed because the man thinks time is better spent on planting paddies, milling grain, selling futures downriver.

Tse-tung squeezes his eyes shut, wishing he could banish the image of his father violating his mother. But yes, the old miser must've torn through his mother, a quick furrow of her rich fields to claim them as his own.

The painful seconds of inaction grow into minutes. Tse-tung lies still beside his bride in the heat and dim light. Neither speaks. They blink and blink, staring at the rough palm boards above them, as if the ceiling might hold some insight into their joint future.

There's a mantra of sorts passing through unnamed woman Luo's head. *Now, now, now.* The rite is unfulfilled. *Yuan fang* is incomplete. It's incomprehensible to her that he doesn't just do it. Her body is seized with terror, with an awesome responsibility unfulfilled, encapsulated in this mantra of increasing fury, ultimately targeted inward, at her own unworthiness. *The rite, the rite, the rite.* She has long since suppressed her fear of the intimate act, to be performed for the first time with a hostile stranger. She doesn't feel any relief, or harbour a secret desire for her new husband to fail. There is too much haze between Luo's young body—wrapped tightly in cotton and entrenched in Confucian responsibility—and the so-called self that might desire an individual way. She cannot imagine a veering from the straight and pointed prescriptions of *yuan fang* or other rites.

Woman Luo, six years older than Tse-tung but still only twenty, has no name, has never had a name, never even imagined a name for herself. She has never met a woman in possession of an individual name. It is impossible for this girl to conceive of herself as an independent actor in the world. She knows that she only has worth as a body engaged in specific duties and requirements. Wash, sow, feed, mill. Earn a high bride price through impeccable manners and abilities. Marry and produce many sons. When she recalls her nightly pain from many years ago, those throbbing explosions centred in her broken toes and arches that sent shock waves up her legs, the months of immobility and subsequent tender steps, and even her wretched and putrid feet when finally unwrapped — the way they glistened with pus in the candlelight — she must also recall her grandmother's whispered reminders about marriage and *yuan fang*, about this night, this very rite. Her grandmother's soothing voice accompanying the terrible sting of the washcloth, the bite of tighter wrapping, the extended agony. "Marriage is the purpose of your life." This rite of *yuan fang*. Everything must be buried away beneath this rite. And then she will have sons. Even the infuriating scratch in her chest, the first tickling of the tuberculosis that will leave her dead in two years, her insatiable need to cough as she lies on her husband's bed, is suppressed beneath her fierce need to complete the rite, as it has been all day. One does not cough in the sedan. One does not cough in the tea ceremony. One does not cough in *yuan fang*. There is no question about that. The pain in her chest is nothing compared with the agony she feels from the complete and total inaction of the boy lying beside her.

An agony that won't abate for the young bride tonight.

The rice paddies of Shaoshan valley are flooded for planting season. Tse-tung has hidden himself on a knoll, in the cool shade of a pine tree, near the old tomb wall. His conical hat and a half-empty sack of young rice shoots rest beside him.

He has been reading and rereading a section of *Water Margin*, his favourite novel, under this tree for an hour. In it, the novel's hero, Sung Chiang, kills his evil blackmailing wife Yan Poxi. Tse-tung has been imagining himself as that noble head clerk, wearing long silk robes, charging through the governor's *yamen* on important business—the kind of man who doesn't let a woman manipulate or corner him. After killing Yan Poxi, who's been threatening to expose his growing relationship with the rebel factions, the hero retreats into the mountains and joins the fabled bandits at Liang Shan Po. Tse-tung admires how Sung Chiang smiles at his enemies and pledges allegiance to the authorities—but when cornered, proves quite adept at double-crossing them. He never has a wrong instinct. Tse-tung decides that he too will be fierce against injustice, generous to a fault, and the model of filial piety.

His gently floating fantasy snags on the barb of reality. He is incapable of filial piety. Neither Sung Chiang nor Tseng Kuo-fan, another of Tse-tung's heroes, the great Hunanese leader who defeated the Taiping rebels and established a new Confucian orthodoxy, would ever have refused *their* fathers. Both of them would have performed *yuan fang* with woman Luo. All the helium of the boy's fantasy escapes through this rough tear, leaving him deflated and limp.

His bowels rumble and he grimaces in discomfort, shifting his weight so he can release a loud fart. The smell is acrid and sharp, product of a troubled body. He can't go on like this, with so much stomach trouble, nausea, exhaustion, and weight loss. He's passed three endless nights without sleep, unnamed woman Luo lying beside him, her legs parted, ready for *yuan fang*. Three nights with only an hour or two of rest. His temples are throbbing and there's a dull ache in his legs.

Now Tse-tung recalls his father's vicious goading at the dinner table. "Why don't you stick her? Look, she's very pretty. It's not like we married you to a plowing ox. It's your duty to make her bleed." After getting no response, his father turned his wrath on woman Luo, who sat curled over her rice, unable to look at anyone directly in her state of constant humiliation. "Make yourself pretty, woman. Smile at the boy. Why don't you show him what you've got? You're not married without *yuan fang*. It's your duty to produce a son."

A patch of dark cloud passes overhead, dulling the midday light. Thunder rumbles in the distance. Tse-tung studies the low cover and guesses that it will pour in a few seconds, a rain lasting three or four minutes at most, and probably ceasing as quickly as it began. This is not unusual for a spring afternoon in Shaoshan. He feels the pressure all around him in the volatile pre-storm air, much like the climate in the village whenever he's present—the incredulous squints and open grins of the labourers and landowners in the tiny shop where he exchanges sugar for pork, and the gossip and laughter at his expense as soon as he leaves. He knows what they're saying about him. "Did you hear that Mao Tse-tung hasn't yet slept with his wife? Impotent Tse-tung."

The rain collapses on the countryside all at once. Tucked under the tree, only sporadic, thick drops pass through the foliage to smack against Tse-tung's homespun clothes. He pulls his knees into his chest and hides his book behind his back. He shakes his head at the dirt, wishing he could disappear, but then chastising himself for that desire. He knows Sung Chiang wasn't as lazy as he is, always reading under a tree. He knows that he wouldn't last a single week in the company of real bandits. No, he would be mocked and forcibly expelled from their hideout. Why would heroic bandits want to have as a brother a little boy who can't even sleep with his wife—no, not even a boy, but a weak, crying girl with dainty hands, a high voice, and an awkward shuffle? All he is missing are the bound feet.

The sunlight cuts through the dark clouds in angled shafts as the rain lessens. From atop his knoll, Tse-tung spies the labourer Wu working a few hundred metres away, standing ankle deep in the flooded field, his back bent as he plants young shoots. The clouds pass and the world floods with light, the irrigation pool sparkling around the rows of young shoots. Tse-tung wonders if Wu can provide him with a path out of Shaoshan, an escape from his humiliation. He grabs his book and tucks it into his large sack, slinging the sack around his shoulder. He puts on his rattan hat and marches into the muck of the rice paddy.

Wu is focused on his planting and doesn't see the boy coming. He only glances up when he hears the suck of Tse-tung's feet in mud. They nod at each other, Wu seemingly indifferent to the youth's presence, and certainly not about to start mocking him openly for his failure with woman Luo. That's good. Tse-tung will show Wu that he's a real man, as capable of working the fields as any stoic labourer. He unwraps a wet cloth around his first batch of rice shoots and withdraws a small spade. He digs a hole in the mud and stuffs the shoot inside. Wu will know all about the nearest Ko-lao hui lodges in Hunan province, as easily half the labourers in the region are members of that ancient and rebellious society, which has long opposed the Manchu rulers of the Qing dynasty, and is clearly modelled after the bandits in *Water Margin.*

The landowner's eldest son and the hired labourer Wu work side by side, each maintaining an efficient pace so as not to be called lazy by the other. Drops of perspiration slip from their foreheads and dissipate in the pool below. Their feet slosh in the mud. The rhythm of planting the rice lulls them both. The humidity is so thick that their repeated motions seem to carve ruts in the air. Tse-tung can't bring himself to ask Wu his question, and yet, if he doesn't, he'll stay trapped in Shaoshan forever, as rooted in the earth as the rice shoots he's planting. The work pains his back, but it's also peaceful and cleansing. Tse-tung counts his shoots and realizes he's planting faster than Wu. That's a good sign; someone who works this quickly might someday become a leader of the Ko-lao hui, just like Sung Chiang. Tse-tung might succeed if he leaves Shaoshan and joins the bandits.

"When's your next trip to Hsiangtan?" he asks suddenly, without stopping.

Wu flashes him a concerned look. "After planting season."

"And then again in the fall?"

Wu stands and scowls, studying the boy. Tse-tung knows that every year, after the harvest and milling, Wu and another temporary worker pack the ox cart with Mao Jen-sheng's surplus grain and lug it along the bumpy road to Hsiangtan, to be sold on the river for a tidy profit. Tse-tung has been managing the family's accounts for the past two seasons. He knows the routine. So what's he doing asking this question?

"I go every fall," says Wu.

"You know many people there?"

Wu tilts his hat, wipes his brow with his sleeve, and resumes planting at a regular pace. "No," he says, peering into the muck. "Very few."

"A lot of workers arrive at that time, don't they? All selling their masters' rice?"

"I stay two nights, then come right home."

"Do you know any Ko-lao hui there?" Tse-tung presses.

Wu stands abruptly, a rice shoot in one hand and a rusted spade in the other. "I don't know anyone," he says. "I keep away from Ko-lao hui."

"But there must be lodges in Hsiangtan. Is it difficult to join one?"

Now Wu steps back in the mud, waving his arms. "I said I know nothing about that. Nothing at all! They're bad people, those bandits. I pay the *likin* tax for your family and I bring your money home, don't I? You've seen the books. I don't smuggle and I don't steal. I don't want any trouble with Ko-lao hui. You understand? So you tell your father that."

Wu resumes planting with a flat expression, as if he had never backed up in terror. The only sign of his distress is that he's working faster, with performed concentration. Tse-tung blushes and tries his best not to alter his pace. The two men stuff rice shoots in their parallel rows. It was stupid to ask Wu about the bandits. Besides the fact that he's acquired no new information, now there's a risk of the labourer gossiping about the eldest Mao son to all his friends, telling everyone in town that impotent Tse-tung is interested in joining Ko-lao hui, news which would certainly get back to Jen-sheng and result in a beating worse than any he's ever known.

But the hired labourer Wu is not so concerned with Tse-tung's ambitions. He couldn't care less about the boy's rebellion against his landowning family, and only wonders who gave him away. Could it have been one of his blood brothers, some smuggler savagely tortured into a full confession by the Manchu authorities? It is useless to ask the questions; there are too many potential traitors. Wu knows countless bandits, and they know him, as he is a long-standing brother of one of the largest and most active Ko-lao hui lodges in Hunan. Each year, during his semi-annual visits to Hsiangtan, he engages in elaborate tea rituals with his fellow members, exchanging secret information by hand gestures, cup positions, and other hidden signs. He sells Jen-sheng's surplus grain exclusively to Ko-lao hui merchants, since they have connections to smugglers along the Xiang river all the way north to Changsha, and thus can avoid paying the hated *likin* tax, which funds reactionary militias aligned with the Manchu government against the Han majority. Wu pockets the money he saves.

Two years ago, on the orders of his lodge's chief dragon-head, Wu embarked on the longer journey to Lu-k'ou during the off-season to help run one of the lucrative gambling houses used to fund the bandits' revolutionary activities. He offered his services as a spy on that trip, informing numerous lodge members of the Mao family's growing wealth, and of Jen-sheng's cruelty to Shaoshan's starving peasants during the famine of 1906, how his master denied them grain in favour of selling the surplus. And on yet another occasion, Wu participated in the roadside robbery of a rich clerk, a plot that involved spiking the porters' wine, like a chapter from *Water Margin*. The labourer knows that any of the dozens of people involved in those activities could have given him away.

Rather than worrying about Tse-tung's adolescent tiffs with his father, Wu is wondering what will happen to him now, and to his wife and three little boys in the next village. Will he be fired, or something worse—arrested for treason and publicly executed? Wu wants to drop his sack of shoots and sprint out of Shaoshan valley, but instead concentrates on maintaining his composure while he works.

Hours pass in silent labour. Tse-tung plants the last of his rice shoots in the late afternoon. His lower back throbs and his lanky legs ache. He might even sleep tonight. He walks with a swishing gait along the dry dirt path between drenched fields. His family's house has been painted a warm yellow, illuminated in the strong golden sunlight and contrasting strikingly with the thick greenery on the hill behind it. Viridescent shoots grow tall in adjacent paddies. There's an enticing scent of hibiscus in the air. The fish pond, sprouting lily pads and open white flowers, is overrun with croaking frogs, audible from a distance. It's deceiving, how peaceful his home appears. Tse-tung shuffles into the courtyard and steps across the threshold.

"Where have you been?" his father asks.

Tse-tung stands in the doorway, clasping his sack and his hat, his pupils yet to adjust to the diminished interior light. He sees only his father's silhouette at the table.

"You haven't done a second of work today, have you?"

The room comes into focus, exposing Jen-sheng and Hsiao, a second seasonal labourer. They are both sitting at the old table wrapping tomorrow's shoots in wet rags. His father's face, thin and sharp, holds perfectly round eyes, dark with anger. His mother and woman Luo are seated on the *k'ang* near the blackwood table with its bronze Buddha, the former mending a pair of Jen-sheng's pants, the latter sewing a new shirt for Tse-tan, who has recently outgrown everything. Woman Luo is quiet as usual, following his mother's instructions and never complaining.

"Lazy, no-good boy," spits Jen-sheng.

Tse-tung throws his father the empty sack, which lands at his feet.

"You think I'm stupid? You emptied it in the pond."

"Planted," says Tse-tung.

Jen-sheng snatches up the sack and looks inside. His black and fractured smile spreads as he discovers Tse-tung's copy of *Water Margin* in the sack, proof of procrastination. He holds up the incriminating text and peers at his son. "What's this?"

"A book," answers Tse-tung. "Filled with words and stories. Ever hear of books?"

"You think you're funny?" Jen-sheng opens the book and studies the text, squinting with incomprehension at several phrases and then shutting it with a thud. "You read this garbage instead of planting?"

"I did my planting. Ask Wu."

"It's time you throw away this shit and do something useful." Jen-sheng tosses the book on the ground. "If you aren't going to read the classics, at least count the remaining shoots and figure out how long it will take to get them all planted."

"Not now," says Tse-tung. "I'm hungry. I've been working all day."

"You can have a bowl of rice. Eat quickly and get counting. Wen!"

Wen Ch'i-mei drops her mending on the floor and scurries into the kitchen. Tse-tung hangs his hat by the door and follows her, passing his taciturn bride, neither of them acknowledging the other. In the kitchen, Tse-tung moves beside his mother, who is scooping a ball of cold rice into a bowl.

"I did my planting," he says to her. "I did it all."

Wen Ch'i-mei hands him the bowl as she glances over her shoulder to make sure they're alone. "Read your book at the table," she whispers. "But don't speak to him. It will make him crazy." She hands her son a pair of chopsticks to punctuate the advice.

Tse-tung returns to the central room, scoops *Water Margin* off the ground, and takes it with him to the table. He's sitting directly across from his father, but rather than looking at the man, he cracks open his book and lays his rice bowl on its edge. His stomach turns, pain gnawing his intestines. He's far too anxious and fatigued to focus on the words, but if he eats and pretends to read, it will have the same effect.

"So that's what you're going to do, huh?" asks his incredulous father. "Read stupid books instead of helping me? No manly work? Makes sense for a girl like you. I guess you'd also prefer to read by yourself than to fuck your wife. Is that right, woman? Does he take his books into bed at night instead of fucking you? Hey, I have a good idea, Tse-tung. When you've finished that book and your tenth bowl of my rice, why don't you take your virgin wife's sewing and finish that for her too? I'll bet you're good at it. It's the right kind of work for you."

Tse-tung concentrates on the printed characters before him, although they've twisted and warped through the haze of his angry stare. What kind of man, he wonders, does nothing when attacked? He steals a glance at Miss Luo, who's blushing and hunched over, her face buried in her sewing. She must think him an ineffectual coward, not so different from the lump of rice in his bowl.

He can't stand it. Tse-tung stands on his chair and reaches up to the drying *chu tin* peppers that dangle from the rafters. Aware that everyone's watching, he picks a long and thin specimen of deep purplish red, sure to be exceptionally strong, and pops the whole thing into his mouth. He chews the pepper and retakes his seat, firing glances across the table at his father to make sure he's noticed, his tongue and cheeks inflamed, his brow popping with perspiration, but still focused on keeping his expression as bland as the rice he now uses to chase away the spice. This will show his father the difference between a coward girl like Luo and a man tough enough to eat a *chu tin* pepper in a single bite.

Jen-sheng leans back in his chair and laughs at his son. "If you think that's hot," he says mockingly, "just wait until it comes out the other end."

Tse-tung leans over his book and blocks his view of his father with a hand on his brow. He pretends to read *Water Margin* as he works the pepper with his teeth. He's sweating profusely, trying to resist spitting the burning mash out of his mouth.

"Oh yes, tough man! Eating *chu tin* like a real son of Hunan. Are you sure you don't need any water with that, Tse-tung?"

"He doesn't need water," says Wen Ch'i-mei, glaring at her husband from her seat on the *k'ang*.

"Look at him sweat!" Jen-sheng says, leaning in so Tse-tung can't ignore him. "Too hot for you, little boy?"

"What are you reading, Tse-tung?" counters his mother.

Jen-sheng grunts and rolls his shoulders. He sits back and grabs a wrapped rice shoot from the table.

"Must be a very interesting book to hold your attention like that," continues Wen Ch'i-mei. "I think you'll be a scholar when you grow up, don't you, Tse-tung?" She turns to woman Luo beside her on the *k'ang* and touches her shoulder. "Hey, you're a very lucky woman, miss. Your husband will be a clerk someday and take you to the *yamen* in Changsha. And from there, who knows? Tse-tung is very smart, as you can see. Maybe he'll go to Peking to work in Empress Dowager's court."

"Shut up, Wen!" shouts Jen-sheng. He's begun to shred the bright green leaves of the young shoot in his hand, scattering torn bits on the floor by his feet.

"When he passes the state exam, he'll work for anyone in China."

"I said shut up. You talk too much, Wen Ch'i-mei!" The family's patriarch, having reduced the rice plant in his hands to a nest of mangled roots, now looks down and realizes what he's done. He drops the remaining bits on the floor and shoots a desperate glance at unnamed woman Luo, hoping she hasn't seen.

"You're always reading, aren't you, Tse-tung?" continues Wen Ch'i-mei. "I'll bet you know Confucius better than anyone in China. I know what's in store for you. You'll pass the exam and work in government, I'm sure of it. You won't stay a farmer in Shaoshan."

Jen-sheng squirms, wrinkles his brow, and spits on the floor. He grabs another wrapped rice shoot, but then thinks better of it and tosses it back onto the table. He stands, puffs his chest, and looks at woman Luo. "Tse-tung," he says.

"Finish these." He indicates the pile of unwrapped rice plants. "I have better things to do," he adds, and leaves the room.

Wen Ch'i-mei grins at Tse-tung, but he only responds by lowering his head deeper into his book. Something's wrong. Wen Ch'i-mei realizes it immediately and her smile wanes. In the past, when they've collaborated on a plan to defeat Jen-sheng, they've shared triumphant looks after the old man has stomped out of the room. Maybe Tse-tung didn't see his father leave, or maybe chewing that pepper has caused him more pain than she's realized.

"It must be nice," Wen Ch'i-mei says to woman Luo, although her gaze remains fixed on her son, "to have a husband who can read poetry. I wish I had a man like that."

Tse-tung covers his ears with his hands. "Leave me alone," he says. "I want to eat and go to sleep."

Wen Ch'i-mei offers a single nod and then turns her attention back to her sewing. Distracted by Tse-tung's strange reaction, she misses a stitch and jabs the needle into her finger. She doesn't yelp; she merely pops the bloody fingertip into her mouth and sucks, continuing to work as if nothing happened.

The combined forces of Jen-sheng's cruelty, Wen Ch'i-mei's ignorance, and his wife's mere presence have so pressurized Tse-tung that he's sweating and feels ready to explode, like a sealed pot of boiling rice. His family is absurd and infuriating. He has to leave this town at once. He has to join the Ko-lao hui. His naive mother claims that he'll pass the state exam and then advance in society as a scholar and clerk, but Tse-tung knows that she's proud of a future that will never exist. His mother knows nothing of the sweeping reforms overtaking China. She was not with Tse-tung last month when he visited his cousin Xilian at the eastern end of Shaoshan valley. Xilian had just returned from an extended study in Changsha's Western school, and told Tse-tung that the traditional Confucian examinations had been abolished two years earlier, meaning that there would be no more free tickets for any of the humbly born in China. *I will never be a scholar!* Tse-tung wants to scream at his stupid mother. *I will never be a government clerk!* But he knows he can't even do something as basic as inform his mother of what has happened in her own country. How could the simple woman understand that incomprehensible revolution? What could he say to her? That his entire education thus far, all the beatings he took at the miserable village school, all his tedious rote memorization of *Three Character Classic* and the standard Confucian texts, all of that, his whole life, was a complete and total waste of time and effort, because there will be no more official state exams? She'd never believe him. Every illiterate peasant in the land knows that the Confucian exam system is the staple of advancement in China, just as it's been for well over two thousand years. Something so primal and predictable as the state exam can't simply be abolished and gone forever. That would be like the sun forgetting to rise. No, he can't say a word about it.

And so, instead of saying anything, Tse-tung burns with rage, furious at his ignorant ox of a mother for stupidly lording a defunct exam over her husband for power. She has no power, and neither does he. His father is sure to get the last laugh.

It's a perfect night in Shaoshan. A cool breeze rustles the trees and keeps the mosquitoes from biting. In the glow of the full moon, Tse-tung discerns the larger pebbles in the path before him, the swishing rice shoots to either side, and the stone bridge over the river. Silhouettes of farmhouses dot the hills along the valley. He is skipping along the path, prowling and playing a tiger, as the river gurgles beside him. A mouse scuttles across the path, but before it disappears into the greenery, Tse-tung imagines pouncing on it, snatching it up by the tail, and gobbling it down in a single bite. He growls, as deeply as possible, although he doesn't sound much like a tiger, and then continues on towards his house on the north slope of the hill.

He is clutching *Words of Warning to an Affluent Age*, borrowed from his cousin Xilian, or rather, pressed into his hand with his cousin's firm command that he read it. The brief passages he skimmed while sitting on a big stone by the river have already inspired him. The book is an uncompromising polemic against the British and the Japanese, how they continue their ruthless exploitation of China's land and long-suffering people, mining the country's wealth, selling cheap cigarettes, patrolling the Hunanese rivers in their brazen gunboats. There are descriptions of wonders scarcely imaginable: ships propelled across oceans by magical steam engines, and small metallic devices that enable conversation between people hundreds of miles apart. Tse-tung is eager to get home and read this book from cover to cover, no matter that it's long past dark and he's expected to rise with the sun. He's amazed that Xilian has learned these things at his school; it's such a different education from the one he's received in the village. Tse-tung would never have been such a nuisance to his teacher and tutors if they'd taught him these modern subjects instead of the same useless Confucian prescripts a thousand times over, phrases and ideas he'd already memorized and could have taught to the others. In Changsha, Xilian says, you can learn mathematics and geography, and they teach you about the governments of other countries, and you learn about the functioning of the natural world.

Tse-tung kicks a stone and listens to it splash into the river off the path. He's tempted by the prospect of going to a modern school, not that it would be easy to get accepted. But Tse-tung also wonders if he really needs more time with books. Isn't he already too placid and quiet, too high-voiced and feminine? No woman wants to marry another woman. He needs to develop his strength, discipline, and rigour. Sung Chiang might have been a scholarly clerk at the *yamen*, but that hero only distinguished himself when he became a man of action, a fighter on the run, a leader of radical bandits. Books are never enough.

As he marches beside the river, his gangly legs bouncing him with each step, Tse-tung oscillates between the contradictory desires of pursuing banditry and continuing his education. He is plagued by rudimentary questions about his own character. Does he love to read or hate it? Does he want to perform *yuan fang* or not? Does he want to fight the world like an outlaw or study it like a scholar? He's always trapped between contradictions, never has an answer, never feels complete.

He walks up the dirt path from the fish pond to his house. The windows are dark, and a cooing dove, having made its nest in the overhanging eaves, silences in honour of his approach. The gravel in the courtyard crunches under his sandals. He can smell traces of ash and boiled vegetables from dinner. Everyone must be sleeping. Tse-tung inches open the front door to prevent it from creaking.

The central room's large table has been pushed aside to make room for a mattress on the floor. In the moonlight, Tse-tung discerns a body, curled and covered by a thin blanket. He approaches, and the person, hearing his feet, shudders and coils tighter, releasing staccato sobs that are muffled by the straw.

"Mama?"

Wen Ch'i-mei throws an arm over her head, covering her face with her bicep. Tse-tung kneels beside her and is about to lay his hand on his mother's heaving back, but she twists away before he can touch her.

"What happened?" he asks. "Are you all right?"

"Go to bed, Tse-tung."

Tse-tung leans back but lingers on one knee, neither standing nor sitting, neither touching her nor moving away. He is startled by his mother's fury, never having heard such bite in her tone. Wen Ch'i-mei squirms under the lumpy cotton blanket, as if to escape the boy's audible breathing, and coils even tighter—like a snake consuming its own tail—but then she thrashes with frustration when the self-consumption proves impossible.

"I said go to bed, Tse-tung," she hisses. Now she drops her arm and turns her head to attack him at full volume. "Why can't you ever go to bed on time, you stupid boy! Can't you see you're not wanted? You never go to bed! You ruin everything! Go to bed! Go! Now!"

Tse-tung jumps up, tripping over his heel and stumbling, dropping *Words of Warning to an Affluent Age.* He crouches and gropes for his book, but in his haste he jams his middle finger against the leg of a chair. He yelps and shakes the screaming finger. His other hand pats around in the darkness for his lost book. He tries not to make a sound when he sneaks into his room.

Behind the closed door, Tse-tung grips *Words of Warning* with both hands. Stunned and confused, his imagination concocts fanciful explanations for his mother's fury. His father's anger and vindictiveness must be the product of a communicable disease, and his ceaseless spitting and frothing has spread the offending plague, so that his mother now lies stricken, racked by the disease's characteristic fever and fury. Or no, he now thinks, his thoughts replacing one absurdity with another, maybe his mother's crazy superstition, her insistent belief in evil spirits, which she has tried so urgently to pass on to him, has proven true. Maybe in vengeance for her child's denial, she's been possessed by a vampire, bent on feeding from the primary artery between them, their sacred bond. Tse-tung stands wondering by the door.

There's only a single small window in Tse-tung's room, but in the strong moonlight he can see his bed. His cotton quilt and fresh pillows lie undisturbed. It takes a moment for Tse-tung to remember that this is strange. An empty bed. Every night, for ten days, unnamed woman Luo has endured her nightly torture of lying motionless, awaiting his decision to perform or not perform *yuan fang*. She has nowhere else to sleep.

The realization dawns on Tse-tung. He raises the book and covers his face, pressing his nose flat. The old miser. Never could resist a piece of fertile ground. Never one to pass over what others have left fallow. Tse-tung drops his book and remains standing by the door, unable to move his limbs.

It feels as if decades pass before he sits. Decades more pass before he lies on the unbroken surface of his bed. His stomach churns and gnaws and he farts a dozen times. His head pounds, the pain tearing around the bone and pulsing above his neck. He forgets about *Words of Warning to an Affluent Age,* but in the days to come and for the rest of his life, that book will remind him of this evening.

He lies on the bed for hours.

In his mind, Tse-tung is on the deck of a boat at sea, cast adrift. He has heard about the sea, its giant waves and its wide horizon, an endlessness that nobody can seem to describe quite to his satisfaction. He would like to be out there on the water, drifting. Although he wants the peace of a calm sea, a storm rolls over his boat in a single blink. Waves rise into swells the size of mountains, rivalling any of those in Hunan. He's in a valley between swells, a cavernous seascape, and now a gigantic wave is about to collapse on his boat. Tse-tung has never seen the sea, and is incapable of imagining it accurately, so the wave is a solid thing, resembling a Hunanese rock cliff, but bigger than any he's ever seen, and it falls upon him in crumbling chunks and boulders, like an avalanche. Although the rock-wave is sure to crush him, Tse-tung stands on the deck against it. A moment before he's engulfed, he dives into the sea and swims deep.

He can imagine what that feels like, as swimming in the ocean can't be much different from swimming in the river. Tse-tung wills himself to breathe under water. When he rises, he discovers yet another wave crashing, again as solid as a mountain, and so he dives deeper still; there's no limit to the power of his lungs. For hours he will fight these mountains, diving, rising, and diving again, until he's exhausted. But the storm passes.

Tse-tung lies on his back and floats, light as a bug on the lily pond, studying the moon out the window. He feels the perfect light breeze and tropical warmth of Hunan in the middle of the night. He tells himself that no man has ever defeated these mountain-waves before. He is sure his daring will be the gossip in cities across China, and that the news will travel through the countryside, across the great river, south to Shaoshan. Everyone will learn of his accomplishment.

When the sun finally rises, and his room is engulfed in pink and yellow and light blue, he allows himself to drift in a tranquil sea, the fish gathering around him in admiration, their fins cracking through the surface of the water. Thousands of mesmerized fish. "Here is the man who has beaten a storm by disappearing into our realm," the fish whisper to each other, and they *k'ou-t'ou* to Tse-tung, although their gestures are halting and absurd and incomplete. Tse-tung laughs at them. "Come, come," he says out loud. "No need for that. You're my brothers. You are family. I will swim with you, and you can follow me forever. Yes, I'll swim all the way to the coast, and by the time I hit land, a million of your compatriots will have followed me."

Tse-tung waits until there's movement in the central room before he rises. The heat of the bright day has already begun to bake the inside of the house. He doesn't hesitate to open the door. The mattress his mother has slept on has been stashed away, and now Wen Ch'i-mei bustles in the kitchen, her pots clanging, cleaning up from breakfast. Jen-sheng eats a bowl of boiled and mashed grain at the table. Unnamed woman Luo, who stands in the middle of the room, a few paces behind his father, with her head lowered and hands clasped, allows a deep and diseased cough to rise from her lungs. Woman Luo's cough shakes her whole body, drawing up a wad of phlegm that she promptly spits onto the ground. It's a terrible sound, and her behaviour is shocking — a breakdown of decorum, an admission. For ten days Tse-tung has heard his wife suppress her coughs, lying in bed beside him or sewing and washing with his mother, and though that fight has caused her obvious pain — a reddening face, a neck tensed to the point of bursting — she has not once abandoned her decorum, not once let him see her behave unattractively. And now this coarseness. He closes his eyes. He is doomed. Woman Luo is doomed.

Jen-sheng turns towards the boy and smiles slyly. "Did you sleep all right?"

Tse-tung frowns and doesn't answer.

"I did. I slept very well. You want breakfast?"

Again, Tse-tung doesn't answer.

"Woman," barks Jen-sheng. "Go tell Wen Ch'i-mei to make the boy a bowl for breakfast."

Woman Luo scurries into the kitchen with her broken steps and nearly toppling gait. Both father and son watch her depart.

"That woman," says Jen-sheng, grinning. "She is very nice. You made a very bad mistake." He points his chin over towards the door.

Tse-tung follows his father's gesture to a pile of crumpled sheets, placed by the threshold to be taken into the courtyard and washed. Stains to be scrubbed by his own mother. Tse-tung tenses his fists.

Woman Luo returns, holding out a bowl of mashed grain. Her eyes meet Tse-tung's for the first time since her initial unveiling. Tse-tung stops breathing, as her stare is no longer dead but as sharp as a tiger's teeth, filled with accusation and disgust. Tse-tung looks at the floor, his cheeks crimson, and he kicks at the brushed dirt. He hears his mother's piercing voice in his head: *Go to bed, you stupid boy.*

Tse-tung's thoughts are lucid, hot, and certain. He understands all too well Confucian law and custom. He knows that he has ruined the life of another human being, that he has dropped woman Luo from the high status of the eldest son's wife to the lowliness of a concubine. She will never be a matriarch now. Any son of hers will forever inhabit a position inferior to Tse-min's or even little Tse-tan's. Her sons will have the low status of Tse-tung's younger siblings and nothing more. He has destroyed her prospects out of cowardliness and indecision. He has ruined this woman by acting like a woman himself.

He is humiliated by his own behaviour, humiliated by the public knowledge of his failure, but at the same time Tse-tung no longer feels any regret or sympathy for his former wife's suffering. The truth is that he never wanted to be pushed into this marriage by the stupid greed of his father or by the small world of Confucian beliefs. And does it really matter what the idiot peasants in Shaoshan think or say about him behind his back? He's happy that it's over. He's thrilled he isn't married. Although Tse-tung has done much worse violence to woman Luo than the pounding he would've given her in *yuan fang*, she's still alive, isn't she? Yes, alive, standing before him. She'll survive. It's just tough luck for her.

Unnamed woman Luo lowers her eyes and holds out the bowl of grain mash for Tse-tung.

Jen-sheng grins. "Take it," he commands his son.

His father is eager for him to eat. It's a new beginning today, and the boy must be strong to face it. Yes, he must eat. He has to work and face the world, no matter what obstacles he encounters. Although it has not been easy for Jen-sheng to deal with a boy as pigheaded as this Tse-tung, this difficult son who fights all the time and counters everything his father says, Jen-sheng is certain that he must learn these lessons if he expects to grow into a real man. He must learn to accept his place if he expects to inherit the farm and keep it growing, keep it earning what it should. Jen-sheng knows this experience will hurt Tse-tung — yes, of course, it hurts right now — but the child will thank his father someday for the instruction, Jen-sheng is sure of that. He will learn what's right and proper from what his father has done. Woman Luo could not be kept waiting any longer. It wasn't right. And now the neighbours need to know it's over. Tse-tung has to learn that he must fulfill his duties. Yes, and now he must take his proper place, and do what's expected of him. And it's not so bad, either, to be the eldest son. He can have his pick of brides, although of course not this pretty woman Luo anymore, but any of the other young jewels in the region. And next time, he won't back down from his duties, because his father will have taught him what's right. And he will stop being so lazy and finally be a man. And he'll settle into his role and plant shoots and work the abacus as well as he should. Someday he will be the master of this farm. Master of all Shaoshan. He will have everything his heart desires. *Yes, you will have everything I have had,* Jen-sheng thinks, as he smiles proudly, waiting for his son to take his bowl of breakfast, *everything and even more, my eldest child, my Tse-tung, my beloved boy.*

LADO'S
DISCIPLE

Soso is lined up single file with the other sleepy seminarians in an unadorned dormitory. Thirty-five miserable teenagers face the doorway, wearing black surplices and cassocks with heavy crosses around their necks. Silence is mandatory. Although the sun has yet to rise, it's already been twenty minutes since the bell's ominous clang woke them. With one plain crucifix on the wall, uniform cots, and wooden lockers, there's nothing to look at while they wait. Soso's thick dark hair is brushed to one side but, like the boy himself, it's begun to rise in rebellion.

Every minute feels like thirty. Seid Devdariani, a sixth-year student with heavy cheeks and close-set eyes that twitch regularly due to his poor eyesight, stands at the end of the line, cursing the delay. He's resting one of his weary feet on a nearby bed. Although Devdariani is the acknowledged leader of the secret socialist reading group, which all the students know is the real education offered at the seminary, he's got a pathetic lack of endurance and no strength. Devdariani sighs as he waits. Soso chuckles and shakes his head at the boy's poorly managed misery. He cannot understand why the other seminarians continue to revere that fool.

There's yellow crust in Soso's tear ducts and bags under his eyes, fuzz on his chin and across his cheeks. As beards are required of Orthodox priests, each of these young men has the beginnings of one. Beneath his cassock, Soso's arm presses Darwin's *Descent of Man* flat against his belly. At least half the seminarians have stashed clandestine books in their clothing — unholy subjects, strictly forbidden — tucked into armpits or balanced precariously on forearms.

At last the obese Inspector, Dimitry Abashidze, lumbers down the hallway to gather the students room by room and heel them into the chapel. He steps into the doorway, a dour frown pulling his lips. His nose is too sharp for so round a face. He has a Russian's rat eyes, Soso has long thought, bulbous and pure black. With his long dark beard and cassock, he could easily be the villain of any anti-Russian novel. Soso has gone so far as to name the Inspector "Black Spot," a dastardly moniker worthy of the scoundrel, but the name hasn't yet caught on with the other students. Abashidze steps into the dormitory and counts seminarians, his lips moving. After confirming there are no fugitives, he nods at the first in line and leads the group into the hall. The students, heading towards the stairway, slip in beside another column of seminarians, occupants of dorms farther down the hall.

Soso marches next to Ilya Parkadze, a fifth-year student nine inches taller, with a thicker beard and clearer skin. Scrawny Parkadze is Devdariani's main supporter in the socialist reading group; he behaves with a lackey's pre-dictability and stupidity. As they march down the windowless hallway, the students are required to keep their gazes forward, their minds meditating on the mysteries of resurrection and the blessed Trinity. The air is thick with soot from the Inspector's kerosene lamp. They can barely see the grey walls beside them. When they reach the stairs, Parkadze shoots a disdainful glance at Soso's left arm, which was damaged by a runaway phaeton when he was a child. His arm has never grown to full size and has limited use. Although Soso's only sixteen, he clasps the railing like an old man, his elbow protruding above the banister.

"Hey, *Koba*," Parkadze whispers, scoffing at the nickname Soso took from a Georgian nationalist novel. "Who's going to fuck a pockmarked, crippled runt like you?"

"Your mother asked me the same thing," Soso answers, without showing any agitation. "Then I fucked her with my cock."

Parkadze open his mouth to fire back but closes it again. It's too risky to respond. They descend three flights in silence. They enter the unadorned chapel and the columns split to left and right. The seminarians line up on either side of a central aisle in seven standing rows. Soso is chanting the entrance hymn in Church Slavonic and enjoying the sound of his own smooth tenor, which has garnered praise from his teachers. Abashidze and the other priests separate from the students, climbing two steps to the soleas and taking their positions before the iconostasis. The Archimandrite Serafim lingers in the sanctuary with the curtain closed while he finishes off the Proskomedia — the ritual of preparing the bread offering for the ceremony.

It seems as if the sole purpose of the slow and monotonous Orthodox service is to bore Soso and his friends. One by one, the seminarians slip forbidden books out of their surplices and crack them open, where they remain hovering unseen at their waists. Soso, who is chanting loudly, opens his Darwin to where he left off. *My object in this chapter*, he reads, *is to show that there is no fundamental difference between man and the higher mammals in their mental faculties.*

Inspector Abashidze periodically searches the students' faces to make sure they're paying attention, but since they are accustomed to his surveillance, they anticipate each of his sweeps by glancing up from their texts, singing heartily, and performing their piety. The Inspector sees someone moving inappropriately out of the corner of his eye and grows more vigilant. His lingering suspicion forces him to watch the seminarians all through the little Litany and the recitation of Beatitudes. Soso gently closes his book and tucks it back beneath his cassock. The endless prayers to the Lord mix together and merge into an extended and dreary moan, exhausting Soso, but also strengthening his resolve. Abashidze's surveillance feels like a personal challenge. Soso sings with real fervour, a few decibels louder than the others. The Inspector has no way of knowing if he is mocking him or just being especially pious.

Something pricks against Soso's ear. He glances over his shoulder to see Parkadze snickering and, a row behind him, Devdariani staring ahead blankly, singing loudly and with too much conviction — an obvious imitation of Soso. Soso glances down at his feet and sees the crumpled piece of paper that hit his ear. He grits his teeth. How dare they mock him! Don't they understand he's faking his performance for the Inspector? Don't they know a trick when they see one?

The morning sunlight shimmers through the old barred window but doesn't do much to light up the gloomy hall. Soso can barely discern the room's corners in the darkness. The most sacred moment of the week is gradually overtaking the chapel—the transubstantiation of the wine into the true Blood of Christ and the bread into His true Flesh—but even that miraculous event can't clear the air of all the dry and peppery frankincense, a scent that Soso will forever associate with unadulterated boredom. Inspector Abashidze no longer feels the need to watch over his charges; they are surely too overcome by the awesome mystery even to consider rebellion. A hymn fills the room. Soso snickers at the way he's once again tricked the stupid priests. He removes his book from his surplice and hungrily devours Darwin. *Terror acts in the same manner on them as on us,* he reads, *causing the muscles to tremble, the heart to palpitate, the sphincters to be relaxed, and the hair to stand on end. Suspicion, the offspring of fear, is eminently characteristic of most wild animals.*

Although it is technically still a seminary of the Georgian Orthodox Church, the priests in this institution are all imported Russians. The sole exception is Inspector Abashidze, an ethnic Georgian with a fervour for domination. The Georgian teenagers under instruction are all too aware of the hundred-year-long occupation of their homeland, the renaming of their capital city from Tbilisi to Tiflis, and the arrogant and patronizing behaviour of any Russian with the slightest bit of power. Never is this general sense of oppression felt more sharply than during weekly Communion. Soso grumbles under his breath as he lines up behind pigeon-toed Nicholoz to approach the ambo, where he will have to submit himself to the haughtiest of masters, the Archimandrite Serafim. Soso crosses his hands over his chest and presses the Darwin text against his heart. He swallows the wine from a spoon and, by rote, kisses the base of the chalice. Beneath his dead, impenetrable stare, he thinks: *I am only thankful you Russian dogs have enough sense to use our good Georgian wine.*

When the service is at last finished, the weary seminarians march up the narrow stairway on their aching legs, their vitality temporarily subdued. Soso limps up the steps — another childhood accident. He eyes the back of Devdariani's head and imagines crushing it with his heel. The boys will now have an opportunity to change before lunch and their single afternoon of freedom for the week, but rather than laughter and relief when they enter the dormitory, they erupt in grumbles and curses. Inspector Abashidze must have left the chapel during the final part of the service: the students' lockers have been searched for political documents or other morally dubious texts.

"Look at this," says one seminarian, kicking a mass of clothing piled on the floor.

"The cunt," says another, riffling through his scattered letters.

Iremashvili, a tall and skinny boy from Soso's hometown of Gori, is pale-faced and frantic, tipping over his mattress.

"Oh, thank God," he whispers. He withdraws a ragged copy of his translated Zola novel and presses it to his forehead, sighing in relief. When he lowers his book, he notices Soso standing by the foot of his bed with his hands on his hips, grinning.

"You didn't leave that here, did you?"

Iremashvili holds up the novel as an answer to his friend. "I thought they'd search us in chapel."

"Then you're an idiot," says Soso. "You think lazy old Black Spot would pass up an excuse to avoid Litany?"

"I know I'm an idiot," agrees Iremashvili. "A very lucky one."

Soso returns to his own wooden locker, where the contents lie scattered around his bed. Abashidze has been disrupting the private items of every student, regardless of his grades or his loyalty to the priests. As the seminary's latest Inspector, promoted from the deputy position, Abashidze has promised Serafim that he will keep a tighter rein on a student body that has become violently rebellious, and has even in recent years produced some of Georgia's most infamous young revolutionaries. The Inspector has rifled through Soso's notebooks, his copy of Xenophon, and his Ilovaiski textbook of Russian history—written with an infuriating, pro-imperialist slant—in search of forbidden texts. Soso's tall black boots have been tossed on the floor, de-laced, their gaping tongues obscenely pulled out over their toes.

"Cocksucker," Soso mutters, although he can't help but grin at the affront. He removes the poem he's been writing from the pages of Darwin's book and holds it high in the air for the other students to see. "Hey, Black Spot!" he calls. "Looking for this?"

The seminarians glance up from their own trashed bunks, regarding his small act of bravery with either mild amusement or indifference. Soso recklessly tosses both the book and the poem onto his bed, in full sight, as a kind of taunt to the Inspector.

He sits on his mattress and shoves the protruding tongues back into his boots. He finds the laces and begins to string them through their holes, chanting in a singsong rhythm:

"Not for all the trees in Eden would I these rugged cliffs exchange,
Nor for paradise undreamed of would I my native land exchange!"

Peter Kapanadze, another of Soso's friends from his hometown of Gori, laughs and slaps his thigh. "Eristavi!" he cries.

"Of course," answers Soso with a grin.

Kapanadze plops down on the bed and joins in the recitation of the famous poem, written by a Georgian count who is admired for his rebellious stance against the Russians and his calls for reform. The two boys chant and sway together with their eyes closed, moved by the verse. Kapanadze, who is also sixteen, but with a trim and muscular body more like a young adult's, wraps his arm around Soso's shoulders and pulls him side to side with the rhythm. Soso looks tiny next to Kapanadze, more like his younger brother than his peer and classmate. Soso tightens his stiff back, charged with the pride of having started a political movement, albeit one of only two people. He opens his eyes and scans the dorm for other recruits while waving his free arm, as if he were spurring a future Georgian national orchestra into playing their patriotic anthem with all the passion it deserves.

"Shut up, Soso," growls Parkadze from his distant bunk. "You pockmarked, one-armed loper."

"Your voice sounds like my farts," adds another seminarian, "when I'm doubled over with diarrhea."

"Fuck you," barks Soso. He pops up from his bunk and points his finger at them. "I chant better than all of you idiots combined and you know it. You're not worth one piece of my shit." As quickly as they have appeared, the popping veins in Soso's forehead recede. He inhales and calms in the span of a single breath. "I wish I had my old slingshot," he says, his tone now more of a jest than a taunt. "A stone in the face is what you'll get when you cross a couple of mountain men like Peter and me. We're true Gori *abreks*, that's what we are!"

Soso sits again, squinting with mirth, and refocuses his attention on his boots. He's oblivious to the smirks of his companions. They know all too well the difference between these boys from Gori and those legendary Caucasian mountain men called *abreks*, resisters of all authority, who are more likely to be Chechens or rugged Islamists than Georgian teenagers at a seminary in Tiflis. Still, most of the seminarians secretly wish they were as brave as Soso and Kapanadze, reciting Eristavi's poem so openly.

Iremashvili, having put on his trousers and his long cotton tunic, stands by Soso's bed passing his forbidden novel from hand to hand as if it were too hot to hold. He decides to tuck it into his pants, pulling his tunic over it. "Want me to help you clean up?" he asks.

Soso, concentrating on his laces, grunts — an animal code that Iremashvili has learned to interpret as approval. Iremashvili gets to work, folding Soso's clothing, straightening his books, and tucking each item back into his friend's locker. He finishes his tasks before Soso is done lacing his boots.

Although Soso's twenty-year-old black boots have distressed toes, the soles have been replaced and the stitching is fully intact. Every time Soso weaves the laces, he extends his arm until the length of each side is balanced and measured against the other. Then he pulls and adjusts them with the same precision that the priests use to prepare the diskos and the chalice, a comparison that doesn't escape Iremashvili's observation.

"Your father's?" asks Iremashvili, nodding at the boots.

Soso glares at him with dull and mute anger in his eyes.

Iremashvili lowers his head and fumbles his too-large hands around each other. He rubs his toes against the dormitory's uneven wooden floor, wishing he hadn't asked such a stupid question. Many times, as a young boy, Iremashvili watched those boots pound against Soso's thin chest and stomp down on his arms, crunching the child's bones. Many mornings when he came by the Djugashvilis' rented room to fetch his friend, he found those filthy boots sprawled by the door, speckled with blood. His gaze would then drift to Soso's father Beso, who, having temporarily returned to the family he tortured and then abandoned, was invariably passed out in the room's only bed, stinking of sweat and cheap wine and kerosene spilled from an upturned lamp.

Soso registers his friend's embarrassment and lets it pass without comment. He shimmies out of his surplice and cassock, relying on his right hand to do most of the work. "Go on!" he barks at Iremashvili, shielding his warped left arm from his friend's sight, although the damage is hardly a secret after so many years in school together. "I'll meet you at the door," he says.

Soso finds a cotton shirt, thin pants, and a pair of socks. Iremashvili backs up and faces another seminarian, who's busy making his bed with the awful precision demanded by the priests, until Soso, fully dressed and sitting on his bed, grunts at him to turn around again. Soso is pulling on his boots and tucking his pants inside them.

"What're you going to do with your book?" Iremashvili asks, indicating the Darwin text on Soso's bed.

"Leave it in my locker."

Iremashvili offers the wide-mouthed astonishment that's clearly expected as his reply. "Soso, are you crazy?"

"What did you call me?" asks Soso, his brow furrowed in anger but his lips rising in a grin.

Iremashvili holds up his hand in apology. "Forgive me," he says. "Koba."

"Don't forget my name."

"But your book," says Iremashvili, eager to change the subject.

"Let them search my locker," says Soso. "I'm not afraid of them."

He picks up his poem, folds it into a square, and tucks the paper deep into the pocket of his pants. He throws the book into his open locker and kicks the top closed, the wood slamming down with a loud crash, startling the few seminarians still lingering in the dormitory. "Christ," one of them mutters. Soso nods at Iremashvili and together they proceed to the stairs.

"What's that you've got this week?" asks Iremashvili once they're in the hall.

"Darwin's *Descent of Man.*"

"I hear it's very good."

"It's clarified a few things," says Soso, grinning. "Now I understand why you look so much like a monkey." He laughs, claps his hand on the top of Iremashvili's shoulder, and gives it a hard squeeze. Iremashvili thinks his friend is going to throw him to the floor or smash his face into the flimsy wall of the hallway — the beginning of a fierce but playful battle, full of cheap shots to the head and sharp kicks to the ribs, exactly the way they used to fight back in their unmonitored days in the dusty streets of Gori. Iremashvili chuckles at Soso's joke. He wants to retort with a minor quip about the simian hair on Soso's ass but thinks better of it, especially with that hand gripping his shoulder. He presses his lips together and says nothing.

In the refectory, there's a giant steaming samovar, a platter of thinly sliced *lavashi* bread spread with honey, and a small bowl of *lobio* beans for each student. Soso lines up, fills his glass, takes away his bread and beans. All six hundred seminarians are crammed into this small, overheated room. They've fallen into a regular seating pattern, so the meal moves swiftly. As usual, Peter Kapanadze and Vano Ketskhoveli are sitting at the end of the long table. They glance up and offer Soso and Iremashvili nods as they approach. Vano, who is stockier and less handsome than his friends, with glasses, a rounder face, and a more prominent brow, is eating his meal one bean at a time in a desperate attempt at making it last. Kapanadze, having just finished his lunch, sighs in frustration, reclines, and pulls on his thick beard. Soso and Iremashvili wolf down their bread in seconds, and most of their beans. The smoky flavour and almost meaty texture of the beans is more taunting than satisfying. The seminary's small rations are intended to teach some stupid lesson about self-discipline or gluttony; none of the students care to remember. A couple of eavesdropping priests march back and forth on the far side of the room like bored prison guards.

"Hey," whispers Vano, "you going to Chichinadze's this afternoon?"

"No," answers Kapanadze. "I thought I'd stay around here today and kiss the Inspector's fat lips."

Iremashvili and Soso laugh over their few remaining beans.

"What do you think?" Kapanadze scoffs, leaning forward and flicking a crumb across the table. "Of course I'm going."

"What's the reading today for Devdariani's group?" asks Vano, his plump fingers tapping the table.

"Why *his* group?" grumbles Soso. "It doesn't belong to him."

"Well, he started it."

"Don't be an idiot," says Soso. "Your brother started it long before Devdariani was here."

"We're reading's Plekhanov's latest," says Kapanadze. "What, you didn't read it?"

"I never got a chance."

"No way you'll find it in Chichinadze's."

"Damn it," says Vano.

"What's the point of even coming?" mocks Kapanadze. "Better to stick your head in the toilet."

Iremashvili guffaws and slaps the wood. Soso gulps his tea and decides that since he can't have a second helping of bread or beans, he'll go to the samovar and replenish his cup. Standing before the serving table, he takes care to smile at the suspicious priest on duty, who's guarding the remaining slices of bread from would-be gluttons. Soso whispers under his breath: "Hope you choke on your louse-infected beard, you brigand." When he returns, his friends are midway through a conversation about their assignment for the socialist reading group.

"Plekhanov's a genius," Iremashvili claims, crossing his arms, leaning back, and playing the authority. "I can't wait to discuss him."

"You should read Marx," says Soso as he sits with his tea. "Plekhanov is only saying exactly what Marx said twenty years before him, except he writes *Russia* instead of *Germany*, so we're supposed to love him more."

"I *have* read Marx," says Iremashvili, stung.

"You won't learn anything new today," adds Soso, sipping his bitter tea. "Not with Devdariani leading the way."

"I thought you two were friends," says Kapanadze.

"Friends," scoffs Soso. "He's an asshole and an idiot."

A commotion arises on the other side of the refectory as Inspector Abashidze lumbers into the room, flanked by two burly priests, and approaches a third-year seminarian who is eating with his friends. The authorities stand sternly before the boy as he holds tight to his bread, his skin paling. Wheezing, Abashidze pushes his glasses up his nose and portentously raises a beat-up copy of a Balzac novel for the entire refectory to see, as if the seminarians should all gasp in horror at the sight.

"What's this?" asks Inspector Abashidze.

"Oh," says the boy meekly.

"Why did I find it in your locker this morning?"

"It isn't mine," says the blinking seminarian.

"Orthodox priests do not read French filth."

"I don't know where it came from. I don't have anything to do with it."

"Then you're as honest as a Jew." Abashidze, as if playing a Roman emperor, gestures with his chin to unleash the two large priests. They clutch the boy's wrists and pull him up from his seat, knocking his bread on the floor, honey side down.

"Wait," says the boy.

The priests yank the terrified student out of the refectory while Abashidze presses his fat hands together to emphasize the piety of his duty. He follows his minions into the hall and then down into the cellar, where the boy will spend the next twelve to twenty-four hours in a tiny room constructed for solitary confinement. No light, one glass of water, and nothing to eat. Only a blanket on the floor and a bucket in which to relieve himself. It's a punishment the seminarians have affectionately labelled "the wolf's ticket." Although there's a certain honour to the sentence — it's seen as a kind of training for their future lives as revolutionary socialists — these seminarians are still just boys who secretly dread the fate. The remaining students murmur and gossip in the refectory.

"Silence while eating!" shouts the priest Alexandre from his march along the back wall. He punctuates his command with a sharp clap.

"Poor guy," whispers Iremashvili. "The wolf's ticket for reading Balzac."

"They're monsters," murmurs Vano.

"He deserves it," says Soso. "The stupidity of stashing a novel in your locker. What did he think would happen?"

"I said silence!"

The students lower their chins and quiet themselves. Soso and his friends pull their chairs closer to the table. "Hey," Kapanadze whispers to Vano, "I heard something this morning about your brother leaving Kiev."

Vano adjusts his round glasses and raises his bushy eyebrows. "Where'd you hear that?"

"From Parkadze and Devdariani. They said he's coming back to Georgia. Is it true?"

"What do those two idiots know about it?" says Soso.

Vano glances from side to side to ensure that no priests are listening. He hunches closer to the table, drawing in the others with the prospect of new information about his famous brother. Lado Ketskhoveli is perhaps the most famous of the student revolutionaries, having once organized a protest so effective that it shut the seminary down for several weeks. Under orders from the Okhrana, the Tsar's secret police—who know all too well how violent students mature into cold-blooded opponents of the Russian Empire—Lado was expelled and forced into exile at the Kiev Seminary. While finishing his studies there, he met and paired up with another legendary ex-Tiflis seminarian, Silva Jibladze, who was in hiding from the Okhrana in Kiev. Jibladze was even more radical than Lado. He'd killed a rector at the Tiflis Seminary with his Georgian sword and then had to escape in the middle of the night. It was said that Lado and the young killer were agitating for revolution with the socialists in Kiev.

"It's true I got a letter from him, yes," whispers Vano Ketskhoveli.

Soso clenches his fists beneath the table, pained that Ilya Parkadze, Seid Devdariani, and Vano all know more about Lado's plans than he does. It doesn't make any sense. Lado always seemed to like and admire Soso, ever since their early days in Gori, when Soso was a child and Lado nothing more than the local priest's eldest son. Why would he convey his secret intentions to cowards like Ilya and Seid, or to his thick and myopic brother—a boy who hasn't even read the most basic Marxist writers like Plekhanov—instead of to the brilliant Soso Djugashvili? Surely Lado trusts him more than he could ever trust Vano or the others. Didn't he once take Soso to the Gori bookshop, pay his lending fee, and even insist on him reading *On the Origin of Species*? Why would he do that unless he understood Soso's potential as a comrade—unless he trusted him? Biological brotherhood means less to a hero like Lado than the camaraderie of like-minded revolutionaries.

"He writes in secret code," whispers Vano to his friends. "For everyone's security. So only I can read it. And I burn his letters straight away."

That's why, thinks Soso, his knuckles turning white under the table. Lado hasn't yet had the chance to teach his other comrades the code. But then how did Parkadze and Devdariani know everything?

"The movement's building in Kiev," says Vano. "He says he's done with his work there. So yes, it's true, he wants to return. As soon as the Okhrana forget his expulsion, he'll sneak into Georgia. In the spring, or maybe sooner. You never know with him. Lado's not one to avoid a risk."

"That's for sure," says Kapanadze.

"He'd come back though it's forbidden?" asks Iremashvili.

"Don't be stupid," grumbles Soso. "Banishment is nothing for a revolutionary. I'd defy the order myself."

"Me too," says Kapanadze.

"Me too," adds Vano, but with less enthusiasm.

"I doubt that," says Soso, glaring hard across the table at the great Lado's inferior younger brother.

"I guess I'd defy it too," adds Iremashvili, although everybody knows he doesn't mean it.

"Lado's not afraid of the Okhrana," says Soso. "He'd spit in their faces, even in jail."

"He'd spit into the eyes of a bear."

"A mother bear," laughs Iremashvili. "And her cub!"

"I'll bet when he comes back, he'll kill Serafim or Abash-idze," says Kapanadze. "Just like Jibladze did. Did he say anything about it?"

"Nothing," says Vano, shrugging.

"He's probably planning it."

"Let him take out Serafim," mutters Soso. "But we should be the ones to take out Black Spot. That'll show Lado our solidarity."

"And for revenge," says Kapanadze.

"We should do it."

"We should."

"They've got it coming."

The big bell clangs in the hall, ending the time allotted for their meal. The priest Alexandre, standing by the samovar, announces that the front gates will soon be opened for the students' weekly free time in Tiflis. The boys clean up their places, rinsing their glasses in a bowl of lukewarm water on the serving table and returning them to the shelf. They trot out of the refectory and approach the doors to the portico, where they wait with a growing congregation of seminarians hopping excitedly from foot to foot. Two attending monks slide the metal gate aside and pry the door open.

After quick mock-solemn bows, signs of the cross, and words of praise for their priests and masters, the four teenagers hurry out of Tiflis Theological Seminary into the brightness of Yerevan Square. Standing on the marble steps, they squint in the midday light. The brightness stabs their eyes after so many days in the gloomy and oppressive seminary. They have exactly two hours before they have to return.

They climb the narrow and steep road into the Armenian Bazaar, chatting boisterously. The tiny street is lined with wine merchants and bakers, their fragrant shops laden with swollen sheep skins hanging from nails, and flatbreads roasting in huge clay ovens so powerful that their heat is felt in the street. The boys laugh and joke as they weave past a couple of itinerant vegetable dealers with wooden trays balanced on their heads, a Tartar mullah in a white turban, and an old, ruined prince with a staggering gait and bloodshot eyes, struggling with the fingering for a common tune on his *duduki* pipe. Kapanadze skips over a mound of camel dung and stumbles against a burly mountain peasant, knocking his shaggy hat off. He apologizes, picks up the grumbling Chechen's cap, and returns it to him.

The group enters a Persian neighbourhood, full of steaming bathhouses that stink of rotten eggs from the sulphuric hot springs. They climb a steep hill, which rises up to Holy Mountain and the ancient, prison-like Metekhi fortress. Vano and Iremashvili scoop rocks from the road and challenge each other to a skipping contest on the cobblestones. Soso lets his friends pull ahead. A little distance is important—essential, even—if he's going to clear his head and prepare himself for Lado's arrival. Soso lowers his eyes and tries to give the upcoming event proper consideration.

He imagines Lado Ketskhoveli—an image in earthy tones, the muted oranges and browns of cheap icons nailed to the chapel walls. Lado's a handsome man, taller than the average Georgian, with a reticent but mirthful stare beneath his high forehead. His beard is thick and full, his moustache wide and curled. He has neither the thick brow nor the burly mien of Vano, his inferior brother. Soso allows himself to imagine a gold-leafed halo painted above Lado's head. The priests may have commanded Soso to revere the living Jesus, even to taste his flesh and blood, but Lado is the only saint whose material being cannot be denied.

Soso recalls some of the parables circulating through the seminary about their exemplary leader. It has been said that Lado, at loose in the city one evening, enchanted, seduced, and deflowered an otherwise chaste Armenian girl in less than an hour. The students still laugh about it. Another tells of how the great Lado, having orchestrated a public debate between himself and a pompous priest, conned the priest into making an illogical and paradoxical statement about morality. It was a trap that proved God did not exist. The priest was so embarrassed by his utterance that he gave Lado the wolf's ticket for three days. And of course there's the well-known parable that Soso first heard back in Gori, the one about Lado's bravery during the student revolt at the end of '93, which resulted in the seminary's temporary shutdown. Lado stood on his chair in the refectory, calling out for other students to boycott their classes until all their demands were met. He insisted that the monks end their constant spying, that the rector fire the seminary's worst offenders, and that the school immediately establish a Department of Georgian Studies with classes offered in their native language. Lado emphasized these points by dumping his entire bowl of beans onto the recently mopped floor. The Sermon of the Beans is what the students call it, and it's far holier to them than Jesus's talk on the Mount.

Lado may be the hero and commander, but every successful movement must be led by more than just one man. He will need a prized disciple upon his return to Tiflis, someone patient and strong, with a firm grasp on the classic literature — a second-in-command who can be trusted and relied upon. Silva Jibladze, the killer of the former rector, is certainly a committed soldier, but he's said to be a lunatic, without the cool head needed for any position of authority.

Lado's disciple. That's what Soso will be. He is sure of it. As he scales the steep street on Holy Mountain, Soso remembers that afternoon last April when he was called into Archimandrite Serafim's office. It was the first time he proved his worth as a revolutionary in Lado's mould. When Soso entered the room, he faced the iron-latticed window framing the greenery of Pushkin Gardens, the austere wooden desk, the Byzantine cross with its top crossbar and bottom slanted bar engraved *INBI*, and the redundant bookshelf, stocked with Scripture ad nauseam. Old Black Spot stood, while the white-faced, white-haired Archimandrite Serafim sat at his desk. Two dour and severe inquisitors.

"Glory to Christ, the Lord and King," said Serafim upon Soso's entry.

"Glory to the Lord," answered Soso, crossing himself and shutting the door behind him.

"Iosif Vissarionovich Djugashvili, sit down."

Soso recalls how he inhaled the fresh spring air seeping through the window. The wind carried on it the faint sweetness of camomile. The high windows in his dormitory didn't open at all. He craved that breeze. It was his first year in the seminary and he'd already been cooped up for months, longing for flowering season, which he'd loved since he was a little boy. As he sat before the Archimandrite, revived by that scent, Soso wanted nothing other than to go outside for an entire spring day, from dusk till dawn, as he did back in Gori, to climb the steep trails of Gorijvari, play in the intricate, linked caves of Uplis-Tsikhe, and swim the river Kura.

"Mmm," said Archimandrite Serafim with approval as he rifled through reports from Soso's teachers. The morose Inspector Abashidze stood unblinking behind the Archimandrite's desk as if he were an Okhrana agent or, with all his girth, the Tsar's own bodyguard. "You are proving to be a very good student, Djugashvili."

"Thank you, Archimandrite," whispered the scrawny fifteen-year-old.

"Your secular history, Holy Scripture, Church Slavonic — all satisfactory."

"Thank you, Archimandrite," repeated Soso.

Serafim, to Soso's surprise, then clicked his tongue with disapproval. "I see your Greek could use some work."

"Yes," said Soso, fighting a grin. "I know it could."

"All in all, very satisfactory," concluded the Archimandrite as he put down the papers and nodded. "Well then, no doubt you know about the problems we've had in recent years. The murder of our last Archimandrite. The unfortunate expulsions of last spring."

"Yes," said Soso. "I do."

"Of the several students behind that most recent disturbance, there was one culprit in particular. Vladimir Ketskhoveli, the student leader."

"Lado," said Soso.

"A boy who won't be giving us any more trouble," said Serafim, half smiling. "But now we've got to contend with his brother, Vano, that one in your year. He's a friend of yours, correct? You were at school together in Gori?"

"Yes," said Soso.

"So you must have known Lado as well?"

"Not really, no. I saw him around. He was older."

"Causing trouble at a young age?"

Soso shrugged and clasped his hands, but didn't answer the question.

"I suspect these things run in the family."

"I don't know if they do," said Soso. "Their father is a priest and very pious."

"Yes," continued the Archimandrite. "But our challenge today is to prevent a repetition of '93. Some bold little Georgian uprising led by the younger brother."

"I don't have anything to do with that."

Soso heard the deference and piety in his tone. It was a convincing performance, but the officials in this seminary never trusted students. The Archimandrite nodded at Soso suspiciously. Inspector Abashidze, always eager to find a liar, chuckled and shook his large head.

"You're a good pupil, Djugashvili," continued Serafim. "We're very impressed. You're a pious and obedient young man, and your performance in the choir has been exemplary to say the least. We think the priesthood will benefit greatly from your service."

"Thank you," said Soso, forcing a smile, trying his best to look grateful for the praise.

"And so we know you'll tell us if this Vano Ketskhoveli imagines himself a hero. If he thinks Lado's rebellious blood flows in his veins as well. We've always trusted our best students to keep us informed. And we're right to do so, aren't we?"

Soso found himself unable to say anything.

"Especially when that student is a half-boarder who has already requested additional assistance with his dues."

Soso lowered his head. He recalled the obsequious letter he had had to write to the Archimandrite the summer before. Even with the help of his mother's wealthier friends and Gori's police chief Davrishashvili he couldn't raise enough money to pay the school's fee. Unlike the other seminarians, with their princely parents and sophisticated backgrounds, he was indeed in debt.

"You should answer when addressed, Djugashvili."

"Yes," said Soso, forcing himself to speak. "You can trust me."

"I'm sure I can."

"That's all, then," said Inspector Abashidze, his flabby arm gesturing towards the door. He twitched his nose—a nervous habit that Soso had seen a thousand times.

Soso stood and managed a smile for the two brazen, blackmailing dogs.

"Glory to Thee, O Christ our God and our hope," the Archimandrite intoned, making a sign of the cross.

"Glory to the Father, and to the Son, and to the Holy Spirit, now and ever and unto the ages of ages," replied Soso, mirroring his master's gesture.

"Continue making us proud."

It was only Soso's first tense encounter with the authorities, but already he had shown all the qualities necessary to become Lado's disciple. He had prepared the priests accordingly with his excellent grades and exemplary performance in choir. He played the model seminarian, showing no apparent desire beyond that of remaining in the good graces of his dear Russian priests. And then, as he sat before them, Soso was meek and pious, angelic and articulate, seemingly willing to rat on his friends and companions if that's what the priests required of him. He'd earned their trust, which showed great skill. Now, as he walks in the city, lost in thought, Soso is sure that Lado will come to appreciate and even rely upon his capacity for deceit.

The boys move into a less populated neighbourhood of houses with larger yards, pet goats chained and bleating, the occasional trellis overgrown with grapes. Iremashvili turns around and notices that Soso has slipped well behind the group. "Hey, Koba," he calls. "Come on!"

Kapanadze spins around and walks backwards, smiling at Soso, tossing a rock up and down from one hand to the other. "Save me, Koba the avenger," he cries in a false, girlish voice. He throws his rock into the street, clutches his breast, and blinks. "Please, Koba, *help* me — I'm Iago and he's Nunu." He whacks Vano on the chest with the back of his hand. "Hurry up and save your friends."

Iremashvili and Vano laugh together. Vano kicks a stone. "Are you or aren't you Koba?"

Although the question stings Soso, his face remains vacant and placid, and his dull eyes regard the reedy boys marching a dozen paces before him. Koba is the hero of *The Patricide*, Alexander Kazbegi's most famous novel, and Soso's favourite. All Georgian boys pretend to be Koba the Avenger during their war games, especially the well-read nationalists like these seminarians, and so it's always been vaguely comic that Soso has tried to monopolize the name of their collective hero.

The others turn and continue forward. Soso keeps his distance until they reach their destination.

Zakaria Chichinadze's small, packed bookstore and unofficial lending library occupies several small rooms on the first floor of an old brick building. Sunday is not a day of business, but the owner knows these students have only a few free hours each week and so he waits for them by the entrance, propping the door open with his foot. Past a row of stacked bookshelves and through a narrow threshold is Chichinadze's dark and windowless office. Its ceiling is far too low for any of the taller Russian Okhrana agents to comfortably stand beneath, but it's perfect for fellow Georgians. The office has a cracked brick floor and a constantly replenished jug of *napareuli* wine, and serves as the secret refuge for seminarians to read their forbidden books or discuss socialism's progress with an eager and knowledgeable elder.

"Good seminarians!" Chichinadze cries, bowing his head in mock deference. He pats each boy on the back when they enter the shop and waits at the door as the shortest and slowest of them, Soso Djugashvili, lopes crookedly in silence.

"Hello, Soso," says Chichinadze warmly, although one glance at the boy's face informs the bookseller that he shouldn't try to touch him.

Soso nods briskly and slips into the store.

With the front door closed so that passing Okhrana officers won't suspect Chichinadze of operating on a Sunday, the boys make themselves at home. As Vano pleads for a copy of Plekhanov, Kapanadze searches the shelves of Russian works for Dostoevsky's *Devils*, and Iremashvili tries to capture Chichinadze's attention by exaggerating the story of Inspector Abashidze's morning search, Soso hides between bookshelves and scans a recent edition of *Iveria* for the poem that he's written. The editor, the famed Prince Chavchavadze, doyen of Georgian poetry, told Soso that he liked his poem, loved it even, but still Soso wonders if the old prince has lived up to his word and published it. Soso eagerly searches the paper and, to his surprise, finds "Morning" in the right-hand corner of the final page.

He rereads his work, his heart pounding with excitement.

The poem's images of roses and larks, violets and nightingales are a Romantic celebration of the Georgian motherland, but they suddenly seem derivative and a bit embarrassing. Still, he can see that his poem has some virtues. The scan of its syllables and the rhymes he worked so hard to perfect hold up. It's a decent poem, he decides.

Most importantly, it's done. Soso is officially a published poet, not so different from the great Eristavi, and only sixteen years old. The thought of his precocious success does not penetrate Soso's mask of equanimity. He stays sitting in the aisle, popping into his mouth the dried cherries and small grapes that Chichinadze keeps in a big bowl by the store's entrance. Although his first poem has appeared in a prestigious newspaper published by the great nationalist prince himself, Soso resolves to keep it a secret. His life as a poet, he has decided, is no one's business but his own.

Kapanadze, clutching Dostoevsky's novel, crouches behind Soso and lays his arm around his chest. Soso is surprised by the firm squeeze. He shuts the newspaper and yanks his small body out of his friend's grip.

"Hey, Koba, lighten up," says Kapanadze, now laying a hand on his friend's shoulder. "I was only kidding back there in the street."

"Get your hand off me before I bite it off your wrist," Soso whispers through his tight teeth.

Kapanadze holds up the offending hand in obedience. "All right," he says. "Right away. I'm sorry, my friend."

While Soso tries to refocus his attention on the front page of *Iveria*, Kapanadze backs away, slips behind a nearby bookcase, and moves into the back office to join Iremashvili, Vano, and Chichinadze. The air inside the store gradually turns blue as smoke from the pipes the owner has offered the students drifts out of the office. Soso remains in the aisle, pulling a variety of texts from the shelves and reading bits and pieces.

An hour slips by. Soso's peers and the bookseller debate the future of Georgia—whether resistance to the Russian authorities should proceed by liberal reforms, as argued by Prince Chavchavadze in *Iveria*, or by revolution, as argued by the International Marxists. When the debate shifts to the status of Mesami Dasi, the Georgian socialist party, and whether Noe Jordania, the party's charismatic leader, is more of a reformist or a revolutionary at heart, the students argue for the latter, using as proof the fact that Lado is planning on joining that secret organization when he returns from Kiev.

It's an unbelievably stupid position, Soso decides. They have no idea what they're talking about. At the mention of Lado Ketskhoveli, he has to cover his ears with his hands and try to focus all his attention on the Victor Hugo novel he's laid in his lap. There is nothing more irritating to Soso than the pompous declamations of boys who will never make it with the great Lado.

Eventually, the seminarians' idiotic banter becomes too much for Soso to bear. He grumbles and curses, slams his book shut, and moves into the doorway. "It's nearly three," he barks. "I'm going back to the Stone Sack."

The air is so thick that the bodies in the back office are

almost silhouettes. Chiçhinadze, leaning on his desk, blows a puff of smoke through his rounded lips and checks the clock on the wall. "Nonsense," he says. "You have at least half an hour."

"Come join us," says Vano, the long pipe in his mouth a ridiculous juxtaposition with his youthful features.

"No, I'm going," says Soso.

"Wait a moment," says Chichinadze. "Do you still have Darwin's *Descent of Man*?"

"Yes, but I want another week with it."

The bookseller nods. "I'll mark it in my ledger. Take your time, Soso."

"Koba," Soso growls.

Chichinadze raises his brow and fights off a smile. "Right," he says. "Sorry."

Soso slips out of the store and marches down the hill towards Yerevan Square. Each step stirs a cloud of dust beneath his sole, as if it were afraid to touch his boot. The dirt rises and swirls in the thin mountain air, only settling on the weathered brick when it is certain the boy has moved on and will not turn back. *At least the dust has the good sense to understand who I am*, Soso thinks as he quickens his pace, stomping harder with each step.

Once returned to the Stone Sack—as all the students call the seminary—Soso lies in his bunk with his head propped on a pillow, reading Charles Darwin. The other seminarians are gradually returning from their free time and assembling in the dormitories. Soso buries his face in his book so he doesn't have to meet their curious glances. He has hidden his forbidden text inside a larger, tedious book on ecclesiastical history.

Abashidze stands in the doorway and scowls. "Absolute silence in study period!" he barks. "Punishable by solitary." He closes the door and locks it from the outside.

The seminarians glance at the door to make sure the Inspector is really gone. A dozen students rise from their bunks and desks to arrange a circle of chairs in the back of the large room. Seid Devdariani pulls his chair into the corner and commands with a sharp whisper that the younger students hurry up and assemble around him. He is stroking his almost full beard and reclining, trying very hard to look like an important revolutionary. Ilya Parkadze positions himself beside the group leader to the right, also stroking his beard thoughtfully. Kapanadze and Vano Ketskhoveli occupy seats to his immediate left. Soso drags his chair into the position directly opposite Devdariani and then sits with his elbows splayed out on the armrests as wide as he possibly can. He stretches his feet to the floor and grimaces. Iremashvili curls like a centipede in the chair beside Soso's.

The students have to conduct their meeting in calculated and practised whispers, just loud enough to hear each other. The dormitory's inner walls stop a foot short of the ceiling, so the priests patrolling in the hallway can eavesdrop on them if they speak too loudly. They have stashed dummy books under their seats in case their meeting is interrupted.

"I take it you've all had a chance to read the Plekhanov," whispers Devdariani, still stroking his beard.

Vano lowers his eyes and murmurs his false affirmation along with the other seminarians.

Parkadze withdraws the forbidden book from inside a folded surplice and hands it to the leader. Devdariani palms the brand new edition with one hand, like the priests with their holy books, rubbing his fingertips on the leather cover and laying it on his lap.

"You have no idea how lucky we are. This text is only just out in Russia. Chichinadze had to send away for it on my request."

Kapanadze can't help but roll his eyes at the leader's pretension.

"I know it must be difficult for some of you to follow Plekhanov's argument," continues Devdariani, "as you're every bit as unfamiliar with subjective Russian Utopians as you are with German Utopians. But let me see if I can't explain the situation in simpler terms."

Soso grits his teeth at Devdariani across the circle. So the leader's going to explain the basic arguments of Marxism in "simpler terms"? To think, last year, when Soso was new to the seminary and far more timid in all matters, that he befriended and even liked this sixth-year student, that he was impressed by Devdariani's wide learning and past friendship with the great Lado Ketskhoveli. He'd even invited Devdariani to drop by his mother's home in Gori during the first part of their Christmas break. What a naive error! Now Soso considers Devdariani just another pompous priest to endure.

Several of the sharper seminarians sigh and shift position.

Although their leader irritates them, it's true that these younger students don't really know anything about socialism. When Devdariani begins to explain Plekhanov's arguments about Marxism in the Russian context, those willing to listen learn something. As the conversation grows more theoretical, more and more of the students wrinkle their brows and lean forward or pull back in their seats, tightening their lips in thought. Mikhail Semenov, a bright second-year student, asks for a brief clarification of human nature as understood by Marx.

"Human nature," explains Devdariani, "is not a fixed and constant thing." He rifles through the Plekhanov until he finds the quote he needs. "Here," Devdariani says, looking at the text. "*He*—meaning Marx—*regarded man's nature itself as the eternally changing result of historical progress, the cause of which lies* outside *man*. In other words," continues Devdariani, "Marx has defined human nature as the *product* of our behaviour and not as its *cause*. Human nature is *variable*. It is conditioned by our economic situation and therefore always subject to change. It is not really a *nature* at all."

"But that reverses everything," says an excited Semenov. "That means the science of human development can only be truly understood from the opposite vantage point. From the external to the internal."

"Precisely," says Devdariani—rather too smugly, Soso thinks.

"So whereas generations have looked to human nature for ultimate answers, Marx has rightfully taken the historical and material condition of man to be the defining factor in human development."

"Yes," Devdariani says, leaning back with satisfaction.

"Keep it down over there," calls Konstanin Feokhari, a grim young seminarian with long hair and a pair of glasses that are too small for his wide face. Feokhari sits with Aleksander Novikov at Novikov's single desk on the other side of the room. These two serious and hard-working students, both top performers in their class, study together, pray together, eat their bread and beans together, always without complaint. Both boys dream of a life in service to the Orthodox Church and neither would dream of joining Devdariani's forbidden group. They are reading and discussing a glorified account of Tsar Alexander II from the seminary's approved history of Russia.

"*You* keep it down," shouts Parkadze, although the two students have been silent until now. "Pious ass-kissers."

Parkadze's insult garners laughter from the other seminarians around him. One member of the group, Doremidont Gogokhiya, pounds his beefy hand on his chair and guffaws with an open mouth.

"You're drug dealers," adds Devdariani, suddenly realizing the social potential in baiting the other two. "Poisoning the proletariat with your piety."

"Shut up, Seid," whispers Novikov.

"Religion's an opiate," Devdariani continues. "You're training to be the capitalist's wine-slobbering, Eucharist-chomping lackeys."

"Godless monsters," whispers Feokhari as he grabs the greasy hair falling over his temples and pulls it down over his ears.

"Get back to your prayers," calls Kapanadze, laughing.

"Never mind them," says Devdariani, turning back towards the group and shaking his head.

"They dream of their heaven," adds Parkadze, still playing the eager apostle to Devdariani's Christ, "but don't give a thought to the salvation of our Georgian workers' souls."

Soso frowns, shifts his weight, and clenches his fists until they're numb. He can't stand this pathetic and timid shouting match. In Gori's ramshackle streets, he broke noses, slingshot cows, set fire to an old prince's apple orchard. Lado too is a fighter, demanding real change from the Russian authorities. These children around him now are nothing more than petty fools. Devdariani and his idiot friends think rebellion is a game, a mere school argument, and a challenge is nothing more than the berating of a couple of easy targets like Novikov and Feokhari. In his sudden fury, Soso feels moved to speak against Devdariani and the entire reading group. He stomps his boot, stands, and shouts: "You idiots act as if Charles Darwin never existed."

The others turn towards Soso in astonishment. He is pacing back and forth on the outside of the circle.

"Listen to yourselves. *Marx has defined human nature as the product, not the cause.* What a load of horseshit! You blabber on and on as if the precious 'human' were some kind of sacred creature, when anyone who's thought enough to read a little bit of Darwin knows that human nature is precisely the same as animal nature at its core. It's just a difference in degree."

"Now wait a minute, Soso," says Devdariani without raising his voice. He sits perfectly still, both of his hands resting on top of his book.

"What, are you a priest?" asks Soso, standing behind his chair and leaning over it to face the leader. "Are you and your little deacon Parkadze here going to explain the gospel to us faithful seminarians? The devil take you both! Someone ought to kick you square in the jaw. And with a vengeance, too!"

"Soso," says Devdariani, holding out a soothing hand and smiling benignly. "I think you've underestimated the intellect of our dear comrade Plekhanov."

"Our dear *comrade?*" Soso makes a show of his laughter. "Is that how it is? If Plekhanov was here, on the toilet, he wouldn't deem your Holy Arrogance worthy of tapping the piss out of his Marxist cock."

A few of the seminarians, including Iremashvili, giggle at Soso's glorious heresy.

"That's how much he's your *comrade.*"

Although Parkadze is red-faced, Devdariani remains calm, his hands still resting in his lap. He waits for the laughter to die down. "You're quite mistaken, Soso," he begins, "if you think Marx or Plekhanov are unfamiliar with the work of Charles Darwin. Both men say that Darwin was *right,* that human nature is not at all special, but rather that it contains characteristics virtually identical with other animals. This difference between man and beast is quantitative, they say, not at all qualitative. So they *agree* with Charles Darwin on the question of human nature."

Parkadze nods and leans back, letting a wide smile spread across his face as he looks at Soso. He mouths the word *runt.*

"I suggest you read your text more carefully in the future, dear Soso. Especially if you intend on attacking the intelligence and diligence of your comrades."

Soso grips the back of his chair. A milky haze encroaches upon his vision, filling the space between him and his older foe. The teeth in the back of his jaw ache. His nails are digging into the wood, carving shallow crescents. The muscles in his hands throb; his fingertips are numb. His body recalls swirling like this once before, digging his nails into another piece of wood, the leg of that lopsided bed in the gloomy Avlabari district as his angry and drunken father, home from Adelkhanov's reeking and half-flooded shoe factory, and having already blown his day's wages on vodka and wine, stood above the writhing boy and punted him with his big boots dozens of times square in the chest. The same boots that are now on Soso's feet. These boots that float through Soso's dreams, alighting here, on the branch of a cherry tree, and there, on the floor, in a pool of blood and mud. He still feels those soul-crushing, body-breaking thuds.

He curls his toes as if the boots have lost their laces and are in danger of slipping off his feet. Soso searches the fuzzy faces of his companions, reading their poorly hidden mockery, their amusement at his idiotic failings, the willingness of these so-called friends to gather themselves in Devdariani's corner as soon as the power shifts. One comment, one mistake, one error, and all is lost. *It's true I read the Plekhanov much too quickly,* thinks Soso, *and far too late at night, and only after studying homiletics and moral theology for god knows how long. I put myself out on a limb by taking a forceful position without proper preparation, without giving it anywhere near enough consideration.*

Soso slides his chair to the side and steps into the circle.

"Here's the truth," he says, the strength of his voice condensed into a fierce and raspy whisper. "You cocksuckers think reading a book or two of summarized Marxism makes you revolutionaries? You think sitting in a circle and coddling each other while discoursing on this or that or the other will give you the courage to lead actual workers into actual rebellion? You think Lado Ketskhoveli would do anything but laugh at this passive, womanly, castrated discussion group? Where are your balls, men? I know damn well as you that Marxism is founded on Darwin's thought. But to sit around here talking about human nature this, human nature that, what's the point of it? Do any of you ladies know what it actually means to live as a man? Because this isn't it, comrades! This is playing a little game. This is what children do!"

Soso storms to his bunk, crashes down, and brazenly opens his borrowed Darwin. He has nothing more to say, not another word for his fellow seminarians. He pretends to concentrate on the book, deciding he'll let them wonder if he's finished with his rant or about to explode again.

Devdariani sighs. After a pause, he speaks again, now

leading the conversation into Plekhanov's criticism of Mikhailovsky, another Russian socialist. The pious boys at Novikov's desk brush their greasy hair behind their ears and return to their more chaste books and thought.

Later, as the students are eating their beans and gossiping between bites, they are conscious of Soso's bulky silence, although they decide to ignore him. Soso continues to brood as he limps up the stairs to the dormitory and again in the communal bathroom as he washes his face in the large basin, the others' laughter echoing off the cheap white tiles. He has neither a word nor a glance for them. Soso is studying a moonscape in the mirror, the hundreds of craters that smallpox has carved into his skin, as Iremashvili and some of the other students furtively glance at him while brushing their teeth.

Only minutes before the final bell and the call for lights out, when the seminarians are supposed to be praying by their beds, contemplating the day that's past and committing themselves to another in the service of the Lord, Soso breaks the invisible bubble he's been living inside for several hours. He walks over to Vano Ketskhoveli's bunk, kneels, and whispers into his friend's thick ear: "As of this moment, right now, you are no longer a member of Seid Devdariani's discussion group. Tomorrow afternoon we will meet in study period and I will begin to explain to you what Marxism is really about."

Vano raises his bushy brow and parts his lips. He blinks and squints; his glasses are lying on the bed. He can't bring himself to speak.

Soso stands and marches to Iremashvili's bunk. He kneels and repeats the firm command in identical language, causing Iremashvili to frown and wrinkle his forehead. "But Koba," he whispers, "Devdariani and Parkadze are final-years. They've studied with Lado. Don't you want to learn from them?"

Soso wraps his thick hand around the back of Iremashvili's neck, pushes his friend an inch or two forward, and squeezes hard enough to communicate the seriousness of his intent.

"Don't you know I can read any book as well as fucking Lado? I'll explain to you all about old Marx and Plekhanov."

Now he stands and makes his way over to Kapanadze's bunk.

Kapanadze, who is kneeling and pretending to pray, begins to listen to Soso's command, but erupts in laughter before he's finished. "You screwed up with the Darwin," he says. "That's all that's happened, Koba. Forget about it and rejoin the group tomorrow."

Soso feels he could bite down hard enough to crack all the teeth in his mouth.

"Devdariani's an asshole, I agree," continues Kapanadze, "but he knows what he's talking about. I'm not leaving his group."

"Yes, you are."

"No, I'm not."

Kapanadze stares into Soso's dull speckled eyes, an act of pure and brazen defiance, which has the peculiar effect of further calming Soso.

"Let me ask you something," whispers Soso. "A clarification, for my benefit. Are you aware that every April the best students in our seminary are called into Serafim's office and asked to inform on their peers? And are you aware that at those meetings there are Okhrana officers present?"

As Kapanadze pales, Soso begins to smirk with unrestrained pleasure.

"No, I didn't think you knew that. Only top seminarians are privy to that kind of information. And you're not one of the best, are you?"

"Koba," Kapanadze says, "you wouldn't."

"What do you know about it?"

Kapanadze stutters and shrugs.

"Seid Devdariani's an idiot with half-baked ideas about Marxism," continues Soso. "He can't abide the thought of someone else knowing more than him or, god forbid, explaining it to the others. No, that devil would rather us wallow in his stupid blunders and outright lies than give up an ounce of his own control. He'd rather corrupt the minds of impressionable students and lead us away from Lado's cause than admit he was wrong. Tell me, Peter, is that Marxist? Is that the collective spirit of the workers? You know damn well it isn't. That scoundrel doesn't understand anything. He's against our...everything! You know it would be a blessing if he were kicked out of school."

Kapanadze sits back on his heels and lets his hands sink into his lap. He looks at his squatting companion with an open combination of bafflement and disgust.

"The second Devdariani loses control, he'll knife his best friend in the balls. I'm absolutely sure of it. He's a collaborator and a criminal. And the same goes for that shit

Parkadze. Time will prove me right. Someone should kick them in the head!"

"Koba, please, that's nonsense!"

Soso's wide smile exposes his clean white teeth — unlikely pieces of perfection in an otherwise scarred and ruined face. "Go ahead and stay with Devdariani's discussion group, you miserable fool," he says. "You'll be in for a real surprise."

Soso leisurely leans his weight onto his right hand and nibbles his left hand's pinky with unrestrained pleasure, his pinched eyes nothing but slits, fanning wrinkles. His joy is wide and pure. He chuckles and spits a piece of chewed fingernail onto Kapanadze's bed. Kapanadze opens his mouth but finds himself deprived of words.

"Or, if you'd prefer, you can join us tomorrow in study period for an honest exploration of the text. The decision is yours, friend. All yours!"

Soso whacks Kapanadze on the back, stands, and returns to his bunk. He winks at Vano and Iremashvili but doesn't look back. The other students watch as Soso closes his eyes and lets his expression fade into serenity, kneeling by the side of his bed, hands locked in prayer. His lips are moving rapidly, but no sound comes from his throat. No one is fooled into thinking that Soso believes in prayer.

Kapanadze takes a moment to wonder if Soso would really do it, and then suddenly he is sure. Yes, Soso would tell the Archimandrite and the Inspector everything; he would betray every single member of that discussion group, just to get back at Seid Devdariani.

There's an itchy patch of skin where Soso has hit Kapanadze's back. He's been hit much harder than this countless times, in the organized brawls of his hometown, but the reverberations from this blow have special power, and they continue inside his chest as if he were nothing but hulled-out skin, less a human being than an empty drum. *I'm bigger than that runt*, he thinks. *I could march across this dormitory right now with everybody watching, pound his pockmarked face, and wrestle his skinny, long-legged body right to the floor.* Although he knows it's true, Kapanadze's legs feel flaccid and weak; he doesn't trust that his muscles are capable of lifting his skeleton off the ground. His cavernous stomach, certainly too enormous to fit inside his body, might even be protruding through a hole in his spine. The vacuum in his guts has pulled his brain into darkness; he's been turned inside out. Kapanadze has never been punished by the Inspector, has never been cast by the wolf's ticket into the darkness of solitary, but he can imagine the stifling claustrophobia of blindness, the anguish of gnawing hunger and interminable boredom interspersed with episodes of real fear. The Okhrana's prisons are even more horrible places, aren't they? Labyrinths of black rooms worked by fearsome men. Week-long tortures that put the seminary's petty denials to shame. The authorities won't be lenient with another reported disturbance originating with the seminarians. The next round of agitators will not get off with simple banishment, as Lado Ketskhoveli did. Kapanadze's legs melt into the floor. Where is his will to stand?

His terror and paralysis will continue tomorrow evening, when his chair is pulled into a semicircle in the corner of the room opposite Devdariani's noticeably smaller discussion group. His back will recall the reverberating thud of Soso's hand against it, and all the emptiness that thud implied. He will sit there in the circle, fumbling with the frayed cotton of his favourite shirt, beside Iremashvili and Vano Ketskhoveli, as gleeful Soso Djugashvili outlines the major points of Darwin's *Descent of Man*. And when Soso condescendingly asks, with a good deal of mirth and mockery, "What have you learned today?" Kapanadze knows he will bow his head with the politeness he usually reserves for priests and inspectors and hear his own foreign voice echoing in reply, "That man's instincts, which are often the same as animals', but only differing in degree, make him quite susceptible to the same forces of nature as other creatures." And Kapanadze will wonder: *Why this colourless tone, this perfect repetition of Soso's dry phrasing, so diligently memorized and copied like a parrot? Is this how I sound? Am I really nothing other than a drum?* Kapanadze will never feel emptier. But then Soso's yellow, tigrine eyes will be directed his way, and Kapanadze will feel a surge of real pleasure — base and simple pleasure, pure animal relief — because Soso, nodding and laughing and pointing at him, will say with glee: "Yes, Kapanadze! I think you're finally catching the spirit of our collective!"

BOTTLE CAP

Rafael sits stiff and straight before the Bunnell sounder, awaiting the evening's final telegraph. It's cooling outside, with a mild breeze rolling north across the hills from the Caribbean, but the thick stone building traps the island's tropical heat. Although he wears a heavy coat and refuses to loosen his necktie, he does not sweat, nor does his posture slacken with fatigue. The nub of his fountain pen presses against his paper at the optimal angle for penmanship. The boy grins and waits. The message will come when it comes. No need to fidget or complain. He is capable of sitting motionless all night if it comes to that.

In the distance, lounging on the church steps in San Cristóbal's main square, a man plays three breathy notes on his accordion. He stops, regroups, and plays the same notes again. The cicadas halt their screeching in wonder at the unidentifiable bird.

Rafael continues to wait. Five minutes, seven, ten — his pen never moves. When the main line relay fires, the local battery is engaged and the Bunnell sounder's brass armature suddenly knocks off an audible series of dots and dashes. He jots down the code without hesitation. Señor Leger, who's spent the past half-hour bent over his desk on the other side of the municipal telegraph office, adjusting springs on a dysfunctional relay, now stands and approaches his young apprentice, peering over Rafael's shoulder to read the Morse code message taking shape on the paper before him.

With a sharp memory and almost a year's worth of experience, Rafael has no trouble converting the rapid code into letters and words virtually in tandem with their sending. The telegraph operator at Santo Domingo's Hacienda Ministry is obviously an experienced sender, uniform with his dots and dashes and spacing between words. A good, clear transmission like this one makes Rafael's job so much easier; he barely has to think. Only a small part of his brain registers the message's content: *under order of president caceres stop begin construction of high road stop local labour required by min of hacienda velaquez stop.* Mostly, Rafael is concerned with the numbers of dots versus dashes in the transmission as a whole. It's imperative that the former surpasses the latter. More dots per day is a good sign, a fortunate omen, and no oranges will need to be crushed to rectify the situation. More dashes, of course, is a bad portent and could be quite serious; for every three dashes in excess of dots, an unblemished orange will have to be crushed, its seeds removed and pocketed, sprinkled across Constitution Street or any number of locations, but only in the moonlight when no one's watching. Even then, there's still no guarantee the curse against him will be voided. Right now the day's tally gives the dots a slim lead over the dashes, but it's too precarious a lead to guarantee victory. This final message of the day could tip the balance. Rafael's heart thuds in his chest. It will come down to the last letters tonight.

With the message almost finished, Leger leans over the table and shakes his head. "Look at that," he says, grinning with unrestrained pleasure. "Velázquez has done it."

"Mmm," mumbles Rafael, his pen still moving. His boss, who has been baking all day in his formal shirt, smells as ripe as an overworked donkey, but Rafael will not let himself be distracted by Señor Leger's pungency or by the conspicuous wet patches stretching from his armpits down his flanks, no matter how disgusting. His mind is focused and racing: *dots plus seven, plus six, plus five, plus six, plus five, plus four, plus three...*

"And it's confirmed by President Cáceres."

"Yes," says Rafael. The body of the message is complete, but still there's the sender's initials, which will determine the entire day's tally, since the dots retain only the slimmest of leads.

"Virtually guaranteed," says Leger.

The sender's signature taps into the relay, through the sounder. *Dash dot dash dot.* Pause. *Dash dot dot dot.* The sounder stills and the gentle clacking of the brass armature is replaced by silence.

JB, writes Rafael. He flips the paper, glances at the table watch, marks his initials and the time, his posture still perfect, his brow and neck clear of perspiration, but his lip imperceptibly twitching with the excitement of the dramatic finish. He can hardly believe that the entire day's tally has come down to a final letter *B*, and that the dash and three dots signifying that letter confirmed a net plus advantage of two dots for the day. He presses his lips together and grins at the good omen.

Señor Leger picks up the completed message and rereads it to make sure he hasn't been deceived, that the Minister of Hacienda for the Dominican Republic really did just order the construction of a high road from Santo Domingo to Azua, which will pass through San Cristóbal and guarantee numerous well-paid, local jobs for at least a year. "Cáceres is a real leader," Leger declares, slapping the paper against the palm of his hand. "For once in this damn country, we've got an honest president."

Rafael nods, but he isn't listening to his boss. He's busy rethinking his future in light of the good omen. Maybe he doesn't have stomach cancer, which has been his vague worry for most of the past month, not that he's shown any symptoms. This omen could mean good health, although it's impossible to interpret its significance precisely. It might also denote a joyous event for this evening or tomorrow.

Leger takes the message across the room and files it into Juan Piña's box. Half the telegraphs in this small rural office are destined for Señor Piña, the government's informal contact in San Cristóbal, the man in charge of executing all state requests, including this present command to gather labourers for the road construction.

"You'll probably take that new road to the capital in the spring," Leger tells his apprentice. "By then the whole trip should take no longer than a couple of hours." He removes his suit jacket from its hanger and slips it over his damp shirt, pulling his cuffs out of the sleeves.

"Not necessarily," says Rafael, who remains seated at the telegraph desk. "The journey will still be unpredictable without a bridge."

"Yes, I suppose," agrees Leger. "But a Haina bridge will come in due time. I wouldn't put it past Cáceres and Velázquez to have one built by the end of next summer. That's the kind of men they are." He grabs his hat and an iron key ring from off a hook, and puts the hat on his head.

Now Rafael stands and straightens his tie, although it's perfectly straight already and needs no adjusting. He runs his hands over his trousers. His back remains as stiff when he's standing as it does when he's sitting. His clothes are as clean and pressed as they were first thing this morning, before the heat set in. "Well," he says.

Señor Leger smiles at the boy and wipes his brow with a handkerchief. "Good work, Trujillo. As usual."

"Thank you, sir," says Rafael, nodding and returning his boss's smile.

"I'll see you in the morning."

"Yes. Nine o'clock."

"I'm sure," says Leger, smirking slightly, since the boy hasn't been late even once in over a year.

"Good night, sir."

Señor Leger opens the door for his apprentice and lets Rafael precede him into the dusty street. Outside, Leger pulls the creaky wooden door closed. He turns the key and shakes it once to ensure it's truly locked. He faces Rafael and taps his hat in parting. "Good night, then," he says, slipping the key ring into his pocket.

They walk in opposite directions. Rafael's commute is a straight shot down Constitution to the town's main square, where his family's big red house sits across from the Church of San Cristóbal. It's a three-minute journey at most. But instead of heading home, Rafael turns off the main thoroughfare and walks towards Padre Ayala on a short, unnamed side street packed with ramshackle *bohíos* on either side. Each makeshift home is roughly constructed of stripped palm planks and cabbage-palm thatch roofs, and the shacks' bright paint jobs of red, blue, green, and yellow do little to mask the essential poverty of their crowded inhabitants. Dark-skinned kids in torn trousers yell at each other in the street or run circles in concentrated pursuit of some fantastic end. Rafael kicks at the dust and searches for any metallic shine. Nothing here but tiny rocks. Smoke drifts up from an open kitchen behind an adjacent *bohío* and the air smells like roasted red beans. He turns down Padre Ayala.

Maybe Uncle Plinio will let me keep this tie, thinks Rafael as he fingers its smooth silk and makes sure it's still tight around his neck. *Or maybe he's bought a new suit jacket for me.* Either addition to his wardrobe would be news good enough to befit the omen. But Rafael knows he can't really predict it. The omen might have nothing to do with his clothing or his health. It might just signify that María waits for him by her house right now with the lascivious intent of leading him into the cornfield. No, omens cannot be predicted.

Rafael is enjoying his stroll in the cooling air, but he

would prefer to be trotting down Padre Ayala on his father's pinto mare. It took him hours of practice in the tall sugar cane and along the bank of the Nigua River to master the art of riding with a perfectly flat back, given the horse's jumpy gait and its frequent missteps. Walking down Padre Ayala can be dignified, of course, but it will always lack the gallantry that every girl, no matter how impoverished or dark skinned, adores and desires. *When a man travels by foot, he lacks chivalrous comportment, thinks this sixteen-year-old boy, which is the crucial component to success.*

Chivalry made the difference last summer, when Rafael started courting María. He presented himself as the perfect image of a man, stopping his father's mare with a tug of the reins and a low grunt, dismounting in one fluid motion, and handing the astonished girl an overflowing armful of bougainvillea. The grand clatter of spurs on boots, the strut in his step, and the tilt of his hat—yes, a real caudillo. And now Rafael recalls María's plump, dark ass, his delicate first touch as he recited some florid verse Uncle Teodulo had him memorize—yes, yes—and then his second, firm squeeze, delivered no later than midnight that night, as María lay sprawled on the dirt in the corn with her skirt hiked up, her panties by her ankles. María. So perfect. A dark indio's sweet molasses skin. He has taken this detour onto Padre Ayala with the hope of spying her full frame through the front window of her family's *bohío*.

Rafael rubs his fingers through his wavy, oiled hair, slowing his pace as he approaches the girl's hut. Although the window is small and the daylight is beginning to wane, he can distinguish a human form inside. He concentrates his energy into a penetrating stare, his eyes dark and full of purpose, a lecherous grin poking out from the corners of his otherwise tight mouth. His fingers tingle with anticipation. In the orange light of dusk, he can't discern any features, but the person inside the little blue *bohío* could very well be his conquest. He slows and shortens his steps. The figure disappears behind the wall. Was that her, and has she seen him? The front door opens and the threshold fills with a large man's frame — Fernando, María's brother. He's tall and fat, sporting a tapered and waxed moustache much like President Cácares's, and he's gnawing on a long root.

Rafael nods a perfunctory hello and quickens his step. This Fernando's got murder in his eye. *My reputation precedes me*, the boy thinks, with considerable pride. *Hey, Fernando*, he wants to say, *put a fence around your sister if you don't want her flowers picked.* Chuckling, the boy taps the thickening fuzz on his upper lip with three extended fingers and peeks over his shoulder to see the large brother, still in the doorway, glaring. Rafael resists laughing and maintains his composure. An impotent sibling is almost as good as a cuckolded boyfriend.

He continues ambling down Padre Ayala, searching for other young girls whose treats he might sample at a later date, when his eye catches a silvery object sparkling in the dust. He bolts towards it. He's still a few feet away when he recognizes the distinctive colours of a Pabst Blue Ribbon. He picks up the bottle cap and turns it over, assessing its condition. There's the usual bend from where it was pried off the bottle, but that's easy to fix. Otherwise, no scuffs.

The paint is intact and the metal is complete. He takes out his handkerchief from an inside coat pocket and stands in the dusty street for a while, polishing the cap into a brilliant shine and surveying his work when he's done. Yes, it's a fine specimen. His sixty-third Blue Ribbon — a slip back into odds. That, of course, changes everything.

He cuts off Padre Ayala and heads towards his home, forgetting the fury of brother Fernando, María's chunky body and smooth skin, and even the omen of dots and dashes. This bottle cap must be integrated into his collection right away. Appropriate adjustments must be made. A failure to do so properly will cancel out the telegraphic omen, replacing that good portent with a violent and destructive one, which couldn't be cured by crushed oranges or sprinkled seeds, or any means other than old-fashioned patience, fortitude, and endurance. The prospect of that failure makes him feel sick. A bad omen could mean cancer, tuberculosis, disasters of human or divine origin.

Rafael hurries along a side road darkened by the shade of an enormous mahogany. When he reaches Constitution, he's only a few feet from his house.

His father, Don Pepé, and his uncle Plinio are sitting and drinking beer in rocking chairs on the front porch, Plinio holding today's copy of *Listín Diario*, which he's had imported from Santo Domingo, as he does at least twice a week. There are only a handful of people in all of San Cristóbal who read the newspaper on such a regular basis. Don Pepé stands as Rafael opens the gate and hurries towards the front door.

"Hey, Rafael," Pepé calls, the anger in his tone undermined by a grin he can't quite suppress. "Come here, son."

Rafael fights the urge to barge past his father and uncle, to hide himself in his bedroom where he can get to work on his collection. He steps onto the porch and stands before his father, his eyes lowered respectfully, his hands pressed to his sides, and his back straight.

Don Pepé grabs Rafael's tie and yanks it out of hiding from beneath his waistcoat. The boy winces at the affront. Ties do not look proper hanging outside waistcoats.

"Is this the one?" Pepé asks Plinio.

"Yes," says Plinio as he rocks slowly in his chair, his fat hand resting on the curve of his protruding belly.

"Rafael?"

"Papa."

"Do I have to tell you this?"

"No."

Plinio slurps from his bottle of St. Pauli Niña and suppresses his own smile. He burps and hiccups, blowing gas from the corner of his crooked lips. *This is ridiculous,* thinks Rafael. *They're not even angry at me.*

"Take it off, Rafael."

Rafael's shoulders sag as he removes the elegant striped tie from around his neck. "I'm sorry, Uncle Plinio," he whispers, as his heavy cheeks dip into a frown. He hands the silken treasure to its rightful owner.

"You have to ask me, boy," says Plinio. "I spent half my morning looking for it." Plinio folds the tie into quarters and tucks it into his pocket.

"I know, uncle. It was a mistake in my judgment. I am sincerely sorry."

"As if you didn't have enough of your own," Pepé says, grinning openly. He fills his mouth with a swig of beer. "The boy's got more ties than I do, and he's only fifteen."

"Sixteen."

"I know that," says Pepé. "You think I don't know that?"

"I know you know."

"I know lots of things. I even remember the day I made you. A lot of hard work that was, for sure. I don't have to tell you how it's done. I remember the details as if it were yesterday. You're sixteen, of course—not fifteen at all." Pepé furrows his brow and twists his lip in a mock expression of consideration. "But I forget which one you are. Not Pedro or Virgilio. Are you the little dark one, Héctor?"

Rafael shakes his head sombrely at his father's joke. "Héctor's the baby in the crib."

"Oh yes. The one who cries all the time. I know him. So you must be the other, Pétan."

"No, Papa," says Rafael, shuffling his weight from foot to foot, thinking: *Is this fucking man just going to stand here and tease me all night? Why can't we end this conversation so I can get back to my room?* It's infuriating, because there's a time limit, after all, for the integration of bottle caps into his collection. Not a second to be wasted.

"Not Pétan?" says Pepé as he squints at his son, his drunk eyes glassy and playful. "Are you sure?"

"I'm Rafael."

"Oh, yes! Rafael. The necktie thief. The powdered boy. The one who always smells like flowers."

Uncle Plinio laughs and rocks his chair as he takes another sip of beer.

"May I go now, Papa? I have important tasks."

"Important tasks!" Pepé cries, laughing. "Well, forgive me, son." He turns to his brother-in-law and adds: "My telegraph son's got important tasks to do here in San Cristóbal."

"Oh, he does, then?" says Plinio as he rubs his belly. He then answers his own question with a nonchalant shrug. "At least that makes one of us with important tasks."

"May I go?" asks Rafael.

"You may go," Pepé says with a casual wave of his hand. He throws himself back into his chair, which rocks to and fro with the collapse of his weight.

Rafael hurries to the front door.

"Hold it!"

The boy clenches his jaw and faces his father with as much equanimity as he can muster. Don Pepé waves him back. Rafael approaches and stands before the rocking chair. Pepé holds out his clenched hand and indicates with his jaw that he's got in his grip a precious gift. Rafael lets his father press the sharp contents into his fist, and then opens his hand to reveal two bright new bottle caps: Plinio's St. Pauli Niña and his father's Malta Nutrine. Rafael's head swirls with excitement and dread. Each one of these bottle caps pushes its brand into the opposite category—odds into evens, evens into odds—as well as altering their relative values, which of course affects their positioning with other brands on the windowsill, and all of this value change needs immediate integration at risk of negating the dots-versus-dashes omen. Rafael's on the verge of sobs, but neither his father nor his uncle can tell from his placid expression.

"Thank you," he whispers, tucking the two new bottle caps into his coat.

"No more stealing your uncle's neckties, *chapita*," says his father. "All right? Now, Pétan's got something important he needs to talk to you about. Go inside. He's been poking his little nose out here every five minutes to see if you've come home." Pepé winks at his son. "Go, *chapita*, go!"

Rafael nods and turns away, secretly enraged by the mockery of that name, and wondering if his father would like those bottle caps shoved down his throat. If Rafael could have his way, he'd banish the word *chapita* from the Spanish language and throw anyone who ever used it into prison for the rest of his life. *By the grace of virgin Altagracia,* he thinks, *how am I ever going to charm an Espaillat, Cabral, or Troncoso—or any one of those fancy girls from the rich families of the Cibao—if everyone in my thick-headed and vulgar clan insists on calling me "Bottle cap"?*

As usual, there's chaos inside the house. The younger boys, Pedro and Pípi, are playing a game derived from baseball in the living room, while their tiny sister Nieves Luisa watches the mischief. The game involves one brother throwing an old tin into the air and the other smashing it across the room with a large stick. Pedro, who's just had the pleasure of a direct hit, which has ricocheted the tin off the wall, is tackled by his brother Pípi for no discernible reason, and is now being punched and kicked as Pípi screams about the injustice of Pedro's play. Another, slightly older brother named Aníbal has dragged a large washing tub, his makeshift terrarium, into the dining room and is trying but failing to force a large snake he's captured to eat a whole frog.

Rafael speeds by the little ones without saying hello. He passes the closed door of his sisters' room, where Julieta quietly sobs — probably lying face down on her bed, as she often does. He enters the sheltered kitchen in the backyard and finds his mother, Doña Julia, and his two older sisters preparing supper. In truth, only his eldest sister, Marína, is helping his mother by boiling and mashing the yucca, while the younger one, Japonesa, passes her time stealing bites rather than working. Doña Julia turns away from her vat of red beans and rice when she hears Rafael enter. She offers her son a smile.

"Mama," says Rafael, holding out his arms.

Doña Julia pulls the teenager into a tight hug and the boy plants a wet kiss on his mother's round cheek.

"I'm sorry, Mama, but I have to hurry off," he says. "There is work I must do in my room before supper."

"All right," she says. "We'll eat in fifteen minutes."

"Perfect."

He nods briskly at his sisters, who grunt in return. Rafael leaves the outdoor kitchen and enters the house, this time heading straight into the bedroom he shares with Pétan and used to share with his oldest brother, Virgilio, before he left home last year to find work in Santo Domingo. He closes the door, removes the three bottle caps from his coat pocket, and sits on his bed. Now he can take a closer look at his compete collection displayed on the windowsill. A quick survey of the Pabst Blue Ribbons, stacked in groups of ten, confirms his earlier guess at numbers. There are fewer Malta Nutrines and St. Pauli Niñas, but they are still large piles. Rafael adds the new caps and makes the appropriate adjustments: re-stacking each brand; making sure the new additions are located in the centre of a stack and not at the top or the bottom; reordering each brand's location on the windowsill if necessary. He mumbles a running commentary as he works, counting out stacks of ten, offering bits of encouragement to the bottle caps as if they were sentient beings. For the first time today, although the heat has slackened, Rafael begins to sweat.

Pétan enters the room, cinching his belt, and shuts the door behind him. Although the boy's only a year younger than his brother Rafael, he stands a good six inches shorter, a plight he tries to rectify with an exaggerated swagger. He stands by the side of Rafael's bed and watches his brother work on the bottle caps.

"Hey, *chapita*," Pétan says. "Stop with that. We need to talk."

"Quiet," says Rafael. "Come back later."

Pétan gives Rafael's foot a light kick.

Rafael turns his sweaty face against his brother, his teeth bared like a dog with its meal interrupted, and says, "I told you to come back later, asshole." Rafael's voice is high and shrill when agitated.

"We've got a job. Listen."

"And don't ever call me *chapita* again."

"Hey, Rafael, listen. We can make some money here."

Pétan sits beside his brother and watches. He knows his brother won't stop fiddling with his damn bottle caps once he's started, but then there's no reason why Rafael can't also listen to the proposal at the same time.

"So Papa was up in the valley last week," Pétan begins, "and he came across a rancher who wants to add a few to his herd. A couple of his old cows died last month and the guy let it be known pretty clearly that he's got some pesos saved. He can buy at a good price, I mean if he gets healthy animals and a good deal. Anyway, I don't know the specifics, but Papa made it seem like it might be worth our while."

Rafael nods to let his brother know he's listening, although most of his attention is channelled towards the bottle caps on the sill. He's pulling down the Daisys and Holsteins and reordering them in stacks of ten on his bed.

"Papa hinted he could sell the man a few good cows with no questions asked," Pétan continues. "Papa said the man was not so interested in where the animals might have come from, and his ranch is up at the far end of the valley, so there's not much chance the new cows'll be parading along the *malecón* or be giving out their address to any of the lucky girls, if you know what I mean."

Pétan tries to raise his grin into a smile, but the effort only lifts half his face and makes him feel absurd. He picks at stray threads on Rafael's old bed quilt.

"So this morning I went for a walk and happened to notice that the Uribe brothers down the river sure have plenty of cows in their field. You ever notice that, Rafi? I sure did this morning. Nice fat cows. They're reproducing well over there. I was thinking they might even have a few too many to take care of. I was thinking they might need some help taking care of all those beasts, and I don't think Papa would ask us any questions if we showed up tomorrow morning with some nice fat animals for him to take up into the valley. What do you think of all that?"

"I don't know," says Rafael. "What do you think?"

Pétan grits his teeth and stares at his brother, who still hasn't even glanced at him. "I think not everyone can find work smacking his dick against an electric line for twenty-five American dollars a month, and that some of us might benefit from a little bit of work every now and then with an older brother's help."

"I see," says Rafael, fitting one cap inside another.

"I think we could borrow a couple horses from Alvarez, then you and me and him could ride out late tonight. That's what I think. Papa'll let you take his horse and then we'll have three."

"I don't need the money. I don't need the risk."

"Well, I fucking need the money, Rafi."

"I'll think about it."

"All right, fine," says Pétan. "But hurry up about it, because if we decide to do this thing, I should get over to Alvarez's place and get those horses lined up before it gets too late."

Rafael whispers something under his breath, but Pétan has the good sense to realize that his brother's secret words have nothing to do with his proposal and everything to do with the weird omens and portents he likes to tie up in those stupid bottle caps. He's sweating and mumbling to himself like a lunatic, and certainly won't waste any time in consideration of his brother's plot. Pétan knows he's just saying he will. Only drastic measures will shake Rafael from his reverie.

"Hey," says Pétan, "smell this." He sticks a couple of fingers underneath his brother's nose and grins his wry smile.

Rafael breaks his concentration and pulls away from the offending fingers invading his treasured personal space. "What's that?"

"You know that girl María over on Padre Ayala."

"What about her?" hisses Rafael.

"The nectar of that flower," says Pétan. "That's what's on my fingers." He sticks his fingers underneath his own nose, inhales, and shakes his head in wonder at the intoxicating scent. "My, my, my. So sweet!"

"You're lying," says Rafael. "Her brother would have killed you."

"No way," says Pétan. "And I might go back tonight for seconds over there."

"You're a fool," says Rafael, his tone rising. He tenses his upper lip and turns back to his bottle caps. "I don't believe you."

"Whether you believe me or not doesn't much affect the sweetness of the flowers of San Cristóbal, eh, Rafi?"

"Get out of here," says Rafael as he fumbles with a stack of ten Holsteins, trying to recall if he's already handled them. "I'm busy."

"So it's agreed? Good. I'll go get Alvarez. Maybe he can come back here with his horses around midnight?"

"I'm not doing it," says Rafael. "They'll catch us."

"They won't catch—"

"I said I'm not doing it. And that's it."

Pétan throws his head back in fury and grunts. "Fine," he says. "Terrific!" He sweeps his hand across the windowsill and knocks over the bottle cap towers, hopelessly mixing their brands, crashing some on the bed, and flinging others onto the floor. Rafael is too stunned to react, but Pétan, realizing he's made an impetuous and terrible mistake, quickly stands and heads for the door. "What, are you so rich and powerful, Rafael," he calls back without looking at his brother, "that you don't want to make a few extra pesos?" He slams the door behind him, rattling the few remaining bottle caps on the windowsill.

Rafael's precious bottle caps lie scattered and disorganized, the new ones unidentifiable against the old—a scrambling that negates the good omen of surplus dots for the day and magnifies its opposite, virtually guaranteeing he'll get cancer or some other illness of slow, withering decline. It's his own fault, really, for having tempted Pétan with that harsh dismissal, for not appeasing his stupid and callous brother as he knew he should have. Appeasement would've shown proper respect for the power of the bottle cap ritual. Instead, he dismissed his work as some minor task that could be completed while holding a conversation. No, he did not protect his treasures.

Rafael's frantic eyes search for the upturned, flipped, and disorganized bottle caps, which are wildly dispersed along the rough tiles, by the closet door with the spiderwebs, and in the dust underneath Pétan's filthy bed. He realizes it will be impossible for him to absorb their images in a single glance as required, let alone to account for their proper positions in relation to one another. His stomach constricts and his dread feels as heavy as an anchor chained to his ankles. The rock in his belly must be the hard mass of disease eating him from the inside. He wants to cry, and he's gripped by a compulsion to powder his brow, which is now so rank and sweaty that he can feel the drops of perspiration clinging to his forehead like the ticks he sometimes picks up in the sugar cane. He tries to whisper to himself, out loud, that it's unmanly to cry, undignified, but any clear articulation of those words is impossible. He moans low like a cow in the throes of labour as the dreaded tears escape down his cheeks.

"Rafael," his mother calls from the dining room. "Your supper is on the table."

He scoops bottle caps off his quilt and piles them in a heap on the windowsill. He jumps up and scurries around, picking the others up off the floor as fast as he can, trying to prevent himself from assessing their condition or registering their brands on the spot. All the while, he's thinking that even if the bad portent proves not to be cancer or some comparable disease, it will be a horrible event, like a brutal beating from Fernando that results in lost and cracked teeth, or a massive, disfiguring gash on his forehead that could never be hidden with powder. He piles the bottle caps he's gathered on the sill and pulls back the bed so he can access the few strays that have slipped to the floor against the wall. These too he stacks.

The spasms in his belly are so painful now that he feels like throwing up. He surveys his work. The sight of all those distinct brands piled together willy-nilly without respect to colouring or condition, without accounting for dates and places of discovery, and, most importantly, not stacked in proper towers of ten weakens his knees and forces him to sit on his bed. His thoughts spiral into a familiar looping pattern of *if, then* statements: *if you don't separate the Malta Nutrines, then the tumour will grow a millimetre per day; if you don't stack the Daisys bottom to top from least to most faded, then the tumour will snuff out your ability to breathe,* and so on and so forth.

Rafael uses his weight to push the bed back against the wall. He knows his family is waiting for him at the dinner table. He doesn't have time to stack the bottle caps in their correct groups, but he wonders if he can't at least separate them from this single, unholy clash of types, origins, and colours. Yes, there's time enough for that. He wipes his brow with his sleeve and focuses on his task.

As Rafael works, he begins to calm down. His breath slows and his legs regain some of their lost strength. He tells himself that things will most certainly be bad for a while, but that he has dealt with bad times before and will have to deal with them again in the future. As he separates the brands, a frisson of unexpected joy tenses his arms. Rafael realizes he's grinning. He remembers that he is a strong and disciplined young man, one who can show fortitude when under attack. If he can survive this sudden misfortune, he will certainly have the strength for other perils thrown his way. He sits taller. He begins to imagine himself wearing a fine wool suit imported from Madrid, seated at the head of a long table of stained mahogany—the kind of majestic table one supposes would be used by a wealthy family in its dining room. He's surrounded by aristocrats and other high-ranking military officials, with oxtail bones on their plates and half-filled goblets of wine and heaping fresh fruit platters placed on either end for dessert, and a Cuban cigar in every mouth. He imagines telling all his cultured guests, who are descendants of the great families of the Cibao, that *a true man is never forged in the ease and luxury of life. No, he is born from hardship and strife, as I have been, from those grim occasions when omens turned against me and called upon the strength of my character. A man,* he tells the rapt guests, *is the product of his own virility and determination. Nothing more and nothing less.* His hands work quickly, stacking and aligning bottle caps. Order rises from chaos before him. Yes, Rafael is man enough to handle any bad omen.

"Rafi," his mother calls. "Are you coming?"

"One moment!"

He has to stop for now. The reorganization is incomplete, certainly not far enough along to reinstate the good omen, but it might be sufficient to ensure survival through his upcoming tough times. Rafael takes care to straighten the quilt on his bed, erasing the wrinkles. He goes to his closet and opens the door so he can compose himself in the small mirror he's installed. Before he sees his reflection, Rafael is struck by the dismal state of his two suits hanging from the bar. Yes, they're clean and pressed and ready to wear, but the fabric of his favourite jacket is distressed on one shoulder, and the knees have thinned considerably on the other suit.

His three neckties hang limply from a single hook. He fingers one tie, made of a rich purple silk with a faint floral print, smooth to the touch. It is probably the best-quality tie in all of San Cristóbal, with the exception of the two dozen or so hanging in Uncle Plinio's closet. Still, he's worn each of his three ties a thousand times, and he can't keep tying the same damn piece of silk around his neck each and every morning. But what can he do? There is no choice. There will be no gifts coming his way any time soon; the bad omen of tipped bottle caps has, at the least, guaranteed that. Rafael's mind races with rough calculations of how long it will take working at the telegraph office before he can save enough money to import another tie from Santo Domingo. Given the hefty percentage he offers his beloved mama each month, and will be forced to continue offering her until his infuriating papa stops drinking and finally humbles himself enough to plead with José at the postal office for a second chance and another job, and of course the absolute fortune that ties cost nowadays, Rafael realizes it will take him at least four months. Four months in three ties is unacceptable. Neither the Espaillats nor the Mejias, who are arrogant and strident in matters of comportment, would ever let one of their prissy daughters marry a boy from San Cristóbal who has only three suits and ties to his name. And there will be no temporary fixes to the problem either, as Rafael will have no further access to Plinio's collection unless he prostrates himself before his uncle like a bitch in heat.

"Rafael!"

"Yes, coming!"

Rafael studies his reflection in the mirror: the slicked-back hair, the fuzz growing on his upper lip, the strength and stoicism of his gaze. The whitening powder has faded since he began to sweat, and now Rafael can detect the slight mulatto hue to his skin underneath.

"We're starting," his father cries from the other room.

"I'll be right there!" he calls back.

He snatches the whitening powder from the shelf in his closet and begins to dust his face. As he works, he thinks: *You are a small-town* campesino *with black blood tainting your veins.* In the mirror, Rafael sees a hick from a lazy family of nothings and nobodies. He knows that he's been plagued by more than just bad omens, more than just the overturned bottle caps of this evening; he's been plagued by the meanness of his birth. He dabs his chin and cheeks and forehead, the excess gritty powder suspending in the air like a thick fog. As he watches his skin whiten into magnificent, matted formality, Rafael silently tells himself that it will take concentrated effort, mammoth discipline and power, and more than a little bit of daring to overcome the curse of his origins and achieve all that he deserves.

He finishes, replaces the powder, and straightens his collar and jacket. He both looks and feels better with this lighter face, with the oil of his skin blotted away. He considers putting on a tie, but decides against it. "Later," he tells his image as he closes his closet door, "you shall wear your very best."

By the time Rafael joins his family in the dining room, the casual meal has lapsed into disarray. Only his mother and two older sisters remain seated at the long table, eating their beans, rice, and mashed yucca. His father and Uncle Plinio have already wolfed down their food and left their bowls on the table for the women to clear. They're now reclining on the worn sofa in the living room, thickening the air with coarse smoke from their cigars, seemingly oblivious to the constant hair-pulling and spitting of Pípi and Pedro on the floor beneath them. Julieta's inexplicable crying has stopped at last, but she's still barricaded in her bedroom and nobody cares enough to investigate how she's doing. In his parents' bedroom, Héctor babbles in his crib. Pétan crouches in the corner with his bowl of beans. Although there's a chair for him to use, he's too enamoured of Aníbal's snake to sit at the table, cooing at the creature with more affection than he's ever displayed to any one of his sexual conquests. When he notices that Rafael has entered, Pétan stands and grins sheepishly at his older brother. There's no use apologizing for his stupidity. He's not the least bit sorry, but he's clearly afraid. Maybe a shit-eating grin will show enough contrition for the powdered boy to change his mind and help him cows at midnight.

Rafael gives Pétan a harsh glare, but relaxes into a smile when he turns towards his mother. "Mama," he says as he stands tall by the end of the table and bows his head, as he would to a matron he'd only just met. "Thank you so much for this meal."

"You're welcome," says Doña Julia. She flashes a sharp

sideways glance at Japonesa, letting the lazy and rude daughter know that she might pick up a few good manners from her gallant brother.

Rafael sits, tucks a napkin into his shirt, and begins to eat his meal, careful to push small bites onto his fork and to chew with his mouth closed. He dabs the corners of his lips with his napkin and requests a glass of water from his brother, if that wouldn't be too much trouble. Pétan passes Rafael the jug and nods formally, as Rafael did to their mother, but he's unable to make it look natural with his omnipresent crooked smirk.

"Plinio told me you took one of his ties again," Doña Julia says as she sits back in her chair at the head of the table and watches him eat.

"Yes," says Rafael.

"You should know better than that."

"It's important I look respectable at work," he replies with a shrug. "It's very important—and Uncle Plinio has the best ties."

"That's true," calls Plinio from the living room. "I do have very good taste."

"Don't steal your uncle's ties," warns Doña Julia.

"I've been over this with Papa already and it's resolved, I promise you."

"Is it resolved?" His mother frowns and shakes her head. "I'm not so sure, Rafael. This is not the first time Plinio's asked you to stop."

Rafael lays his spoon down gently and stares hard at his mother. "Thank you for your concern, Mama, but I tell you once and for all, the problem has been resolved. I promise you it will not happen again."

The intensity and seriousness of Rafael's expression is enough to make Doña Julia turn away, raise her hands, and refrain from questioning him any further.

Rafael finishes his beans, cleans his lips, and folds his napkin into a perfect square, which he lays on the table. Doña Julia, Marína, and Japonesa gather bowls and carry them into the kitchen. Only when they've left the room does Rafael stand and turn to his brother Pétan.

"Go to Alvarez," he says. "Tell him midnight, by the stable."

Pétan raises his brow in surprise but wastes no time in questioning Rafael's change of mind. He trots to the front door, grabs his hat, and leaves. Don Pepé watches him go but looks back at Rafael when he's gone.

"Your brother's sure in a hurry," he says wryly. "What's the rush?"

"Papa, may I ask a favour?"

"Of course."

"I would like to borrow the mare tonight, if you don't mind."

"Uh-oh," says Uncle Plinio with a grin. "Your boy wants the mare..."

"What's the matter, *chapita?*" teases Don Pepé. "Have you got your eyes on a new girl? Going to chase her down on horseback? That's good, but are you sure you know what to do when you catch her?"

"You should show him how to do it," laughs Plinio. "You're pretty good in that department."

"That's right. Bring her over here first and I'll show you how it's done."

"I can handle that part on my own, Papa."

"Just be careful not to leave too much of your powder or perfume on her panties," says Pepé.

"The poor girl's father will have no trouble discovering the culprit," laughs Plinio.

"I'll take precautions," says Rafael.

"Of course you can have the horse," says Pepé. He sips his beer and adds: "Take her all night if you want."

"Thank you, Papa," says Rafael, offering another of his little nods.

"You're welcome, good sir," says Pepé.

As the men continue sucking their cigars, Rafael returns to his bedroom to prepare for the raid. In addition to certain precautions that must be taken, he feels it's important to be presentable whenever he steps out of the house, even on a clandestine mission in the dark of night when the last thing he wants is to be seen. Moreover, although it's too late to reverse the bad omen, he'd like to spend some time fixing the bottle caps and getting their order right. Alone, blissfully alone, he's able to fill hours with his work on the windowsill.

Pétan returns at some point, but Rafael has no idea how long his brother has been gone, or how long he's been focused on his task. Pétan doesn't approach the bed. Instead, he stands near the doorway and says: "Midnight. It's settled." When he leaves the room, he closes the door quietly, knowing that the wisest thing to do is give his brother some time and space to finish with his bottle caps.

When Rafael's work is completed, he stands and stretches, and then surveys with pride his caps on the windowsill. He's no longer sweating or agitated, but his shoulders ache and the muscles along his arms feel depleted, as if they're hanging off his bones. He leaves the room to gather and warm some water so he can take a sponge bath. When he returns with the filled tub, Rafael strips to his underwear and sprinkles a few drops of orange blossom bath oil in the water, a tincture he acquired from Cucho's mother on the pretext of it being a gift for a girlfriend, and which he keeps stored in the back of his closet behind a pile of socks. He moves his sponge in tight circles across every inch of his chest, arms, and legs, enjoying the pungency of the orange blossom oil, a sweet scent that's laced with a fecal tang of indole, which he can't identify but loves.

When he's sufficiently clean and fragrant, he stands in the doorway of his closet and tries to choose which of his three suits will best serve his purpose. Once he's made his choice, he grooms the fabric meticulously for any particles of lint or dust and lays the suit on his bed without wrinkling it. Now he stands in front of the mirror, slathering his chest and neck with a potent cologne, which cost him almost two months' salary. He puts on his shirt and suit, fusses tirelessly with his favourite purple tie, and combs his hair several times, using copious cream and considerable force. His goddamn hair won't lie flat. He can't seem to remove the kink. *It's the fucking Negro blood,* he thinks as he lowers his comb. *Always worse in the humidity.* Rafael is so maddened by his curls, so disgusted by the faint dark hue in his cheeks, that he can't at the moment maintain his self-deception that darker-skinned Dominicans—himself included—have Taino Indian rather than African heritage. No, it's obvious this evening: he can see a slave's residue in the bones of his face.

He has already powdered himself, but it hasn't been enough. He lays the comb aside, dabs his pad in the whitening powder, and applies another thick layer to his cheeks, forehead, and neck. He's gritting his teeth and patting his face hard with the makeup pad, wondering all the while why his pure-blood Spanish ancestor couldn't stop himself just that once from ramming his cock into a black girl, as if those Haitian temptresses weren't enough trouble already with their constant encroachments on Spanish land, their barbaric jungle religions, and their incomprehensible, mashed-up excuse for French.

Soon enough, the powder's thickness has worked his skin tone back into a safer colour, and Rafael is now able to empty the rage from his eyes, leaving only a smouldering sexuality. Rafael knows he might encounter a potential conquest at any time, even in the dark of night while wrangling horses. He imagines a young beauty enraptured with the intensity of his stare, and is confident there is no longer any outward sign of his fury.

Pétan, who has been waiting outside their shared bedroom door for an hour, picking his cuticles and fantasizing about the ways he's going to throw around his wealth, enters the room at eleven-thirty. He stands by the door, his hands clasped before him. "Almost there?" he asks his brother.

Rafael massages the knot of his tie one last time, moving it a millimetre to the left, and turns towards his brother. "Meet me at the field in fifteen minutes."

"I'll wait for you here," says Pétan, his hands clasped before him, his back slightly bent, trying his best to be subservient although it goes against his every instinct. "You look almost done."

"No," says Rafael. "It's better to leave town alone. You go first. I'll meet you soon after."

Pétan grins. "Always think of everything, eh, Rafael?"

"Fifteen minutes."

"I'll be there," Pétan says, and slips out of the room.

Rafael picks up his old leather saddlebag and takes it into the dining room. His family is asleep, except for his father, who's out drinking and cruising the town, picking up girls. He removes the board of punctured plywood covering Aníbal's terrarium and grabs the long but harmless brown snake by its tail. He turns his head in disgust as the snake tries to coil against him. Rafael snaps his wrist a dozen times. He opens his saddlebag, drops the dead snake inside, and then goes out back to the kitchen to wash his hands three times in rapid succession, mumbling an inaudible mantra of his own authorship, similar in structure to a paternoster. He decides to leave the plywood ajar so Aníbal will think his pet has escaped. His crazy brother will be furious, Rafael knows, and would probably cut Rafael's throat if he discovered who killed his snake. Rafael wipes his hands on a towel and then picks three oranges from the tree in the yard, sniffing each one quickly before he tucks them into his coat pocket. He goes back inside, picks up his saddlebag, and buttons it closed. He snuffs the oil lamp and leaves through the front door.

A cool breeze rustles the trees in the temperate, cloudless night. The streets are empty at this hour, easy enough to navigate with a quarter moon and innumerable stars. He's walking down Constitution to the field at the edge of town where San Cristóbal's better families board their horses. Rafael removes an orange from his pocket and, while he peels it, thinks that there's no way Pétan was telling the truth; María would've been disgusted with a shrimp like him, and it didn't even smell like her on his fingers. No, it was some other girl the rascal had seduced and taken advantage of. Pétan was just lashing out, the impetuous bastard, not so different from what he did with the bottle caps. Rafael drops the peeled orange on the street and steps on it with his heel. He bends down and retrieves a handful of seeds from the mash of juice and pulp. As he peels his second orange, Rafael can't help grinning at his younger brother's audacity. There are qualities to admire about Pétan — he's determined and impassioned — but still it seems certain that his brother is mentally sick. For ruining his bottle caps and destroying the good omen, the shrimp cannot go unpunished. He needs to be reminded of the correct pecking order in the Trujillo family — namely, Rafael's position at the top.

The street curves and transforms into a country road with wagon ruts and tall grasses growing on either side. Rafael slows, giving himself enough time to crush the two remaining oranges and to tuck their retrieved seeds into his pocket. As he approaches the field, he spies two silhouettes, one taller and one shorter, Cucho Alvarez and Pétan. They have bridled the trio of horses and now clutch the reins, waiting for him. Pétan is bouncing on his toes. Rafael stops ten feet away and pretends to draw a gun on his friend.

"Stop, thief! Drop the reins! Or I'll take off the top of your head."

"Go ahead and shoot," says Cucho, grinning. "You won't hit me."

Rafael laughs, goes to Cucho, and hugs him in a firm and manly embrace. Cucho's a beefy seventeen-year-old with widely spread, bulging eyes like a pug's, thick shoulders, and popping biceps. He wears a tight linen shirt with the sleeves rolled up three-quarters and a cowboy hat. Cucho looks like a thug, but he's got a soft voice with hints of a lisp, and he can't stop himself from smiling most of the time. Rafael takes a set of reins from Cucho's hands.

"Cigarette?" Cucho asks, offering him one from his pack. Rafael shakes his head no.

"I've got Papa's horse ready," says Pétan. "Go on and take her."

"No," says Rafael, smiling at his brother. "This is your plan and you deserve the honour. Why don't you ride Papa's mare for me?"

Pétan grins and raises his brow in mock hesitation. "All right," he says. "If you insist." He snorts, puffs out his chest, and spits in the dirt, empowered by his brother's unexpected gesture of goodwill. Before Rafael has the chance to change his mind, Pétan flicks his cigarette into the field, mounts the mare, and gives her a little kick. The horse bucks once, nearly throwing Pétan, and then prances round the field until she calms down.

"Well," says Pétan once he's regained his balance and puffed out his chest again, "what are you waiting for?"

Rafael is careful to mount his horse in one swift motion, as he imagines a trio of gorgeous young women watching him move. He fixes on his saddlebag and unbuttons it. The boys kick off towards the river, their horses galloping hard, sensing their riders' excitement. It's not a long distance to the Nigua, but the brisk exercise of a sprint feels necessary for these would-be thieves. The wind relaxes their taut nerves. The boys slow their animals as they approach the banks of the river, and line them up in single file. The horses snort and huff as they lower themselves two feet into the shallows at the river's edge. The gurgle of water buries the steady clop of horses' hoofs; any hired *campesinos* on patrol tonight won't be able to hear them approaching.

"Cucho's got the clippers," says Pétan as they splash along the river, now riding beside each other.

"Good," says Rafael. "Cucho gets to work on the fence while Pétan and I rustle the cows."

"How many are we going to take?" asks Cucho.

"I don't think Papa can lead more than a dozen to the valley," says Pétan, "or he'll get noticed. A dozen sounds good."

"Let's be safe," says Rafael. "Six to eight."

"Oh, come on," scoffs Pétan. "Are you that much of a coward? I'm trying to make some money here."

"You can still make money with eight."

"I'm taking ten," says Pétan.

"Ridiculous," counters Rafael. "There's no need."

"Let's take nine," says Cucho, finally weighing in. "But only if they're together. If scattered, we stop as low as six. I want to be in and out of that field in no more than five minutes."

Pétan pulls his horse to a stop, sucks in his cheeks, and straightens his back. Rafael knows that his brother is emulating the images of Simón Bolívar he's seen in school books and on posters, but Pétan's fat nose and squat stature couldn't be more of a contrast to the great liberator's streamlined mien. "It's my plan," Pétan says. "I'm taking ten to twelve and that's final."

Rafael also sits taller on his horse. "Pétan," he warns.

"No," says Pétan, glaring at his brother.

"If you threaten me, Pétan, I'll turn this horse around. I'll just go home, you understand? I'm doing you a favour here. I'm already pushing the boundaries by letting Cucho say nine. We're taking six to nine cows, *nine* at the most, and only if we can, and you'll agree to that plan or you'll be hitting that field all by yourself. And if that's your choice, you really are an idiot. I'll wish you the best of luck."

Pétan spits into the dirt and refuses to budge his horse.

"If there's any trouble," says Cucho in the soft voice of a peacemaker, "I say we cross the river and head into the cane. Abandon the cows."

"There won't be trouble," says Pétan as he kicks his horse forward. It seems the change of subject has given him a more or less dignified way out.

"If everything works, we'll drive the cows north a couple of hours," continues Cucho. "Store them at my cousin's place."

"Agreed," says Pétan.

"Then get back to San Cristóbal before dawn."

"No problem," says Rafael, kicking his horse on.

They ride in taut silence for a few minutes, gripping their plodding animals with their legs. Crickets chirp faintly all around them, but otherwise the only sound is the soft sucking click of hoofs cupping the shallow water. The stillness of the night makes these boys feel like screaming.

"Fuck," says Pétan. "I need another cigarette."

"Here," says Cucho, passing him one through Rafael.

"Don't worry so much," Rafael advises his brother as he hands over the cigarette. "What happens, will happen. It they catch us, it's fated."

"Well, they sure won't have trouble following us once they get downwind," says Pétan, grinning. "The smell of flowers trails for a mile."

Cucho laughs, open-mouthed, and then takes off his hat to point it at Rafael teasingly. But Rafael doesn't seem to notice Cucho. He focuses his glare on his brother.

"I mean, come on, Rafi," continues Pétan. "Why are you wearing all that shit just to go rustling?"

"Shut up, Pétan."

"A silk tie? Are you serious?"

"Your brother wants to look good for the cows," smirks Cucho, unable to resist. "Smell good for them too." He puts his hat back on his head.

"Oh, they'll love you tonight," says Pétan. "We won't even

have to wrangle them at all. No, they'll get all hot and follow you straight out of the field."

"He's a bull, your brother," laughs Cucho. "All he needs is horns."

Rafael relaxes into his saddle, stiffening his chin against their teasing, riding with more dignity than ever. "Be quiet, you idiots," he says without raising his voice. "We're almost there."

The boys lead their horses out of the water and through the tall grass, approaching the Uribes' field. Cucho dismounts and advances to the fence. He locks his clippers around the barbed wire, but just before he makes the cut, he turns to Rafael for advice. "You think we can get them upstream? Or should we move north and cut the fence there?"

"No," says Rafael, who has pulled his horse up to the fence. "Here's fine. The cows can handle the current."

Cucho nods and cuts the first wire. There are four thick strands, each pulled taut between the trunks of trimmed but living trees, planted at fixed intervals. The wires are gouged deep into the bark and don't give easily. It takes Cucho a few minutes to cut through all four. Beneath the crickets and croaking tree frogs, the boys can hear the rushing river and the huff of the horses' breathing. Pétan mumbles a curse. After the first cuts are made, Cucho pries back the wires, giving the Trujillo brothers enough space to enter. "Go," he whispers. "Be quick." Rafael and Pétan trot into the field as Cucho shuffles over a few feet to work on another four cuts, which will open a section large enough for the stolen cattle to pass through.

The Trujillo brothers ride side by side through the grazed field, squinting in the darkness. Any figures they might see, bovine or human, will be silhouettes in the moonlight. The gentle roar of the river fades and they're left with only the shrill stridulation of the crickets.

"There!" says Pétan, pointing to a clump of cows huddled around the base of a sapodilla tree. "Fat beauties, like I promised."

As the boys trot forward, a couple of sleepy cows raise their heavy heads to stare indifferently at the intruders. Another two sit motionless in the mud. There are eight altogether in this group.

"Let's get them going," whispers Rafael.

"Wait," says Pétan, circling nearby on his jumpy horse. "They're not enough."

"They're good," says Rafael. "Let's go."

"There's another three there," says his brother, pointing to a second grouping a hundred yards off. "You stay here and I'll bring them over."

"Pétan, we agreed."

"I'll get more," says Pétan, already kicking his horse into motion. "Wait here."

Rafael grumbles as his horse, sensing his distress, skitters on her hoofs and nearly bolts. He calms the beast down with a few pulls on the reins. "Shhh, shhh," he whispers in the mare's ear. "Don't worry. I respect the omen."

The nearest cow turns its broad face towards Rafael, chewing her cud. He studies the animal. It's a wonderful creature, projecting pure strength while maintaining absolute stillness.

The cow's bulk makes it look impenetrable, but at the same time its spirit radiates serenity, fortitude, and harmony. Rafael hears Pétan grunting in the distance, having some trouble spurring his additional acquisitions into motion. He decides that he has a minute or two before his brother returns. Although he knows he shouldn't dismount in the middle of a raid, Rafael can't help slipping off his horse and moving beside the cow. He has to touch it.

His manicured fingers run along the animal's smooth tan hair, pressing against the firm wall of muscle beneath, as stable and true as any cathedral stone. He pushes his face close to the animal's hide and lets his cheek absorb the warmth. He moves around back of the cow and thumps her high rump with his open palm. She's a well-bred specimen, tall and strong and full — God's majesty blazoned in living flesh. All the idiots in San Cristóbal and in each small town across the pathetic and lazy Dominican nation could learn a thing or two about dignity if they'd only look hard at the noble creatures dotting their landscape. Rafael knows they don't. When they look at cows, they see beasts of burden, living capital, nothing more. That blindness, he decides, is the product of the Dominican spirit having been impoverished and enslaved for far too long; people are incapable of awakening to the truth when they are ensnared in their hopeless circumstances. Rafael can sense the power inherent in these animals. That very same power and dignity is latent inside him. What the people will never see in cows, they'll see with perfect clarity in Rafael Trujillo.

Rafael smiles as he strokes the cow's back. Could he keep

this creature for himself? It's a possibility too wonderful to imagine. If he could, he would clear some land in these hills and let his cow graze, mating and multiplying, transforming this sleepy shithole of a town into the greatest cattle region in all the Americas. Yes, Rafael's husbandry would make San Cristóbal legendary for its meat and milk and cheese. And while the fancy Cibao girls would at first never look at him in this vulgar part of the country, no matter how much wealth he acquired, he is certain that after several years of work San Cristóbal would be considered the new Cibao, rival to any piece of land in the Vega Real. Then the girls would fight each other to be close to him. *Oh yes,* he thinks as he strokes the cow, *if I gather enough of these wonderful creatures around me, I'll have no trouble snatching up one of those rich whores as well.*

The ground begins to vibrate beneath Rafael's feet. The cows shift their weight and a couple of them gaze up into the blackness of night. Rafael freezes and drops his hand. The thundering hoofs are growing louder each second. They've been discovered. This must be what the omen predicted. He pulls himself onto his horse and gives it a swift, double-pronged kick.

A shot cracks through the singing crickets, followed by a stranger's gruff voice commanding them to halt. Rafael doesn't wait for his brother, although he's certain Pétan will abandon the cows and ride close behind him. His horse tears across the field towards the cut fence. The warmth of the night air rushes over Rafael's oiled hair, and his favourite silk tie snaps sharply over his shoulder. Another gunshot cracks. It seems fainter this time, because the roar of his gallop overwhelms his ears. Pétan shouts a sharp *eyah!* to his trailing horse, but Papa's mare, as Rafael knows, will never reach the speed of Alvarez's. It hardly matters; neither can outrun the guards. No, the Uribe brothers or their hired help have real quarter horses, well-bred and fed, genuine runners.

Rafael glances over his shoulder and sees the outline of their pursuers in the moonlight, gaining ground. It's time. He reaches into his saddlebag and grabs Aníbal's dead snake. It's too dark for any horse to see it on the ground, but at close proximity she'll know exactly what it is. Rafael pulls on his reins, letting Pétan's horse slide a few feet closer to his. Holding the snake by its tail, he shakes it before the pinto's eyes, and even lets it smack against her nose and bridle.

The startled mare throws her head, shifts her weight, and bucks wildly, launching Pétan into the air. The young teenager is too shocked to scream. His mare, in a panic, continues to buck and neigh long after her rider has hit the ground and begun to writhe in pain. Once the panic is out of her system, the mare trots off into the field with her ears pressed flat.

Rafael charges on without glancing back. Cucho, having heard the shots, has already escaped, but at least he finished cutting away a section of the barbed wire before his departure. Rafael's horse gallops through the opening and into the long grass. With one kick, the horse and rider wade across the shallow Nigua. When he reaches the far bank, Rafael steers his horse to the northeast, where he will disappear into the cane or the more distant and expansive fields of corn and yucca, only doubling back when he's far from the ranch. He rides on at a furious pace for a few hundred yards, letting his horse slow from a gallop into a canter when he's sure he's in the clear.

Rafael is hidden in a field of tall cane, the sugar plants rising above his head and swaying in the breeze. No one's going to search for him here, and even if they did, they could never find him in the dozens of rows. Still, Rafael continues the canter. The guards are probably kicking Pétan by now, he realizes, grinning at the thought. It serves his brother right, that arrogant runt, for calling Rafael *chapita*, and for brushing over the bottle caps with a flick of his wrist. Now Pétan has become like the stack of caps, tumbling off Papa's mare as it were a windowsill.

Rafael slows his horse to a gentle trot and imagines taunting Pétan directly. *What, didn't you know that Papa's old mare was terrified of snakes? Did I forget to inform you of that? Well then, my apologies, Pétan. But I'll tell you what, if it makes you feel better, why don't you confess the names of your co-conspirators to your captors? Go on, don't be afraid, tell them everything. Say you were working with your brother, Rafael Trujillo. Tell them twice or three times, even—insist that it's true—and then watch the Uribe brothers raise their skeptical brows. Listen to them laugh at your claim. Listen to them say: "You mean that saint who works with Señor Leger in the telegraph office? He was with you? Are you sure? Or are you really that jealous of your brother, Pétan? You think we're idiots here?"*

Rafael laughs at the imaginary exchange. He can hear Pétan's voice insisting to the Uribe brothers that it wasn't just him, that he was raiding the cows with his brother Rafael and Cucho Alvarez, that the three must be punished together or not at all. How regrettable that Pétan doesn't have any of Cucho's horses with him to prove his claim. And how regrettable that Rafael will already be fast asleep when the Uribe brothers arrive at the Trujillo home to investigate his claim. Regrettable, indeed. *And regrettable,* thinks Rafael as he smirks in the cane, *that you didn't properly read the omen before you, Pétan, although its presence was obvious in those sprawled and toppled stacks of bottle caps. How regrettable that you have neither the discipline nor the determination nor the fortitude to handle your bad luck. Yes, it is regrettable, Pétan, that you're a fool who hasn't the wisdom or pluck to lead other men, although it is perhaps better for you to learn your place now rather than later, when the consequences will no doubt be more severe.*

Rafael pulls on the reins of his horse, bringing the animal to a stop. As he listens to it heave and snort with exhaustion, he straightens his tie and tucks it back into his waistcoat. Pétan will be angry for a while, but that will hardly matter. When the next opportunity arises for him to make a few pesos off Rafael's effort, he'll forgive his brother. Rafael removes a comb from his jacket pocket and passes it through his ruffled hair. If he decides to speed up the process of reconciliation, Rafael can throw his brother a few pesos at the end of the month. Pétan is cheap and vulgar that way. And if he continues to make a fuss, if he's really that angry and vindictive, Rafael might offer him María as a gift, and let the poor fool exhaust himself fighting off her maniac brother. He can be benevolent; he doesn't have to cling to any one girl. There are plenty of beautiful flowers all across the isle of Hispaniola for a young man as handsome, clever, and resourceful as Rafael Trujillo.

Rafael puts his comb away, reaches into his pocket, and withdraws a handful of orange seeds. One by one, he tosses the seeds into the dirt. Any bad omens can be appeased, he believes, as long as one knows what to expect and is prepared. Tonight, Rafael succeeded with only a couple of hours' foresight and a few minor preparations. How could cancer ever strike a man who sprinkles his orange seeds properly? No, he has nothing to fear. Bad omens can't touch him. So let the dashes surpass the dots and let the bottle caps be upended. He will wake up early and stand firm every morning and don his very best suit. And he will find a way to get that fourth tie soon enough. All it takes is money. He will buy this land around him, buy the Uribe cows and a brand new suit, and then all the young women in the Dominican Republic and nations beyond will sell their own mothers just for the chance to touch him in his bed.

"You're Rafael Leonidas Trujillo Molina," he says out loud, and nearly laughs at the sound of that splendid name.

He tosses his last few seeds into the cane beside his horse and wipes his hand with a handkerchief. "Rafael Leonidas Trujillo Molina," he says. There is such rhythm to those words, such mystical power within. He kicks his horse into motion, trotting back towards the river. "Rafael Leonidas Trujillo Molina," he says once again, and then once more, knowing full well he'll never tire of the sound of that name.

INCENSED

The skinny sixteen-year-old in a long nightshirt climbs out of bed. He plucks the ten-Kronen lottery ticket from the notebook on his dresser. His pale blue eyes stare at the card no bigger than his palm, rereading its eight-digit number and studying the bold icon of the twin-headed eagle of the Hapsburg state. Adi's future depends on this little piece of paper.

He climbs back into bed and sprawls on the quilted bedspread. Paper is a fragile medium for such a historic transmission. He could easily rip his ticket to pieces. He wonders where it would go, the victorious spirit inside it, the awesome power to transform a life. Would it disappear altogether and cease to exist, or would that disembodied spirit float into the air of his closet-sized bedroom, drift out of his window, above the courtyard filled with early summer flowers, and, catching a current, would it surge high in the air, swirling and turning flips, before gently floating down again, only a block or two away — *perhaps no further than Mozartstrasse, there's the fickleness of fate* — into the recently purchased card of some unworthy farmer? Yes, that's exactly what the spirit would do, fall into the crumpled ticket at the bottom of a filthy rucksack, belonging to a muddy farmer who's come into town for the day to sell turnips. Or even, God forbid, into the ticket of a Czech weaver. The spirit of victory is a capricious vagabond, easily driven from its proper home by human free will. This is something Adi knows for certain. To avoid altering history, he must protect the piece of paper in his hand.

He lays the ticket on his bony chest and tries to feel its weight through his cotton nightshirt. He's certain he can feel something. It must be the spirit. Yes, when he wins the lottery, that spirit will leave the ticket, enter him, and be his forever—a victory designated for Adi alone.

There's a timid knock on his closed bedroom door. Adi rises and opens it without saying a word. He stares down into his mother's blue eyes, as wide and round and icy as his own. Klara, who is almost a foot shorter than her son, stands on the threshold, her cheeks and lips twitching, her hands squeezing together. She says she's very sorry to disturb him and that she doesn't mean to bother him, but it's already two in the afternoon and he's been in bed all day and she thought he might be hungry. "It's important for a growing young man to eat," she says, staring nervously at her son. "Always you have to eat in order to stave off further illness," she adds, crossing herself inadvertently, "and to keep your strength."

Adi mumbles his consent. His mother is intertwining and releasing her fingers in front of her smock. "There's roast pork and potatoes and green beans on the table," Klara says. "And how's your breathing today? Any return of dangerous symptoms?"

It's a question she asks every day. In response, Adi manufactures a few abrupt coughs and tries to imagine the burning in his lungs, the pain he never really felt, not even when he dropped out of Realschule on its account. He tells his mother he's quite well, thank you. "Just the usual tickle," he says, the result of scarring acquired during his lung infection.

"Are you sure?" Klara asks. "Nothing more than a tickle?"

"Nothing else, I assure you."

"All right," says Klara. "That's good. I'm sorry to have disturbed you." She scurries away towards the kitchen.

Adi decides to eat before starting his work. He returns the ticket to his dresser and ventures into the kitchen, his long nightshirt almost touching the floor. He sits at the little green table and looks out of the window into the meticulously tidy courtyard, all flowers in pots and well-swept cobblestones. The air is thick with pollen, hints of manure and tobacco. A pungent tinge of fermenting hops emanates from the breweries. His mother is standing by the sink, washing dishes that are already clean, peering over her shoulder at her son.

"Are they roasting tobacco today?" Klara asks. "Is that what's in the air?"

"I don't know," says Adi. "I thought it was father's pipes."

He stares down at the food on his plate, the muscle striations of a pork chop, the pink juice that seeps. He cuts and forks a piece of meat, but as he chews the rich morsel, he has to resist the urge to gag and spit it back into his napkin. He pictures the corpse of a pig with its throat cut, its blood pouring, the purple, glossy viscera lying in a heap outside its carcass. He imagines its bones roasting on a fire and feels the meat inside his mouth, knocked around by his tongue and teeth, lubricated with his saliva. Yes, the flesh of a pig that once wallowed in its own shit. Adi distracts himself with a second helping of beans. After he wins the lottery, he will hire a cook to make only what he wants.

When Klara finishes the dishes, she wrings out her cloth and wipes the counter. Adi watches her clean the handles of all the cupboards, even the ones that haven't been touched. She opens a drawer beside the sink and removes a velvet rag that she will use to polish the eighteen pipes mounted against the back wall. Adi's dead father's pipes retain their scent of putrid tobacco even though they haven't been used in well over two years. Klara removes a large one, polishes its meerschaum bowl and the lips of its mouthpiece, and replaces it on the rack. She makes sure it's straight before moving on to another. Adi can't understand why she takes such care of these pipes, even here, on Humboldtstrasse. Does she think her husband will come back from the dead to reign over this apartment? Does she expect him to demand clean meerschaum? Is she still that afraid?

Adi stands and pushes his chair to the table, leaving his meal half finished. Klara asks if he's got any plans for the day. It's a timid question, but there's a hint of accusation to it. Adi knows all about the heated conversations Klara has had with Angela, his older half-sister, and with Leo, Angela's husband, in his mother's bedroom. He eavesdropped on them from the hall. Angela and Leo demanded that Klara put more pressure on Adi to establish himself in a trade, the only proper thing for him to do now that he's dropped out of school.

"No plans until evening," Adi tells his mother, glaring at her in defiance. "I'm busy with my work."

"Adi," Klara whispers.

He throws his head back and groans. "Mother," he says with a sigh. He stiffens as he approaches her. "I have explained to you many times that the production of great art is a fickle, haphazard, and mysterious process. It cannot, in any way, be compared to other kinds of work." Adi takes Klara's trembling hands and holds them still. "It is a terrible mistake to judge an artist by the same standard as one would judge an artisan."

"But why can't you find a trade," Klara responds, her wide eyes moistening, "and still work at your painting, like Gustl with his music? Your father—hallowed be his memory—would not approve of this behaviour. He would not have liked it one bit."

Adi releases his mother's hands and steps back to face her. "My dear mother," he says, with firm but condescending sweetness, "Father so prized efficiency because his job required that particular skill of him. It's the same for all those customs officials. Time itself is the gold standard whereby their every action is judged. If a case is processed quickly, it's a success, pure and simple! Efficiency, for that whole lot of bureaucrats in the civil service—why, it's the only means for them to determine success or failure." He retakes his mother's hands and kisses two of her fingernails. "Not so with art," he says, his blue eyes bulging at her. "Not so with art!" Repeating the phrase with greater animation makes it sound all the more convincing.

Instead of being soothed by her son's explanation, Klara lowers her head and starts to tremble and cry. Her hands shake in his grip. Poor little Mother is so like a bird who's struck the glass, or perhaps fallen out of her nest onto the busy street below, just a delicate featherlight bird, soon to be crushed under the boot of an oblivious passerby—unless, of course, Adi scoops her up and protects her, nurses her back to health. He squeezes his mother's fingers and forces her to look up at him.

"I will tell you a secret, Mother," he says.

Klara sniffles and swallows, but listens.

"I will tell you a secret at the risk of tempting fate," he repeats, his eyes growing wider. "I will tell you a magnificent secret."

Adi releases his mother's hands and disappears into his room. Klara brushes away her tears with her knuckles and waits for Adi to return. When he does, he is holding his lottery ticket.

"Here," he says, handing it to her. "You see?"

Klara stares at the card with its embossed digits and the Hapsburg icon, unsure of what exactly she's supposed to see.

"I have won," says Adi, tapping the paper. "The lottery."

Klara's childlike face opens in astonishment. "You have?" she asks, her voice rising to a cry.

"I have won the lottery," he repeats, now pressing his lips together and letting his eyes widen.

"You've really won the lottery?" Their faces are moving closer and closer together with each iteration of that magnetic statement. "Are you certain?"

"I've won!" he says again. "I was in bed this morning with that ticket on my chest and felt the spirit of victory inside it. I felt its weight. I felt it on me. I have won the lottery," says Adi. "I assure you. I guarantee it."

"Oh, Adi," Klara says, bursting into tears again. "Oh, Adi."

Adi wraps his arms around his shaking mother and holds her close to his chest. Tears have begun to stream down his cheeks as well. "It's happening, Mother," Adi cries. "It's happening, right now. I've won!"

"Oh, my Adi," Klara whispers through sobs. She clings desperately to her son, pressing her small body against his, as if she's terrified of what will happen to him when she lets go.

A few minutes later, after his mother has gone, the frantic teenager, assured of his own victory and heroism, sits alone at the little desk in his bedroom and extracts sketch paper. Where will he begin? He closes his eyes and focuses his concentration. When he opens them again, he begins to draw the bridge he's designed to span the Danube, wide as Vienna's Ringstrasse and lined with mythological statues. It will connect the Hauptplatz to the green hills of Urfahr, replacing the present iron monstrosity, which is completely impractical for modern Linz, as it is not much wider than a single horse-drawn cart. Today's version of the bridge adds nothing to his basic design, conceived months earlier.

He soon tires of architecture and decides to execute a few pastoral paintings. He's not very interested in these, but he'll need them for his entrance portfolio for the Viennese Academy of Fine Arts. Using watercolour and a postcard as a guide, he paints the hills around Linz, a field by Pöstlingberg in late afternoon, the shadows long in the yellowing sky, and a couple of peasants tending sheep. He's humming Elsa's motif from *Lohengrin* while he works. He finishes the first painting, makes a second, and a third. His strokes are short and serious, although he's not really focusing on his craft. He's imagining the astonished faces of the Viennese academy's instructors, how they'll shake their heads and raise their brows and whisper excitedly to each other: *Look at Hitler's pastorals! He can whip them off, just like that, one after the other, without stopping!* And when those flabbergasted teachers think they've seen it all, the full range of his talents, he'll knock them out with his plans for the new Linz opera theatre.

"Victory is a spirit," he'll tell his instructors. "When it's inside you, you cannot be defeated."

Hours pass and the light softens. It is nearly four-fifteen. Adi goes into the bathroom, shuts the door, and runs the water until it's hot. He studies his reflection in the mirror, his long face and bulging eyes, his gaunt and sallow cheeks. A mop of black hair falls over his pasty forehead. His brow is as bulky as an ape's, and it recedes ridiculously. His nostrils are so cavernous that two snakes could slither inside and make themselves at home. Who knows how much dripping snot is stashed up there? His nose is horrible, prominent and protruding. He twitches the fuzz above his lip, wishing it were thicker. He wets his washcloth and scours his face, careful to remove every flake of dry skin.

Now Adi must address the problem of his teeth, which are yellow and rotting, especially the bottom ones. A few are turning black. What a pity. He needs to practise smiles that will keep them well hidden. He tries several options, but there's really no hope. It's the same conclusion every day: he must raise his chin slightly, smiling only with his eyes. Stefanie does not need to see his teeth.

His mother has laid his shirt on his bed, as requested, pressed and clean, crisp and white. He puts it on and fumbles with his silver cufflinks, ties a red and gold cravat, and then dons his best suit, which shows signs of wear at the elbows. He tucks the notebook and lottery ticket into his pocket, along with a recent drawing he's made of his future apartment's interior, folded into a square. When he emerges, his mother is waiting for him in the living room, standing beside his little sister, Paula. It's nearly five o'clock.

Adi nods coldly at Paula. She nods in return, a half-step hidden behind her mother. A pretty girl of nine with the Hitler family's big blue eyes, timid by nature, and dour, Paula wears the dress uniform of her elementary school, from which she has recently returned. Klara is gently and absently stroking the girl's straight hair.

"The opera?" his mother asks.

"Yes, of course."

"Go get your brother's money from the can," Klara tells Paula.

The girl scurries into the kitchen and searches under the sink for the tin stuffed with Kronen. As she does, Adi and Klara wait beside each other, fidgeting on their feet, glancing alternately at the carpet and the wall.

"Oh, Adolf," Klara whispers, her voice almost breaking.

"Mother, please. I'm an artist, you understand. That's all there is to it."

He glances at the large portrait of his father on the side wall. Alois Hitler, in his official, double-buttoned customs jacket, has a low and bulging brow, a bulldog face, and a wild moustache with side whiskers like the emperor's. The portrait has been recently dusted, no doubt that very morning, since Klara cleans house daily, without exception. In the image of the dead customs official Adi sees disdain for artistic greatness, for the fancy suits of those without station, for the dandies' leisurely nights at the opera house. Adi makes a point of keeping his expression still while staring into his father's eyes.

Paula returns with three Kronen, two for his ticket, one for his evening snack. His daily allowance. She hands the money to her mother, who in turn hands it over to her son. Adi nods and slips the bills into his pocket. Paula runs to the coat stand by the door and removes his summer overcoat, his ebony walking stick, and his silk top hat.

He takes the coat and slips it over his shoulders like a cape. "Thank you, *Fräulein*," he says to his little sister, nodding formally. Paula beams. He removes black kid gloves from the pockets and makes a ceremony out of pulling them on. He lays the top hat on his head and gives it a little tap. Then, at last, he takes his ivory-handled walking stick from his sister. Resting his weight upon it, he steps one foot forward and raises his chin, striking a dramatic pose. "Well?"

Klara presses her hands together, her face opening into a wide grin. Paula giggles beside him. Adi doesn't hide his bad teeth.

"What's tonight?" Klara asks.

"*Lohengrin.*"

"Again?"

"Again."

He touches the rim of his top hat in parting, as befits a dashing bohemian. His mother closes the door behind him. He swings his walking stick in circles and descends three flights, down to Humboldtstrasse, clicking his heels on each step and humming Siegfried's horn theme from *Götterdämmerung.*

Linz is warm and full of colours on this cloudless evening in early June. The street is crowded with horses, carts, and pedestrians. Civic workers plant flowers for the city's annual summer festival. Children in knickers play with a ball. A drunk staggers and sings a garbled Hungarian song. Adi walks over to the Hauptplatz, where gentlemen sip drinks at cafés and eat early dinners of bratwurst and beer. Crowded streetcars rumble in their tracks. When two young lieutenants pass Adi at a leisurely pace, their sabres trailing like tails, he glares at the lazy Austrian oafs who don't have anything better to do than loiter in the Hauptplatz. He leans against the fence at the large Trinity Column in the northern end of the square and checks his pocket watch. Just after five.

Right on time. He withdraws his small notebook from the inner pocket of his suit and opens it to his poem "Hymn to the Beloved." With a pen, he marks little ticks beside a few words, as if he were still composing it, imagining the sight of his own forehead wrinkled in concentration. He's a rakish figure, is he not, standing beneath the gigantic column with its cherubs and clouds and radiant sun, with his overcoat on his shoulders, his top hat and walking stick? He whistles as he waits.

The winning number will be in tomorrow's newspaper, and then his photograph, an image of the victor, will appear the day after that. When the reporters come to him with their petty questions about money, he will unveil his great plans for the new bridge to Urfahr, for the lengthening of the marble frieze on the Landesmuseum, and for the cog railway climbing the Lichtenberg to a new hotel of Italian Renaissance style.

The square is alive with activity—policemen patrolling; civil servants returning from work in groups, laughing and packing their pipes; farmers loading their remaining flowers, vegetables, and leather goods into carts—but Adi doesn't see Stefanie or her mother. They should have appeared by now. Realizing that he might have better luck if he wanders on the street, Adi leaves the towering column and approaches the old cathedral, scanning faces along the way.

Out of the square, on the Landstrasse, shoppers, diners, and amblers present themselves in their finery for their late afternoon strolls. Adi's ebony walking stick clicks on the cobblestones. A horse and cart clomp by. He nods to the driver. Still no sign of her. When he reaches the end of the commercial district, he crosses the street and marches back on the other side, his overcoat swishing behind him as if he were a count.

At last, as Adi nears Schmiedtoreck, he sees Stefanie approaching on his side of the street, walking arm in arm with her mother, as usual. No doubt the sight of young Adi in her peripheral vision has set her heart racing. Her seeming lack of interest is just an act of saving face. Adi stiffens his posture and tries to appear bored by the activity, as if he were, in principal, above the trendy fashion parade on the Landstrasse but had deigned just this once to enjoy its simple pleasures.

Stefanie is tall and slender, with dark brown hair pulled into a bun, chubby cheeks, pouty lips, and light blue eyes speckled with flashes of aquamarine, like opals. An ethereal motif could accompany this walk of hers down the Landstrasse. He can almost hear her pure and radiant voice singing of loneliness and salvation—*Einsam in trüben tagen hab ich ze Gott gefleht*—a prayer that leads to his arrival, just like the hero and heroine in *Lohengrin*. As she moves closer to him now, only a step or two away, Adi raises his chin and closes his mouth, smiling with his eyes. But now a horse neighs in the street and offers a half-hearted kick back to the loaded cart it's hauling, and the stout driver clicks at the nag and mutters bland obscenities. Stefanie and her mother, both expressionless, with nothing more than the mild curiosity of any common pedestrian, turn to regard this amusing exchange between a beast of burden and its master. Adi and the girl pass each other on the sidewalk without making eye contact, and now she's behind him, moving away, and his stick is continuing to click on the stones as the distance between them grows.

Adi blinks rapidly. He's marching past suited gentlemen and ladies in their finery, but the faceless figures all blur together in a stream of copious fabric. Adi stares up into the darkening sky, his cheeks stinging. It's only one evening, of course, and it doesn't matter. Their love can't be obliterated by a single missed connection. The proof of their bond is in the way their glances have locked, here, on the Landstrasse. Not tonight, of course, but other nights, many nights, dozens of times, always in passing, sometimes with a short nod, sometimes a semi-smile. Although they've never spoken to each other, not even a simple hello, Adi's body has quivered with the vibration of their kindred spirits united. The crests and valleys of Stefanie's feelings are synchronized with his own musical emotions, albeit played in different octaves. He has heard the Wagner in her head, harmonizing with the Wagner in his own.

Adi's glassy eyes stare at nothing, oblivious to his surroundings. If Stefanie does not hear their music tonight, that can only be because her mind has been poisoned, must have been poisoned, by the cacophonous Magyar influences in their cursed empire. All that Hungarian smugness. The spirits of the perfumed and arrogant lieutenants passing Stefanie in the street emit an awful white noise, a screech that accompanies their oppressive floral scents. How can a true Wagnerian soul be anything other than an undertone in all that Magyar-Czech garbage? Stefanie's spirit plays an optimistic and ethereal note, quiet and easily missed, but drawn long as it rises into a swell. Her tone is so pure it can fight through noise. And tomorrow, when Adi wins the lottery, when the spirit of victory merges with his own, he will be able to play his musical motif so loudly and clearly that it will obliterate the lesser tones played by inferior souls throughout the city of Linz. He will approach Stefanie's mother and declare his love — and how can she not hear him then? The harmony played by the two Wagnerian lovers will ring out to the world.

He continues north on the Landstrasse then veers west onto the wide Promenade. The road narrows and transforms into the gloomy Klammstrasse, where the plaster facades are chipped and stained by ash and smoke, the street caked with dried dung. Adi pauses before his friend's small and dilapidated Baernreiterhaus, the dangling sign above its storefront reading *Kubizek Upholstery*. He removes his kid gloves and sticks fingers into his mouth, emitting a high and short whistle Gustl will surely recognize. He pulls his gloves back on, wiggling his fingers for effect, and waits with his hands pulled behind his back. Only fifteen seconds later, he's grumbling and kicking the cobblestones. At thirty seconds, Adi is pacing back and forth on the street in fury, prepared to kill his only friend for not responding. "Damn lazy Gustl," he tells the spring air.

A small bell rings, the front door opens, and Gustl emerges from the shop, his clothes white with dust. He jogs up to Adi, who is now standing with his chin raised and one foot forward like a statue. The powder has turned Gustl's curly dark hair grey, which, coupled with his meek demeanour, makes him seem older and more distinguished than his sixteen years.

"Are you finished?" Adi asks, not bothering to hide his disgust at his friend's appearance.

"I'm afraid not," says Gustl. "I don't think I can come today. You have no idea how busy it gets at this time of year."

"No idea," Adi scoffs.

"I papered five rooms this morning, and now I'm restuffing a horsehair mattress which has to be finished by—"

"Leave it for your father," Adi commands. "He's the upholsterer. You're the artist."

Gustl lowers his head in shame. His sleepy eyes have heavy lids that never open wide, which gives him a tranquil and satisfied appearance, as if he were an aristocrat incapable of being upset by common problems. "But I don't think I can—"

"*Lohengrin,*" Adi interrupts. He pounds the tip of his walking stick against the stone and then smacks it against his heel. "The performance will begin promptly at half past seven, whether you're in the audience or not. I suggest you tell your father that you're done for the day."

Gustl nods, knowing there's no choice but to comply. As Gustl scurries back into the store, Adi removes his top hat and uses his handkerchief to wipe away the sweat he's generated while waiting. He grumbles as he folds it into a precise little triangle. He adjusts his overcoat and tucks the handkerchief into his pocket. Gustl trots out again, brushing powder out of his hair and removing his dirty jacket.

"Come upstairs," he tells Adi. "I need to change."

Adi follows him through the side entrance and up the narrow and creaky staircase to the Kubizeks' second-floor apartment. Frau Kubizek, who stands at the kitchen sink shucking beans for dinner, turns to greet them. The small apartment smells of boiled pork. As Gustl takes his one good suit from the bedroom and disappears into the bathroom to wash and change, Adi remains in the entrance, holding his top hat against his chest, bowing at Gustl's mother.

"Greetings, esteemed Frau," he says, as if the woman were a baroness.

Frau Kubizek wipes her hands on her apron and steps away from the pile of green husks to greet her son's friend. She embraces Adi's shoulders, kissing both of his cheeks. "How is your mother?" she asks.

"She is very well, thank you, Frau Kubizek. I will be sure to let her know that you have inquired into her health."

"Yes, please do."

"And how are you, Frau Kubizek?" says Adi, smiling with his lips pressed together. "Enjoying this lovely spring weather?"

"Yes, yes," she answers.

"You must be looking forward to the flower festival and parade this weekend, are you not?"

"Why, yes, I am. Very much. But we're all looking forward to it, Adolf, aren't we?"

"Yes, Frau Kubizek, we are."

The squat, heavy-set woman stares into Adi's huge blue eyes. She smirks and shakes her head. "My, my," she says. "Always the polite young man, aren't you, Adolf?"

Adi smiles and nods in agreement, although he can't help but feel she's making fun of him.

Gustl emerges from the bathroom, wiping the furniture dust off his face and out of his ears with a wet washcloth. He's wearing his black suit and pale yellow tie, but he hasn't put it on straight. "I'm sorry," he says. "Almost ready." He throws the washcloth into the sink and fidgets with his tie while moving towards the door.

"And how's your father?" Frau Kubizek asks her son with a glare.

"Fine," whispers Gustl.

"Are you certain he doesn't need any more help tonight?"

Gustl stutters as he stands by the door, but can't give her a definite answer. The weight of his mother's stare, combined with her question's sharp tone, seems to press down on his shoulders and hunch him forward.

"Pardon me, Frau Kubizek," Adi interjects, stepping forward into the centre of the small space, which the Kubizek family use as their dining room, entrance, and kitchen combined. "It's *Lohengrin* tonight. Of course, you understand it's absolutely essential for your son's development as a musical artist to see that particular work by the Bayreuth master as many times as he possibly can, whenever and wherever it might be performed, no matter the cost to his friends or family."

"My son's development as a musical artist?" Frau Kubizek says, her smile growing wider.

Adi steps closer, his eyes so intense and full that Frau Kubizek retreats a couple of steps, her bum pressing against the sink. She closes her mouth.

"I need not tell you, Frau Kubizek," says the fiery but still scrupulously polite guest, "that our dear Gustl has talent, which does not appear with any frequency in men. When a person has that blessing, he also has a certain responsibility to seize and develop it. It would be criminal of you, Frau Kubizek, and criminal of Herr Kubizek, and even criminal of Gustl himself, to forsake or ignore such a gift. It would be like spitting into the face of fate, would it not? *Lohengrin* is about to be performed in our fair city. That is more important than upholstery. Gustl will benefit by attending the opera this evening. He will grow and mature immeasurably from the experience, and I am sure he will then learn to seize his spirit and harness his considerable power of creation. You must let him go."

Frau Kubizek is holding an unopened bean husk with two hands as if it were a life preserver. Her eyes are wide and her brow is raised. "My, my," she says, amazed. "In that case."

Gustl lingers in the doorway, pale and terrified. Never in this lifetime would he speak to his strict mother in such a manner. If he did, Frau Kubizek would darken with fury and, in a single phrase, banish her son to his bedroom for the rest of the night. But when words of bald defiance originate with Adi, they never seem rude, rather they have the persuasive force of truth. His tone is firm and clear and direct. His phrasing exudes confidence. When Adi speaks, his gigantic eyes seem to draw in and hypnotize Frau Kubizek Still, his friend's audacity makes Gustl uncomfortable.

Adi touches Gustl's arm and leads him out of the apartment. "Goodbye, Frau Kubizek," he calls over his shoulder.

"Bye, Mother," whispers the pale son as he disappears through the doorway, dragged by his friend.

"Come on," Adi commands once they've descended the stairs and re-emerged on Klammstrasse. They are moving towards the tree-lined Promenade. "If we hurry, we might still catch Stefanie in the Hauptplatz before she's returned to Urfahr." While he's not exactly running, Adi's walk is so quick and determined that Gustl has to jog just to keep a few feet behind.

Soon they're back on the Landstrasse, moving north towards Urfahr. Adi slows and begins to measure his steps, casually swinging his ebony stick so as not to seem desperate or excitable. He removes his handkerchief, wipes his brow, and returns his hat to his head. Gustl, huffing through lungs damaged by upholstery dust, at last catches up to his friend and marches by his side.

"Infuriating, this evening," Adi says as he tugs his handkerchief back into his pocket. They enter the narrow Schmiedtorstrasse, heading north towards the Hauptplatz. "The spirit buzzing between us — charged, tonight, charged — and we would have exchanged a glance — yes, I'm absolutely certain of it — were it not for a nag, of all things, neighing and kicking in the street, distracting Stefanie at the one moment she needed to keep her wits about her. Poor thing must be crushed. I'm certain she's thinking that she'll have to wait until tomorrow to see me again."

"Mmm," Gustl says, fighting through the burning pain in his lungs. He has made an effort to make some sound just so his friend will know he's listening.

"A grey dress tonight," Adi says. "No doubt the closest thing she could find to white. With her hair tied back as usual, and—hear *this*, Gustl—she had it wrapped up with a golden cord. Gold, like Lohengrin's chain to his swan boat! And guess what else she's got in her bun tonight?" Adi is peering at his friend, impatient for the answer, but young Gustl can only shrug. "A flower, yes, of course, always that, always a flower, but that's not what I mean. Something else. Guess!"

"I don't know."

"An oak leaf!" cries Adi. "You see? What tree does Elsa von Brabant stand beneath when Lohengrin arrives to save her that first time?"

"Oak?"

"Yes, of course, oak!" Adi's yellow and black teeth show themselves in an open smile. "Knows her role, of course. Stefanie has read my mind. No, more than that—we're thinking the same thoughts!"

"Are you certain it was oak?"

"Yes, yes!" shouts Adi, waving his stick in the air and shaking his other fist. A passing pedestrian pulls a smouldering pipe from his lips, which are hidden beneath a *kaiserbart*, and turns to regard the frothing teenager. "Or, if not," qualifies Adi, "the closest thing to it. Oh, she knows *Lohengrin*'s performed tonight. And she knows how important it is, in our brief passing, to harmonize with the master's spirit. She knows, because she has the same idea as me. Exactly! We are kindred spirits. We can sing our duet without ever exchanging a word!"

They stop before the baroque cathedral at the entrance to the square. Adi stands before the building, his feet straddling its symmetrical line, so that if anyone notices him, it will appear as if the facade's twin square towers, topped with onion domes of copper, were constructed as mere frames for his figure. Gustl picks persistent furniture dust from the depths of his ear and holds out his fingertip to regard it. Adi searches for Stefanie amongst the strollers in the distance.

"Where is my Elsa?" he wonders out loud. "I absolutely must speak with her."

Gustl wrinkles his brow in silence, wondering what will happen if Adi finally does speak with his beloved. If he asks her why she chose to wear that particular grey dress, or the golden cord and leaf in her hair, will he fly into a rage, one of his astonishing screaming and shrieking fits, when he discovers that her reasons do not entirely mesh with his? What will he do if he discovers that she is not at all playing the Elsa to his Lohengrin? Gustl is uncertain that Adi could handle such an attack on his convictions. It would be much better if he were at least somewhat prepared for the possibility.

"You know, it is possible," Gustl whispers, "that Stefanie's not so interested in Wagner."

Adi clenches his teeth at his friend, gripping the ivory handle of his stick with such strength that Gustl fears, for a moment, he's about to whack him with it. "You don't understand," Adi whispers. "How could a child like you understand the meaning of our extraordinary love?"

"I'm sorry. Adi, please, I didn't mean to offend—"

"Didn't mean to offend?"

"You're right," says Gustl, who's even more stooped and submissive now than he was with his mother. "I don't understand. I don't see how it works between you and Stefanie. I am beneath extraordinary love. Maybe you can clarify it? Do you communicate your thoughts to her using just your glances?"

Adi hesitates, raises his chin, and touches his cravat. "We are both infused with the same spirit. Don't expect me to explain it." Now he pivots and marches back up the Landstrasse, away from the Hauptplatz, away from the possibility of encountering Stefanie again, abandoning Gustl by the cathedral.

Is that it? wonders Gustl, for what must be the hundredth time in their friendship. *Will I ever speak with Adi again?*

"Come on," Adi shouts back at him, his overcoat swishing and snapping with each step. "We must secure our positions in the theatre."

Having worked all day, Gustl could use a sausage and a beer, no more than a fifteen-minute stop at the Café Baumgartner, and they certainly have time before the performance begins, but he's not going to make that request. He probably won't have a chance to eat until he gets home, which will be late. Gustl often doesn't have a meal on his evenings out with Adi, since his friend can't eat once he's got worked up. No wonder he's so skinny, with a nearly concave chest.

Adi rounds the corner onto the Promenade, marching towards the Stadtheatre, Gustl following. The box office is open, but instead of approaching it, Adi stands across the street from the bland structure, which cannot be distinguished from neighbouring apartments, rubbing his chin and contemplating its architectural form. He's studied this building a thousand times and has offered his opinions of it nearly as often, but still he feels he's never said enough about it. His face reddens, fury overwhelms him, and Adi is moved to give to Gustl his full critique. He is spitting while talking, and shaking his fist, demanding to know how the idiots in charge of this city could expect anyone to take Linz seriously when this empty and styleless monstrosity remains the home of its culture. "Vienna will always be the greater city," Adi laments, "even with its bastard Hapsburg buildings, as long as Linz is endowed with this dreadful structure while Vienna's got the Hof." Gustl murmurs his agreement, although he's never himself seen the capital's great imperial opera house. "No," says Adi, "we Linzers must resist the urge for Gothic revival. I myself will tear down this blight and, like Theophil Hansen, build the greatest neoclassical opera house in all of Europe."

"Yes," says Gustl, "you've shown me the plans."

Adi is pacing now, pointing out the locations for the Ionian columns, the domed ceiling, the twin statues of

Bruckner and Wagner that he's designed to flank the central staircase. "Statues of actual artists," he continues, "should be erected in the street as a means of inviting Linzers inside." Only when the spectators have crossed the great threshold and entered the magic zone of the auditorium, only then will the citizens see Adi's true, crowning achievement: the hundred statues of notable figures from every German opera of any worth whatsoever. Adi takes off his top hat and laughs, but resists the urge to throw it into the air and catch it. "Come on," he tells Gustl, waving him forward as he crosses the street. "I'll show you everything."

They buy their cheap two-Kronen student tickets and proceed into the auditorium's Promenade, the standing-room-only section. Fortunately, it is located directly beneath the royal box, an exceptionally good spot to hear and see an opera. The two young men position themselves on either side of a large wooden column, so they can lean on it and rest during the long performance. There are only a handful of other people in the audience thus far. Adi excitedly returns to his designs for the new theatre, describing the romantic flourishes he's devised for each interior statue. For an hour he catalogues his entire plan, down to the minute details. The theatre gradually fills. Gentlemen escort primped ladies into their seats. Students, in shabby and threadbare suits, crowd into the Promenade. Adi's rant garners occasional bewildered stares from the students around him, until the lights fade at last and the overture to *Lohengrin* rises out of the orchestra pit.

Adi grows silent, his breathing slows, and his eyes widen.

His expression slackens, and the rigidity in his arms and legs softens. He looks like a child. He rests his walking stick against the column. He lays his top hat on the floor between his legs. He forgets Gustl, forgets the building, forgets his grand plan to rebuild everything. Although the sets are wooden and poorly painted, and the singing is at best passable ("provincial," he would say), it's still Wagner's world being created before him, with Elsa, sweet Elsa, his very own Elsa, appearing in white just as the music softens. She's come to answer the terrible accusation against her, to bow her head and pray for a Christian salvation, and to call forth a mysterious saviour. *I am your saving knight*, thinks Adi. *And you are my Stefanie.* The trumpets blast, followed by a charged silence, and then Lohengrin appears *in splendour shining*, as the stage directions—which Adi has read many times—instruct. *A knight of glorious mien.* Adi gasps. Nothing feels more real to him than this moment. His inner world has been made concrete on stage. He is witnessing everything he believes in and feels, everything he cares about. Tears are streaming down his cheeks. Lohengrin's swan is papery and fake, but his armour is silver and radiant, and he carries a glittering shield. As he sings for Elsa's hand in marriage, Adi's lips move along with the singer's and his throat fights an urge to sing the tune. *My guardian, my defender!* sings Elsa in reply. Adi is sure that someday Stefanie will say the same to him. And now comes Lohengrin's dire warning: she must never ask whence he comes, or what his name is. *Yes, it should be like that*, thinks Adi, *no need to discuss my history, no need to discuss my past, not with the spirit of victory propelling me forward.* Adi hums audibly. When Lohengrin and Frederick fight, Adi moves his hand back and forth as if he himself were wielding the sword. A student standing beside him gives him a nasty glare.

Adi is too exhausted to wander into the lobby during the long first intermission. Instead, he leans against the wooden column. Gustl asks his opinion of the production, but Adi, with his yellow teeth bared and his hands waving in annoyance, shuts him up. When the opera continues, Adi continues to live each gesture on stage, suffering all the twists and turns of Wagner's world as his own. The second intermission is worse than the first. Adi keeps his eyes closed so he won't have his bliss interrupted by Gustl's stupid questions or by the idiotic expression of some dolt in the Promenade.

Adi hungrily absorbs the wedding description that begins act three, since he plans to reproduce it in detail when he marries his beloved. Under a brilliant moon, Elsa and Lohengrin's duet brings tears to his eyes, and he whispers, along with the knight, his favourite passage in the opera: *Say, does thou breathe the incense sweet of flowers?* When Elsa asks the forbidden question and Adi, enraptured, feels the tragic fall of the eternal couple, his already damp hair saturates like a mop. Will Stefanie betray him? Do all women ultimately betray their men? Lohengrin is stepping onto his boat and leaving his beloved forever. Yes, a fitting end. Adi quietly sobs. The lights come up to applause and flowers, to five or six ovations, before the audience filters out of the auditorium. Adi remains motionless, staring vacantly at the fallen curtain, until long after everyone has departed. Gustl waits for his friend by the door to the Promenade, his hands cupped before him.

They are well out of the Stadtheatre when Adi finally speaks. "Let's go for a walk in Urfahr," he says. "I want to see 2 Kirchengasse."

Gustl stutters the first syllables of a refusal but decides to suck his protest back. It's nearly midnight and he's exhausted. He'll have to rise early in the morning to upholster with his father, but any excuse would be read at best as a meaningless annoyance and at worst as a grave insult.

"Come on," Adi says, pointing his ebony stick at the suburb and swishing his overcoat behind him. He marches north towards the iron bridge. Gustl abandons resistance and follows in his wake.

Now Adi has sufficient distance to discuss the production. "Several of the singers were miscast," he begins. Gustl, who readily agrees, is eager to delve into the criticism with his friend, as he has harsh words of his own about the woman playing Ortrud, but just as he's opening his mouth to speak, Adi starts to rant. "In Vienna," Adi says, waving his walking stick in the air, "Anna von Mildenburg was near perfect as Ortrud. And Erik Schmedes was a genius who put our town's Lohengrin to shame. And until I hear my dear Stefanie's voice—which, I can assure you, Gustl, will have the right ring to it—there will be no singer worthy of Elsa other than Frau Lucy Weidt." Gustl murmurs tepid agreements and follows him onto the bridge, envious of Adi's glamorous stay in the capital but not eager to hear about it. Other than a couple, walking arm in arm in the distance, they're alone.

The Danube flows black beneath them. Were it not for the river's gurgling, and the nutty-sweet scent of the cowslips sprouting along the banks, it would feel as if they were traversing a bottomless pit. There are several lit windows and bright street lamps on the other side, but otherwise Urfahr is darker than Linz. Adi lowers his stick. His voice loses its screech. He releases the tension in his shoulders and stops talking about the production. "Yes," he says, his voice quiet and calm. "It's good, out here, in the open." They cross the midpoint of the bridge. "It's better over here."

Gustl understands that their conversation about *Lohengrin* is finished, even though he hasn't had the opportunity to say a single word. In silence, they leave the bridge and turn right on Linke Donaustrasse. Adi quickens his pace and removes the folded drawing from his inner jacket pocket. He takes a left and then a sudden right down the sleepy Verlängerte to arrive at Kirchengasse, with Gustl trotting behind him. Frogs croak nearby on the grassy shores of the Danube. There is not another person on the street.

Adi and Gustl are standing across from number 2 Kirchengasse, regarding the darkened apartment windows on the unlit second floor. Adi unfolds his sketch and holds it before him. He shrugs off his overcoat, which falls in a heap on the cobblestones beside his ivory-handled cane and top hat. "There," he says, a nod of his head indicating a corner room. "That's my studio. And here it is, fully furnished." His thumb smacks the drawing. He's designed, for the parlour, a matching gilt wood armchair and sofa with low-relief classical scrolls, claw feet in front, sabre legs in back. Adi has forgotten the source material of the design and now considers it entirely his own. "We'll have bucolic murals in the hall and the main sitting room. I'll paint them myself." He marches towards the other side of the building. "That's your studio there," he says, indicating a window with his chin. "I've put in a Bechstein grand, unless you'd prefer a Bösendorfer."

"You prefer the Bechstein?" asks Gustl.

"Yes, of course," says Adi, annoyed. "German pianos are superior."

Gustl studies the window of his future studio. Its north-eastern exposure will give it the inferior view of a few green fields in the distance and, if he stretches his neck, a thin slice of the Danube cutting north. Adi's view, in contrast, will be magnificent. From his northwestern window, he'll survey the nearby Pöstlingberg mountain and the more distant, larger Lichtenberg. From his southwestern window, he'll gaze out over the Danube and most of downtown Linz, including the cathedral, the iron bridge, and the train station.

"Once we move in," says Adi, "the city will have no choice but to build my new bridge. And expand the sidewalks on Kirchengasse. We'll need a fixed procedure to manage our guests. They can't just come whenever they fancy to disturb us while we work. Our chatelaine must be schooled in handling interruptions. She'll have to be our watchdog."

Gustl nods and tenses his lips. "And where will she live?"

"Her room's right here." On the drawing, Adi shows Gustl the space he's reserved for a live-in caretaker and patroness.

"The maid's quarters?"

"Look at the bed I've designed." Adi indicates a standard piece of neoclassical furniture, with each of its four posts resembling a Roman column and a large painting of cherubs on the headboard. "Women prefer pieces in this style."

"Mmm," says Gustl.

"An older lady, don't you think?" Adi is searching the starry sky for an answer.

"I would think," says Gustl.

"Someone who's already seen it all and wants nothing more from life now that she's reached her later years than to care for and protect her two young artists, her two national treasures. Hitler and Kubizek, the jewels of Linz!" Adi laughs and shakes his drawing at the apartment building.

"Shh," whispers Gustl. "People are trying to sleep."

Adi flashes him a stunned and furious glare. "And they should be proud to wake for us!" His lips are quivering, and he's on the verge of tears. "My God, Gustl, if you aren't willing to commit and embrace our gift—"

"No, no!" Gustl cries, waving his hands. "That's not what—"

"I'm sure I'll have no trouble whatsoever finding another young musician with the courage to accept—"

"I'm committed. I'm committed."

"Maybe without your talent, but still—"

"I assure you." Gustl grabs Adi's hands and presses them together, crumpling the drawing. Gustl's head is bowed towards his shorter friend.

Adi sighs and blinks, managing to fight off the tears. He yanks his hands away from Gustl's, folds the drawing, and returns it to his pocket.

"I'm sorry if I offended," whispers Gustl.

Adi has already picked up his walking stick, overcoat, and top hat. He turns from Gustl and cuts north on Schulstrasse, weaving through the sparse buildings in the centre of Urfahr until he reaches the semi-rural Aubergstrasse, all the while muttering under his breath. Gustl, who's running beside him, catches only a bit of his tirade—a quick reference to Stefanie, a blanket curse against humanity. He has followed Adi many times on this route to the foot of the Pöstlingberg, and knows better than to speak until his friend has calmed down.

They pass a field of sleeping cows, their bells clanging in the light breeze, and a villa with white flowers in boxes, visible in the moonlight. There is a patch of uncut forest, thick with Norway spruce, silver fir, beech, and giant oak. When the incline suddenly steepens, Adi stops muttering. He slows his pace and relies on his walking stick. Now they have left the farmhouses and picturesque villas behind. The path narrows and roughens, winding through groves and copses. They are climbing the mountain in single file, Gustl huffing and wheezing behind Adi, his bad lungs almost unable to handle the work. He clutches his ribs and sweats, trying to keep up. Adi plods steadily, refusing to slow for his struggling friend, his legs churning and his overcoat swishing behind him. The steepening path turns rocky and unstable, with tree roots and stones as their steps. The moonlight is all they have to guide them. Adi, who has been whistling the wedding march from act three, stops and removes his top hat, and wipes the sweat away with his handkerchief. He puts the hat back on and drives himself forward. Gustl loosens his tie and opens his tall collar, his shirt drenched with sweat. In the darkness of the forest, Gustl trips on a rock and tumbles, bracing himself with outstretched palms. He yelps and curses as he lies on the ground, shaking his raw hands. Adi stops and peers over his shoulder.

"Are you all right, dear Gustl?" he asks.

His friend, blowing on his scraped palms, nods solemnly. When he realizes he can't be seen, he mutters, "Yes." Gustl grins in the darkness, surprised and pleased by Adi's unexpected change of mood, his sudden concern for his *dear* friend.

Near the top of the Pöstlingberg, Adi veers off the main path and cuts down a less worn route, a short, steep decline through coniferous trees. The forest ends at a rocky cliff. Adi takes off his hat and lays it on the rock. He puts down his walking stick and exhales loudly, his hands on his hips. "Our city," he tells Gustl, who has pulled up beside him. "Our magnificent Linz!"

Darkness limits the panoramic view, but with sporadic lights in windows and moonlight reflecting off the river's prominent curve they can make out just enough of the city for their trip to have been worthwhile. Adi sits on the rock ledge, his legs dangling over the side, and Gustl sits beside him. An owl hoots and bats dive at the boys' swinging legs. Adi stretches his arms into the air and sighs. Mountains seem to have a calming effect on him.

"It's not just for me, you understand," Adi says, a few long minutes after their arrival, "that I encourage your musical study. Persuade you to play the truant with your father. Or move into Urfahr. Of course, I'll benefit, but it's not for me. I don't think I'm wrong to say I've detected in you, Gustl, the overwhelming desire to dedicate yourself to art. But you lack the will to do it on your own."

"I have the will," Gustl protests. "I am always studying. And I play everywhere I can. The Music Society. The Symphony Orchestra."

"But there's a line, you must admit, between the hobbyist and the artist. You haven't the will to cross it on your own."

Gustl broods for a moment. There's some truth to what Adi says. Although Gustl has felt bullied all night by this frothing and belligerent dandy, and although he didn't want to follow Adi up the mountain, or hear his lecture on Linz architecture, or his criticism of the opera, now he's strangely touched. Gustl's anger abates as he remembers that Adi thinks well of him, and often considers his dreams along with his own.

"I am correct, of course."

"Yes," whispers Gustl.

"You should study in Vienna. The conservatory there is the best in the world."

"Believe me, I know that."

"Well, then? You should go."

"My parents would never let me."

Adi chuckles at his friend's timidity. "Leave that to me," he says.

"They won't let me go, I promise. They'll think it's foolish and frivolous."

"You don't understand." Adi removes the lottery ticket from his pocket and hands it to Gustl. "Remember, I will win the lottery tomorrow. My destiny will be fulfilled. No one will be able to say anything against me. The victorious spirit will be in my blood."

"The lottery," Gustl says quietly, turning the paper over in his hands.

"You'll join me in Vienna when I am at the Academy," says Adi, snatching the ticket back from his friend. "Unless, of course, that's not what you want…"

"Oh, it is," Gustl cries. "It is."

The heels of their shoes click against the rock. A cool breeze sweeps across the mountain, shaking the needles on the trees behind them. A few crickets chirp in the fields far below. Gustl opens his mouth to speak, but stops himself and looks at his hands.

"One thing's certain," says Adi. "That bridge to Urfahr is an ugly blight. A triviality planned by idiots. It will have to go. That will be my first task."

"But Adi," says Gustl, "what if there's no money?"

"There will be plenty."

"The lottery was today," Gustl blurts, pulling a small piece of newspaper from his pocket. "It was today. I forgot to tell you. I'm sorry, I…I clipped the number from my father's paper, and I meant, I…Here, I have it, here."

Adi snatches the paper from Gustl's hand. He reaches into his pocket for his lottery ticket and hunches over, comparing numbers. Back and forth Adi's eyes travel between the paper and the ticket, the veins on his neck bulging.

"Well?" asks Gustl. "Did we win?"

He hears his own question, hears its pessimism, and trembles at the inevitable consequences. It was a reckless inquiry. His stomach drops and blood floods into the space behind his ears.

For a moment, Adi sits motionless and stunned. When he revives, he tucks the piece of newspaper and the ticket into his pocket. "You," he whispers, beginning to shake a fist. "You and your money. To hell with it, and with you!"

"Me?" says Gustl.

"Why must you try to defeat every project of mine before it's even had a chance to blossom?" Adi's standing now, snatching his accessories off the rock. "I won't listen to you for another moment."

Adi drops the top hat on his head, wraps the coat around his shoulders, and grabs his walking stick. Gustl wants to speak, wants to say something, anything, to appease his friend, but Adi is already marching up the incline to the main path.

"Adi!" he cries.

"Get away, Gustl. Go back to your damn upholstery!"

The hint of abandonment is enough to pull Gustl off his perch. He ascends the hill and catches up to Adi. "I didn't mean to suggest it isn't possible—"

"Oh, but you did," interrupts Adi, halting on the spot, his enraged blue eyes bugging out of his head. "You did! And I'm telling you right now that not only is it possible, this plan you think so funny, not only is it possible, but I can also guarantee you that it will happen. Yes! It will happen! It will happen!" With each repetition of that phrase, Adi whacks his foot with his walking stick. Gustl squints to prevent the shower of spit from getting into his eyes. "Go home, Gustl. I have ten thousand plans to prepare this evening, and I can't do any of them with your incessant comments of money *this* and money *that*." He is pointing the walking stick down the mountain towards the city.

Gustl wipes the spittle off his face but doesn't move. "Will you come tomorrow, after work?" he asks.

"Why should I?" Adi adjusts his cravat and twitches the few sparse hairs sprouting from his upper lip. "Go."

Gustl nods, knowing that it is best not to speak, best to avoid Adi altogether when he's worked himself into this mood. Gustl should fly down the hill, rush back into the city, and climb into bed as soon as possible. He has to get up early. He can only hope that by tomorrow Adi will have forgotten about the lottery, forgotten his friend's indiscreet comment and question, and that maybe they can start afresh. "Good night, Adi," he says.

Adi strikes a practised pose, his two hands resting on the ivory handle of his cane, his right foot placed forward, his cheeks taut, and his top hat tipped back to expose his prominent forehead. He coldly watches Gustl disappear down the path.

All is lost. He will not be able to rent that apartment on Kirchengasse. None of his architectural plans will come to fruition. And how can he go home to face his mother after all that he's said? No, she's too fragile to withstand it. Adi's despair is so intense at this moment that he wants, under its dark spell, to rip the flesh off his bones, to toss chunks of it into the dirt, to grind it with his heels and pulverize it into pulp. Anguish clouds his vision, narrows it to a single point. A rabid impulse pulls at him: to run down the mountain, climb the rail of Linz's iron bridge, call out his love for Stefanie, and hurl himself into the Danube.

Adi snorts. "Well, then," he whispers.

He charges down the mountain. He has been abandoned and forsaken by the spirit of victory. Halfway down the path, he veers onto an alternate route that will take him west to the Danube. It's rockier and steeper at first, but the road at the bottom of this path crosses through the countryside, avoiding the buildings of Urfahr. Adi will follow the riverbank all the way to the iron bridge. He refuses to be calmed by the crunch of sticks beneath his feet, by the way the moonlight, cutting through trees, streaks into beams and pools of brightness all around him. The path levels off, the trees open into a field. He rushes down a long dirt road towards the Danube, the full moon and the mountain rising behind him.

Adi reaches the narrow dirt path that winds through long grasses, unkempt bushes, and wildflowers lining the undeveloped north shore of the river. The water gurgles and flows nearby. The iron bridge spans its breadth in the distance. He will end this life of defeat. He will damn Stefanie with his final words.

He catches a whiff of something sweet, an odour he recognizes, which flares his nostrils and bites his eyes. His throat constricts and he sniffs quickly, like a dog. The odour reminds him of that night, on his recent trip to Vienna, maybe his second or third day in the city, his secret adventure at three in the morning before he returned to his godparents' flat. He'd just witnessed a glorious production of *The Flying Dutchman* at the Hof, and had passed an extremely happy hour studying the new buildings constructed around the Ringstrasse. Curiosity got the best of him. That district was nearby. He ventured into the dark and narrow Spittelberggasse, thinking it important for a man to see the Sink of Iniquity for himself. Prostitutes stood with arms on their hips in dimly lit doorways of single-level houses. Others sat at vanity tables in well-lit rooms, perfuming themselves with flowery odours. That same smell. *This* smell. Men watching them paint their faces through giant windows. They wore stockings on their long legs, partially open corsets, and scarlet dresses with shoulders exposed. Up and down the Spittelberggasse, Adi walked, three times, watching gentlemen in frock coats stopping at the windows—*so much for dignity! the frauds! the charlatans!*—to chat with the ladies as if they were grocers, as if all those men were there to buy nuts or potatoes. He saw the men disappear into the houses and the windows blacken after them. The so-called gentry of a decaying Hapsburg state.

Adi is grinding his teeth together and clenching his fists as he moves along the dirt path. If he could make the world's laws, he would outlaw that demonic profession entirely. Perhaps even outlaw the physical act itself, whenever it's divorced from true love, because it degrades the flame of life, reduces all that's holy into a smouldering and acrid garbage fire. Men slipping their thick and hardening slugs into whorish bodies. Penises covered with sores, dripping yellow pus. Lacerated skin, head-bobbing palsies, shuffling lunatics with frothing lips. All that insatiable lust. And the women, those unforgivable women. Nature intended them to be chaste and pure, but instead they harbour beneath their stockings and obscenely stilted dresses wet and rank cunts, filthy holes, red and infected. Those dark women with dark skin and dark hair. What's the source of this pestilence? Adi doesn't know.

He tries to picture a prostitute's room, her secret lair, the mess of clothes on the floor of her closet, the used dishes in a makeshift kitchen, the food stuck to the plates. Red lights in every lampshade to better cover the grime. Nicks in the wall and hopping lice. Filth from a parade of men's shoes tracking in manure from the street. Sheets stained with muck and shit. The word *scheisse* lingers in his head, satisfying, succinct. He sees a naked gentleman in this room, lying on his back, his quivering voice asking for the whore to squat above him. He watches her do as he requests, stand above him, naked as a child, facing the wall across the bed, her buttocks hovering above his face, one foot on either side of his torso. She is squatting low, just as he requested — *yes, just that, and lower, lower, please.* It's more than a request — it's a plea, a desperate plea. His face is mere inches away, and his eyes are like cameras clicking. He is watching, waiting, anticipating, as she grunts and pushes and digs her fingers into her flesh and spreads her cheeks and, as he requested, as he pleaded for her to do, shits on his face.

Adi gags and heaves in the grass. The disgusting things that men demand. What kind of a diseased city in what kind of a diseased state produces such terrible desires in men? Bent over a pine sapling with his hands on his knees, he's waiting for the nausea to pass.

He stands and walks briskly, kicking the grass with each step, moving towards the bridge that will end this life of suffering. That maddeningly sweet odour grows stronger and more familiar, ever more intense. He stops and squints in the darkness, searching for its origin. Spiky purple wildflowers grow in the field, along the path, and down by the shore. He can't identify them. He's ignorant when it comes to nature, has no idea what anything's named in Latin or in German, but he does know that those flowers, those spiky purple flowers, are the source of the powerful smell. His salivary glands are squirting. His mouth is wet. He recalls a syrupy texture on his tongue—sticky, viscous, sweet—with a hint of that floral odour. Yes, the old jars of his father's honey.

Now he's frozen in place. Now his nose is raised. Adi is squinting and curling his lip, transfixed, standing by the north shore of the Danube. He's immersed. The bugs have halted in mid-air, the wind they've been riding on is frozen, the spinning of the earth has stopped. He's walked right into this and can't take another step. He's imprisoned, caught in a loop, and he can't move. The honeyed odour thickens his throat, makes him feel as if he can't swallow. The particular smell of his father's flower honey.

He recalls Leonding, seven years earlier, how his father, recently retired, donned his customs jacket each morning as the sun was rising, even though he'd nothing to do in those days but walk along the dirt road to the field of purple flowers where he kept his beehives. Father sitting on his three-legged stool, smoking his thousand pipes, puttering with bees in that field near the woods where nine-year-old Adi played with his friends. Adi recalls the endless war he waged, with mud on his cheeks, knees scuffed, heart pounding, holding his favourite long stick, cut from a pine tree and stripped of needles, that stick he used for a gun. He is still running through that forest with his stick, his surrogate gun. He leaps into the stream bed, rattling machine-gun fire with puffed cheeks, leading his platoon of Boers forward into battle. He shoots three Englishmen, and two of them fall abruptly in the water, convulsing and dying while Adi watches. The third remains standing until Adi throws his gun down, screams frantically, and waves his fists. *I shot you! I got you! You're dead, so lie down!* He persuades his terrified companion to fall into the mud and die.

"Adolf," calls his father.

Out of the forest and into the flowers. Standing inside that field of flowers before his pot-bellied, pipe-smoking father, hives of bees flanked on either side of him, he is unable to move. Father picks up the stool, gathers his jars of honey, and puts them in his rucksack, the smoke pouring from his pipe like a chimney—no, a dragon. "I want you home in twenty minutes for your school work before supper."

"Twenty minutes."

The boys are gone now, have been gone for quite some time. His father is gone too. Adi is alone. Now he's Old

Shatterhand, the greenhorn, hero of his favourite Karl May novel, cutting through the field to save Winnetou, an ambushed Apache prince. Adi swishes through tall flowers, spots the attacking thieves, and shoots two through the heart. He runs to Winnetou. The Apache prince holds his sister's head, tears streaming down his face, and he's muttering that she's *dying, dying, dying.* Nsho-tshi, the beautiful Apache princess, sees Old Shatterhand, the only paleface she's ever trusted. *Revenge me,* she says, before she closes her eyes forever. "I will revenge you," says Adi to the corpse. "I will never forget."

It's too dark to see anything. Evening has crossed the threshold into night. Revenge will have to wait until morning. He leaves his rifle-stick by a burnt tree, as he always does, and hops through the field, past the hives, towards the dirt road. It's a five-minute walk to the cemetery wall and their house across the street, but it takes him two if he runs. The front door is open. He skips across the threshold, plotting tomorrow's adventures.

Alois stands waiting in the living room, sucking his pipe, smoke slipping out from either side of his mouth. The Alsatian stands beside him with its ears erect, aware of this situation's severity and wanting to be a part of it. Alois holds the birch stick, rubbing its bark between two fingertips. "I asked you to come an hour ago," he says, without anger in his voice, not even a hint. "Do you think your superior in the civil service will tolerate you arriving even ten seconds late, let alone a full hour?"

"I'm not going into the civil service," says Adi flatly.

Alois frowns, all jowls and brow, holding the rod and smoking.

"I'm not," repeats Adi, his big blue eyes on his father.

"Uncle," whispers Klara to her husband, the meekest of protests. She hunches by the fireplace, picking at her fingernails, almost entirely hidden in shadow. Little Edward, who'll be dead in just over a year, with bubbles of snot protruding from his raw and red nose, clutches his mother's apron with both hands.

Alois couldn't be calmer. He's a big man. A strong man. He knows how to wield a stick. It comes down hard on Adi's shoulder. The boy winces and curls away. The stick falls hard on Adi's back and he falls to his knees, his teeth clenched, his curled back exposing a hump between his shoulder blades. Alois imagines a target. The stick comes down again and again. The Alsatian grunts and longs to woof, but knowing the stick himself, he resists the temptation. The thwack of birch hits meat. Adi's face is tucked into his hands, but his little body's a thudding, muffled drum. He emits a few short squeals in high pitch. The birch is mechanical, powered by a smoking engine, regular in strength and speed and direction. Its motion is precisely vertical. Blows connect every two point three seconds. This beating could be plotted, graphed, and analyzed as a simple statement, a grammar in gesture rather than words. A sentence designed to communicate one simple fact— *the good boy is not late*—a statement lacking malice. The odour of lavender honey, on his father's hands, arrives in a wave with each blow. *Say, does thou breathe the incense sweet of flowers?* sings Lohengrin to Elsa. Alois's bulldog eyes are blank. He's calm and easy with this work. Adi's battered skin numbs between the shoulder blades. Half his brain settles into the musical rhythm of the factory's drone or the metronome—yes, like crude Czech music. A regular polka, one thwack to commence each bar.

Lavender flower. French honey. Father's favourite flavour.

"Uncle," whispers Klara, too softly for her husband to hear.

A folk song played on a child. He lives inside that song, as united with its rhythm as any accordion or drum. Gustl has told him that Stefanie likes to dance. There's a cellist in the Linz symphony who is friends with Stefanie's brother, and Gustl asked him, on Adi's behalf, and the brother said as much. She loves to dance. So, very well, then. Let her dance to this. Let her hold some fancy lieutenant's hands, and twirl and dance to this.

The birch stick rises and suspends in the air. Alois holds back, wipes his brow, lowers his arms, and rests the stick against a chair. With his squat forefinger and thumb, he tames his windswept whiskers. The Alsatian barks, no longer able to resist, and for the first time this evening Alois shows his teeth. His foot kicks out to the side, striking the dog in the ribs and pushing him off balance. Wordless, he clears his throat and goes, although Adi can't see where. It could be into another room, or out into the road, in the darkness, ambling towards the inn for a pint or two. Klara descends, scoops the boy into the rickety wooden chair, and curls him on her lap, although he's too big for such babying now and his gangly limbs can't be contained. Adi's blue eyes open and close in regular rhythm, every two point three seconds. Edward's terrified shrieks fill the otherwise tranquil room.

His mother whimpers as if hit herself, so meek it's unbearable. She gingerly touches her son's wounded back. Adi's cotton shirt, already muddy from the river, now reddens in a couple of places.

He's blinking and blinking, a rhythm lodged deep, as he stands in a field of flowers. The spirit of victory has been torn from his ticket, flogged, and shredded. He removes the ticket from his pocket, rips it up, and tosses the bits of useless paper to the ground. His body is meat. After it's been dredged from the Danube, someone could slice and roast and tenderize it, crack the bones and eat the flesh. The wind picks up across the river, sweeps across sleepy Linz, across the empty Hauptplatz, all the way here, to the wild riverbank in Urfahr, where it rustles the lavender around him, unleashing that irritating and incensing smell. Insects revive, the earth spins. Adi, in his despair, steps towards the iron bridge.

ACKNOWLEDGEMENTS

Many books were used in the making of this one. Although I won't name them all, I am particularly indebted to several biographies, including *The Ghosts of Kampala: The Rise and Fall of Idi Amin* by George Ivan Smith, *Pol Pot: Anatomy of a Nightmare* by Philip Short, *Mao: The Unknown Story* by Jung Chang and Jon Halliday, *Young Stalin* by Simon Sebag Montefiore, *Trujillo: The Life and Times of a Caribbean Dictator* by Robert D. Crassweller, and *Hitler: 1889-1936* by Ian Kershaw. I also used the speculative psychohistories *The Psychopathic God Adolph Hitler* by Robert G.L. Waite, *The Mind of Stalin* by Daniel Rancour-Laferriere, and *Mao Tse-Tung: The Man in the Leader* by Lucien W. Pye. Other helpful sources were *The Young Hitler I Knew* by August Kubizek, *Cambodia* by David J. Steinberg, *Marriage Laws and Customs of China* by Dr. Vermier Y. Chiu, *Prologue to the Chinese Revolution* by Charlton M. Lewis, *Stalin* by Robert Service, and *Lugbara Religion* by John Middleton, as well as the documentary *General Idi Amin Dada: A Self Portrait*, directed by Barbet Schroeder.

I'm also indebted to many flesh and blood people. I am particularly thankful for the insight and support of Ava Roth, Martha Magor Webb, and my editor at Goose Lane, Bethany Gibson.

The story of the red ants in Burma was adapted from a similar tale told by John Nunneley in *Tales From The King's African Rifles.*

The poem by Raphael Eristavi, "The Land of The Khevsuris," is taken from *An Anthology of Georgian Verse,* translated by Venera Urushadze.

1. Are Piatigorsky's imagined early lives for these infamous figures believable?

2. How might Idi's mother, the soldiers, and the major have influenced Idi's decision to become a leader? How might their influence have been a corrupting as well as a motivating force?

3. Sâr's struggle between desire and shame persists throughout his story; even at the end, his apparent certainty is laced with doubt. Do you think he will return to the dancers' house and let his desire win, or will his shame prevent him from repeating the mistake?

4. Is Tse-tung's struggle with his father merely a display of his internal character? How may it also help to shape him into the figure that he eventually becomes as both a great leader and a devastating dictator?

5. Why does Tse-tung fail or refuse to engage in *yuan fang*, in other words, to consummate the marriage?

6. Soso sees himself as powerful and superior to the other seminarians despite his physical and financial limitations. Do you see this self-assessment as accurate, or is it misleading?

7. In what ways does Rafael use the omens of his superstitions to make events happen in the way he expects them to happen? Does he ultimately believe in them, or does he merely use them to explain his actions?

8. In what ways do secondary characters such as Gustl and Iremashvili provide support for their friends the main characters? Do they also hinder them?

9. Do nicknames like Adi and Soso make it easier to sympathize with the characters? If so, in what ways does this help or hinder the reader's interpretation of the stories?

10. There are numerous differences between the lives of these future dictators. Are there any similarities between some or all of them? If so, do these similarities prepare them for their positions of rule?

11. Do the actions and decisions of these dictators in their early years occur as a result of their character or do they form their character? Might they also show some redemptive traits?

12. How do determination and leadership manifest themselves in the main character of each story?

13. Are the characters defined more in their moments of weakness or their moments of strength? Which of those are their strongest traits, according to Piatigorsky's writing?